"YOU'RE ONLY YELLING AT ME NOW BECAUSE YOU'RE SCARED."

Sebastian's voice lowered even as hers had risen. "I won't be blamed for your fear."

"I wouldn't be experiencing this fear right now if it weren't for you." Even the usually calming patchouli scent of Dana's and the gentle trickling sound of the water fountain couldn't calm Angie's anger.

Sebastian opened his mouth to say more. She prepared to lash out at whatever he had to say…

And then her stomach growled.

The sound was loud and very obvious in the quiet store.

His lips twitched. She tried to keep scowling but his expression made her tension break, and she ended up rolling her eyes.

"It's been too long since I ate," she said, almost defensively.

"And I promised to feed you and then didn't." He shook his head, a smile breaking over his gorgeous face and loosening all the tightness in his shoulders. "Ah, Ang. I've missed you so much."

Her heart tightened. "Even this? Even all the fighting."

"Everything." He raised his hand as if he'd touch her but stopped himself, fisting and relaxing his hand at his side instead. "But I've especially missed your appetite."

Bone Lantern Witch

Spiderweb Witch

Storm Shadow
Witch

Darkling Mist
Witch

Apocalypse Witch

BONE LANTERN WITCH

A DEMON WITCH NOVEL

KAT SIMONS

T&D PUBLISHING

Published 2021 by T&D Publishing
Cover design: © 2025 T&D Publishing
Interior book design © 2025 T&D Publishing
ISBN-13: 978-1-944600-41-9 (Trade Paperback Edition)
ISBN-13: 978-1-944600-42-6 (Large Print Edition)
ISBN-13: 978-1-944600-43-3 (Hardback Edition)

This is a work of fiction. All of the characters, places, organizations, and
events portrayed are either products of the author's imagination or are used
fictitiously. Any resemblance to actual persons, living or dead, business
establishments, events, or locales is entirely coincidental.

First printing T&D Publishing edition: September 2021
Second printing: December 2025
For information, contact T&D Publishing: https://www.tanddpublishing.com

Bone Lantern Witch

To my infinitely patient family, in this infinitely weird period of history. Thanks for understanding why I occasionally needed quiet time.

CHAPTER ONE

$\mathcal{A}$ngela Jordan fingered her pentagram bracelet and stared at the natural V-shape formed by the split trunk of the small oak tree. She'd tried not to look, had managed to avoid looking on accident for years. But this tree sitting innocuously along the path from the Mosholu entrance in the New York Botanical Gardens had caught her off guard.

Or maybe her guard was down because of why she was here.

She rubbed the dangling silver pentagram charm in slow clockwise circles, pressing into the pattern with each pass over the top of the dime-sized disk. She took a step toward the tree. A slight tremor from the charm stopping her. The scent of sulfur and heat burned her nostrils, a sharp contrast with the cool autumn air. Ordinary, mundane humans walked behind her on the paved path, ignoring her, unable to see the horror she watched between the oak's trunk.

They were all so luckily innocent, she thought, as a demon from the hellscape noticed her.

She froze. Even her fingers stilled on the pentagram. Her heartbeat pounded. Panic she hadn't felt in months rushed through her blood stream.

If she could just stay still enough, maybe it wouldn't realize she could see it, maybe it wouldn't know.

The creature swiveled its head and flicked the air with its forked tongue, its red-eyed gaze narrowing. Its skin was the color of rolling volcanic lava, hard sections of black covered its chest and thighs, under that a luminous red and yellow glow. It hissed, though she couldn't hear the sound yet, revealing rows of shark-sharp teeth.

She tried to swallow without making any movements, not while it was looking at her. She failed.

The demon raced across the burning, charred land. Charging her. Barreling toward the rip she'd created between its realm and hers. It ran on all fours, even though it was vaguely human shaped, its spiked tail high behind it.

A lesser fire beast. Not the same species exactly. Not the same one as that night.

But the same hellscape.

The same realm.

She held her ground, unable to move even if she'd wanted to, glued by panic and fears she'd worked for almost two years to overcome. The stink of sulfur intensified, along with the burning smell of oak. Ash coated her tongue. An illusion she couldn't ignore.

The demon hit the tree and reached through the split in

the trunk, grasping hands tipped with impossibly long claws stretched toward her. She could hear its screams now, so high-pitched the sound ripped across her nerves, piercing and sharp. Its mouth stretched and distorted with its cries, taking shapes no being of this realm could manage.

Laughter and the chatter of a child moved behind her. The real world. Oblivious to the nightmare trying to reaching them. They'd see it if it got out, if any of the beasts escaped. The humans would see it.

And they'd know she let it free.

Angie folded her hand around her pentagram charm, encompassing the white beads of the bracelet itself where it hung loosely around her wrist. The charm burned coldly in her palm, the sensation a reassuring jolt of reality and sanity. A soft breeze moved through her hair, ruffling the baby hairs on her forehead, making her hanging moon earrings tinkle lightly.

Unless she was working, she didn't wear the stereotypical trappings of a psychic and witch. Not what mundane humans expected. No flowing skirts and excessive silver jewelry. No braids or patchouli-scented perfume. Today, she wore her comfortable camouflage—jeans and a t-shirt, hiking boots and a light autumn jacket. Only the pentagram bracelet, which she never risked taking off, and the earrings—a present from her brothers to represent her love of astronomy more than her witchy gifts—even hinted at her lineage.

None of it revealed her most horrible skill.

The sounds of the demon's screams got louder, a hissing and screeching that raised the hair on her arms. Behind it, more demons noticed the breach. Noticed her. They piled against the thin barrier, pushing through the V made by the oak's trunk like a writhing mass of snakes about to spill into this world.

A tug on Angie's jacket made her breath catch. She sucked in cool air, swallowed her screech, and glanced down.

A little girl, maybe five or six years old, looked up at her with wide eyes and a shy smile. Angie heard the screams of protest from the oak, the sounds piercing her skull. She smiled at the little girl in her unicorn t-shirt and pink ballerina skirt. The gold plastic crown tucked into her tightly curled black hair glittered in the autumn sunlight.

When the girl tugged Angie's jacket again, Angie bent lower so she was eye level with the child, moving her big purse to one side so it wouldn't get in the way.

"Are you a model?" the girl asked, her whisper not very quiet.

Angie chuckled. "No," she said. "Are you?"

The girl giggled and bounced on her toes. "I'm gonna be," she confided. "But right now I'm a princess."

"Yeah you are," Angie said. "And a beautiful one at that."

The girl's mother spotted the conversation and hurried over. "Sorry," she said. "I hope she wasn't bothering you. She's convinced you're a model."

"No problem." Angie waved to the girl as her mother pulled her up the paved road toward the children's section of the gardens.

The scent of sulfur had faded, leaving only the faint spoiled-egg taste of it in Angie's mouth.

She glanced at the oak from the corner of her eye, not making the same mistake she'd made earlier. She could still see the faint glow of the hellscape beyond, but the barrier between realms had solidified.

No demons would be climbing through today.

She pushed her hair out of her face, letting the breeze cool the sweat at her temples. When she felt settled, she tugged her jacket sleeves down, covering her bracelet, though she curled her fingers up into the sleeve to brush the charm one last time. She adjusted her purse at her hip, straightening the strap over her shoulder and across her chest.

Then, letting the fresh scents of green grass, damp earth, and the faint smell of hot sauce from the food truck at the front of the gardens clear out her senses, she moved on, studiously ignoring all the natural Vs formed in the trunks of trees.

ANGIE MET HIM AT THE PAVILION IN THE DECORATIVE conifers section of the gardens. Here, dozens of varieties of pines filled the rolling hills, scenting the air. Angie loved conifers. Very few of them grew with split trunks.

"How many times do I have to tell you I'm not doing this anymore," she said as she approached the loan man sitting inside the gray stone pavilion.

The open top let light spill across his face, making him look younger than his almost forty-three years. His short dark hair was still free of any hint of gray, his brown skin smooth, no creases or laugh lines around his dark brown eyes or full mouth. Sometime in the last year, he'd gone from clean shaven to a dark mustache and goatee-style beard, also without any gray.

Sebastian was a demon hunter, though, and they never looked their age. It wouldn't matter if he was forty-three or sixty-three or even eighty-three. Demon hunters remained exactly the age they wanted to stay. They willed away the process of aging the way they willed away demons called to this realm.

A demon hunter's will was an awesome thing to behold. A rare trait in humans, that kind of will. Rarer still that innate skill put to good use. And it was a trait fewer and fewer possessed with each passing year. Still, there were enough to keep the demon realms at bay. For now. It was their job to fight the fights and keep this world blissfully unaware of the threat.

At least, most people were blissfully unaware.

She refocused on Sebastian. He wore jeans and a burnt orange sweater that served to both honor the season and show off his broad shoulders and strong physique. The color suited him. Even without the softening glow of the afternoon sunlight, he would look good, though. A gorgeous, stunning man in his prime.

Her chest ached. She ignored it.

As she sat next to him, cradling her overlarge faux-leather purse in her lap, she reminded herself, again, demon hunting was his job. *Not* hers.

He studied her, his head tilted to one side as his gaze traveled over her face, lingering on her eyes, her lips. "You're looking good, Ang," he said, his voice deep, the English accent prominent.

She gestured at the surrounding trees, ignoring the compliment and the way his voice always sent a little tingle along her spine. "The Botanical Gardens was an interesting choice. Unless we're here for a specific reason. Either way, the answer is no."

He grinned, quick and sudden, an expression that gave him a boyish charm. That smile had always gotten her into trouble. "Maybe I just wanted to see you again," he said.

"If that were the case, we could have met for a coffee in a crowded café in the city. No reason to get me out here where no one will overhear our conversation."

"I could have kept anyone from overhearing our conversation even in a crowded café," he reminded her.

"We both know you didn't call me for a friendly reunion." Unfortunately. She swallowed that response. "Or anything else personal. We both know this is business."

In the first six months after they'd broken up, when she'd been determined to be done with demon hunting because it had nearly killed her, he'd come to her several times in New York, trying to coax her back into his world. She'd made the mistake of following him into two more hunts before she'd put her foot down for good. Two more hunts she should never have been involved in after…

She let out a long breath. "I'm not dealing in your business anymore. I can't do it again, Sebastian. I can't."

His smile dropped away. "I wouldn't ask if it wasn't

necessary. I don't like putting you through this any more than you like going through it."

She snorted. "Right. Which is why you keep dragging me back in."

She'd been trying to put the demon world behind her for almost two years. She'd worked hard to settle into a life without demons and hunters. Or at least, she'd tried to.

She hadn't seen Sebastian in a year and a half, after yet another hunt went horribly wrong for her. She'd finally, finally demanded he not contact her again unless it was an emergency. The last year and a half had been one of the most peaceful, uneventful times in her life. She'd loved it.

She wasn't going to give that up now, just because he flashed those gorgeous dark eyes at her. No matter how easy it was to ignore the hint of red in their depths. No matter how easy it was to fall back into the old ways, the old feelings.

"Ang," he said, drawing out her nickname. He held out his hand, palm up. "I tried to stay away. This time I really tried. But there's no one else like you in this world. And I need your help."

She let out a huff of a sigh and looked out over the trees, keeping her gaze on the solid trunk of a pine just down the hill from them. She'd known, when he texted her out of the blue, she'd known it would be something like this. Some demon related issue.

"No," she said without looking at him. She could still taste the sulfur and ash in her mouth from the earlier incident. That realm… The reminder helped her hold firm. "No, Seb. No more. Not ever again."

"I told her you wouldn't want to be involved," Sebastian said quietly. "I had to ask."

"Aidan?" Angie shook her head. "Of course."

Aidan was one of the oldest and most skilled demon hunters to walk this realm. No one was sure how old she was, or how long she'd been fighting demons. Just that she was still alive when so many others weren't. She was a legend among demon hunters. She was the hunter who'd found and trained Sebastian.

The hunter who'd rescued Angie from herself.

"You weren't her only option," Sebastian said. "Just a more straight-forward choice than any of the others left to us without you."

"I'm not going to ask," she said firmly, still not looking at him.

If she asked what the problem was, what they wanted her to do, she'd be halfway to giving in. She wouldn't be able to hear about the trouble and ignore it. He'd gotten her before with that trick. Better not to know. Better to stay ignorant and let the hunters handle it themselves.

"It's okay, Angie," he said, his voice quiet. "We'll save the child without you."

"You son of a bitch," she hissed. "Son of a bitch." She glared at him, her jaw tight. "I hate you for this."

He nodded. "I know."

"Bastard." She wrapped her fingers around the pentagram on her bracelet. "Tell me."

CHAPTER TWO

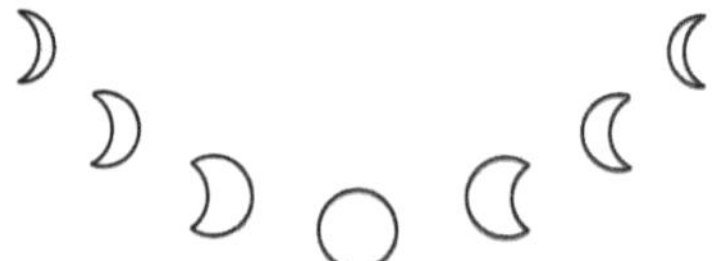

"She's twelve and she's been missing for two days," Sebastian said.

Confirming her worst fears. Angie could no more turn away now than she could have ignored the little girl in the pink tutu earlier.

"I really hate you," she said again. "You think she's in a demon realm?" The girl could survive in one, maybe, depending on the realm. But only for so long. And only if the demon who took her wanted her to.

"We know her asshole father bargained her away. He's all regrets and excuses now."

"They always are," she muttered.

"But by the time we reached him, his daughter was gone. And he's asking us to get her back."

That was…strange. "Wait, did the demon take her, or did she run away?"

"Her father doesn't know. That's why we need you," he said.

"Have the bastard father call the demon again," she said. "Force the demon to tell you."

"Demons lie. Even to us. Or twist the truth."

And those lies and twisted truths could put even a demon hunter into a bad position, weakening their will. Especially when a child's life was on the line. It had happened before. Cost hunters their lives over the years. Children in danger were a weak spot for all of them.

Probably because a lot of demon hunters had been that child in danger.

"What is it about bargaining away their own kids," Angie muttered, not expecting an answer. There wasn't an answer. Some people were just horrible horrible humans and didn't deserve kids.

"We just need you to take a quick look," Sebastian said. "There's every chance she's run away. The father says he didn't go through with the ceremony, but he did activate the circle and left it active while he walked away from it."

"Stupid," Angie said, clenching her fists. "Does he think the demon talked the daughter over the threshold while he wasn't paying attention?"

"He doesn't know. The circle was still active when he came back to it after he couldn't find his daughter. He doesn't know what happened."

If the demon had taken the girl behind the father's back, the father wouldn't receive his part of the bargain. Though, without the ceremony being formally completed, the demon might not have been freed from the bargain either, even if it had taken the sacrifice. That all depended on the initial deal.

"From what I gather from her bastard father," Sebastian said, his deep voice harsh, "she's 'too clever and smart for her own good.'"

"He said that?"

"And then tried to backtrack and make it seem like he was complimenting her."

"So, not really one of the ones who regrets his bargain, then," she said, a deep well of hate settling in her gut.

This was one of the many reasons she didn't want anything to do with the demon hunting world anymore. Too many of the people who summoned demons, the ones who bargained for wealth or power or other greedy rewards, they were the worst of humanity. She hated dealing with them. She already had a pretty cynical view of humanity, thanks to her skills as a psychic. She didn't need the added knowledge she picked up dealing with the demon world.

"Aidan thinks the girl has run away," Sebastian said, "and the father wants her back to fulfill the deal with the demon."

"And you?" Angie turned to face him.

"I agree with Aidan."

"Then why find her? Why not let her stay hidden from the asshole trying to sacrifice her to a demon?"

"To ensure her father, or anyone more dangerous, doesn't find her first. The bargain has been made. We need to keep her safe until the demon can be vanquished."

"If you're sure she hasn't been taken already, why come to me?"

There was no point to her looking into a demon world for a girl not there. And it was safer for all involved if she *didn't* look into a demon world. When they noticed, when they realized she'd opened a way for them to get out, they always tried to take that opening. And closing the breach between realms wasn't always as easy as it had been that morning.

"We'd still like to check," he said. Then, with a shrug, "And we'd like you to…meet the father."

Ah. She straightened, rocking back a little as she realized what they really wanted from her. "You want me to read him if I can. You want me to go around his place touching things to figure out what happened."

Relief made her slump. This was something she could do without fear, without serious and dangerous repercussions. One of her primary witchy skills came in the form of her psychic talents. She read by touch. Physical contact brought up images of things that had happened or were happening under the surface. Sometimes even of things that might happen in the future, though that was always more ephemeral —as future predictions naturally were.

She'd needed years and years of training and practice to control her psychic gift. These days, she only rarely touched things and got readings on accident. Though it still occasionally happened with people, it was rare she picked up random impressions from objects. Which was fortunate or she wouldn't have been able to live in New York City.

Now that she controlled the gift, she used it in her business. Those who came to her for a psychic reading were looking for future predictions. Using what she could pick up of them and their past from an initial handshake, she used her knowledge and understanding of people—earned with a Bachelors and then a Masters degree in psychology—to "predict" their future. Mostly, she was a counselor for troubled souls, a way for them to put their current issue into perspective. She just used a less conventional method than most therapists.

Sebastian nodded, and some of the tension crinkling the corners of his eyes eased. "Yes," he said. "We'd like you to use your psychic skills first. I understand why the other… skill is dangerous. I won't ask that of you unless it's absolutely necessary. Not again."

The last time he had, the last time she'd looked into a demon realm on purpose, she'd nearly died. Again. After that, she'd walked away from demon hunting forever.

Or at least, she'd intended it to be forever. She thought she'd finally gotten forever when she didn't hear from Sebastian for a year and a half. She thought she'd put her feelings for him aside, managed to let the anger and fear overcome the love, and settled into as normal a life as she was likely to lead. With no demons. And no demon hunters.

She'd been wrong.

And now, here he was, dragging her back into his world. She had very mixed feelings about seeing him again. Unfortunately, not all of those feelings were anger. Damn it.

She pursed her lips and stared down at the grass. "I charge for this kind of thing, you know," she said, stalling.

She'd help. He knew she would. There was a young girl's life in the balance. Still, it didn't seem wise to just buckle and do as he asked without at least some push back. Just because this request wasn't likely to get her killed, didn't mean his next request wouldn't. This was how those first six months after she'd tried to leave had gone—he'd ask, she'd cave, she'd get hurt and tell him it was over again, he'd ask again, and she'd give in again. She couldn't let that pattern start all over. Not after she'd finally found some peace.

"We'll pay you," he said, "but I'm not sure you'd trust our money."

There was a note of amusement in his tone, a teasing lilt that brought back too many memories. She ignored the giddy dance in her stomach.

"I'll give you an hour," she said. "Find what I can, tell you what I pick up." She faced him, met his dark eyes without flinching from the hint of red in the depths—a sure sign of a demon hunter, that little flicker of red. Someone who didn't know better could almost convince themselves it wasn't real. She knew better. "Then I'm done," she said firmly. "For good this time. This is it, Sebastian. No more. And I won't deal with the demon or its realm. I tell you what I can pick up from the father and his home, but then I'm out."

"Fair enough. I'll take what I can get."

She ignored the potential double meaning in that last sentence. "Will Aidan be there?" she asked.

Seeing Aidan would raise memories better left buried, memories already too close to the surface for Angie's mental wellbeing. Seeing Sebastian again was hard enough.

"She had to leave for another job, something more… immediate."

Angie nodded in understanding. Aidan had been "called" to a hunt. How that worked, even the demon hunters couldn't entirely explain. They got a sense they needed to be somewhere and they went. Hopefully arriving in time to fend off a demon on the verge of escaping the bonds of the person who'd summoned it. Hopefully.

"So it's just the two of us," Sebastian said. "Like old times."

"No," Angie said, pointing a finger at him. "Not like old times. Never again like old times."

He raised his hands, palms facing her, a defense and a surrender. "I get the message, Ang. I won't push. This one hour of your time and I'll leave you be."

She nodded, ignoring the twinge of regret, the nostalgic longing that wrapped around her heart. Nope. Not this time. Not *again*. One hour. One hour to discover what had happened to the girl. One hour to help Sebastian save her.

And then Angie was done.

CHAPTER THREE

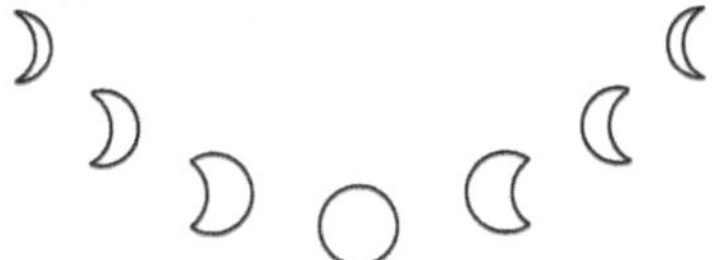

artholomew Grant's home was a massive, five story townhouse on the Upper East Side of Manhattan. The kind of home only the very rich could afford to own. In Manhattan, it wasn't the initial cost of a place that got to a homeowner. It was the annual taxes and maintenance fees. You had to be able to keep the place up over time. And that took money.

Which meant Bartholomew Grant had plenty of the stuff.

"What the hell did he bargain with a demon for?" Angie asked, scowling up at the red brick building.

Beautifully carved stonework edged the front door and formed decorative highlights against the bricks, giving the place a lovely elegance not seen in modern buildings. The steps up to the front door were bracketed by carved red marble. The door itself had a vaguely medieval feel to it with its solid oak construction punctuated by wrought iron accents and hinges. The wrought iron balconies along the lower levels were crowded with planters filled with flowers on their last gasp before full autumn took over. High up, the roof was circled by stone balustrades, through which Angie could just make out more greenery. A roof garden, most likely.

The place was gorgeous from the outside. An enviable home on a street lined with fabulously impressive homes.

"He hasn't actually told me," Sebastian said, his gaze also on the house. "I've a few guesses, though."

"Do I want to know?"

"Probably not." He flashed her a look from the corner of his eye, a slight smile tugging at his mouth. "Though I suspect you'll know more than me in short order."

"Ha." She snorted. Then straightened her shoulders. "Let's get this over with. I skipped lunch, and I'm hungry."

He gestured for her to proceed him up the stairs. Always the gentleman, she thought with a suppressed smile.

Sebastian pressed the doorbell. They only waited a few seconds before a dark-haired woman answered. She took in Angie with a sweeping, assessing glance that revealed nothing except polite curiosity, a reserved inquiry into Angie's business without having to say a word.

Then she spotted Sebastian and her entire body language changed. Her shoulders sagged, her expression softened, and the neutral line of her lips pursed into a fretful mew.

"Mr. Sebastian," she said. "I'm so glad to see you again. Come in. Come in."

"Carmen," he greeted. "How's everything been?"

"Not good, Mr. Sebastian. Not good. He's very angry.

He's trying to pretend it's worry, but—" Carmen pressed her lips together and glanced over her shoulder, falling silent.

Sebastian didn't push her, his gaze also moving toward the interior of the house.

"We'll do what we can, Carmen," he said. "May we see him?"

"Of course, of course," she said, gesturing them inside. "Please. This way. He's in the downstairs study."

They followed Carmen down a long narrow hall, past a staircase with highly polished wooden rails that snaked around to the second story. The inlaid wooden floors were also polished to a glossy shine. The art on the light-green walls consisted of tasteful, muted landscapes. A Turkish rug in light blues, greens, and golds ran down the long center of the hallway, quieting their footsteps. A few polished dark wood tables lined the hall, one held a simple brass lamp, another an empty blue Venetian glass bowl, another was bare.

The place was very…neutral, Angie decided. Not a lot of personality. Like something in a magazine, cleaned and tidied to photograph. There were no family pictures on the walls or tables. No shoes on the floor. No mugs or cups or soda bottles. No dropped books, or pieces of junk mail on a table. No signs of a kid even being in the house.

She realized with a maid there wasn't likely to be any random untidiness on the main floor, where the family might have visitors, but still. The place didn't *feel* like a home. Even the smell was pretty bland and neutral. Clean and with a very faint undertone of bleach cleaner. Not even a nice lemon-scented wood polish.

The nothingness of it all made her jumpy. She followed a step behind Sebastian trying not to shiver. She didn't have to touch anything for her psychic senses to read this house's "public" aura. And its public face said, "Façade."

Carmen led them to a door at the back of the house near a window letting in the late afternoon sunlight. Angie could just see a walled garden behind the house and down a level. A real luxury in Manhattan, even for a wealthy townhouse owner. She made an attempt to swing close to the window to get a better look—she loved gardens even if she had to be careful around trees—but they were too far away for her to see more than just a little bit of green against the red stone walls.

At the closed door, Carmen knocked so quietly, Angie was surprised anyone inside could hear. Through the door, Carmen said, "Mr. Grant? Mr. Sebastian is here. He would like to speak with you."

Angie didn't hear the response, but Carmen must have because she opened the door and stood back to let them proceed. She gave Sebastian a significant look, a steady gaze that said more than anything she'd said aloud, and then she turned and disappeared down a small stairway hidden behind a wall panel Angie hadn't noticed.

Angie didn't speak as they moved into the darkened interior of the study. She let Sebastian take the lead, hanging back to assess her surroundings. The study itself was as neutral as the hallway had been. The bookshelves lining one interior wall were floor-to-ceiling and made of lovely dark wood. Glass fronted doors covered the lower three shelves.

The top four remained open. The shelves were filled with books, but they were all leather-bound matching sets, like volumes of law books or academic digests. She wasn't close enough to see the titles, but it was obvious there were no paperbacks, and she doubted much of it was fiction, even classics.

Except for the one wall of shelves, the rest of the room was open. The windows opposite the shelves were covered by thick blue curtains that were closed to the afternoon sunshine, though a line of light managed to sneak through. The floors were the same inlaid wood as outside, but the rugs here were small circular things set at various points and surrounded by chairs, establishing three smaller sitting areas. The wall opposite the door had a brick fireplace, but it was obvious no one had used it in years. Inside the grate, an arrangement of fake flowers filled the space.

There was a two-person couch next to the fireplace. And a small desk in front of the bookshelves, though there wasn't anything but an ornamental desk lamp sitting on the desk, and the chair behind it looked less than ergonomic.

All for show. Again, nothing personal. Nothing that might reveal the lives of the people who lived here. A place to take visitors and guests, a façade to hide behind.

And what, she wondered, did Mr. Bartholomew Grant have to hide?

Grant sat in one of the more comfortable chairs in a grouping of three near the window, though his back was to the thin strip of light. That position, with the curtains drawn, made his face difficult to see clearly.

A deliberate ploy, she suspected.

He gave the impression of being tall and broad, his shoulders spanning the width of the chair, his physique thickly muscled with maybe a few extra pounds hidden beneath an expensive, well-tailored suit. His hair was a light shade of brown and cut very short. His features seemed pleasant enough, if shadowed. His skin was pale, but whether he was unusually pale from his current situation or just naturally that pale was hard to tell. His age was impossible to discern in the dark lighting, but if he had a twelve-year-old daughter, she'd guess at least mid-thirties. His suit was dark, the shirt under white, and his tie was as dark as the suit with no obvious pattern in it. He rested his hands on the armrests of the chair and Angie noted very long fingers.

For some reasons, the sight of his hands bothered her, made her instincts jumpy again. Why, she couldn't be sure. But she trusted her instincts implicitly. She kept several feet of distance between herself and Grant. Without conscious thought, she tucked her fingers under her jacket sleeve to brush against the pentagram hanging from her bracelet.

"Mr. Grant," Sebastian spoke first. "May I introduce my colleague, Angela Jordan."

"Ms. Jordan," Grant said without moving anything but his gaze toward her. "Thank you for assisting us. I assume Sebastian has…filled you in."

He wasn't asking a question. Still she nodded. "It would be helpful to me if I can have access to your daughter's bedroom."

Grant cut a look to Sebastian. Sebastian met the gaze

without a flicker of emotion. Grant leveled his gaze on her again. His eyes seemed overly pale in the faint light coming in from the slit in the curtains. Pale but bright, with dark brows raised over them—a sharp contrast to his skin's pallor. His eyes were almost watery and yet sharply focused. Not the sort of person whose gaze was comfortable when directed at you.

"Are you another demon hunter?" Grant asked quietly and bluntly.

For some reason, the bluntness surprised Angie. She'd assumed he'd want to dance around the obvious, given his comments up to now.

"I'm not," she said. "I'm a psychic." At least that was why she was here. He didn't need to know anything more than that.

"I don't believe in psychics," he said.

She smiled. "That doesn't really affect my abilities, one way or the other, Mr. Grant. And if you'd rather I didn't help you find your daughter, I can leave." If they were going to be blunt…

"I'm uncomfortable invading my daughter's privacy by letting a stranger into her room," Grant said.

She had to work hard not to react to that. He had offered his daughter up as a sacrifice to a demon, but he was uncomfortable invading her privacy? Right.

"I can attempt to pick up something from items you have down here. A coat maybe? Something she's worn recently. Perhaps Carmen can bring something down from her room that she's in regular contact with?"

In all honesty, Angie didn't want to invade the girl's privacy either. She wanted to find her and ensure she was safe from any and all demon-dealing people in her life. But Angie knew exactly how much she could pick up with her skills, and she was reluctant to "see" that much about someone without their permission.

It was one of the reasons she'd spent so many years training this particular skill. She still got readings occasionally just by brushing up against someone, but only if that someone had some sort of tie back to her or someone she cared about. With absolute strangers, it took effort to read them now. An effort she could dampen if needs be.

"I'll have Carmen show you to my daughter's room," Grant said. "The sooner she can be found the better."

Angie kept her expression neutral. The change in his attitude could give her whiplash if she wasn't careful.

His lips lifted in a slight smile. "You aren't intimidated by me," he murmured. "Are you, Ms. Jordan?"

"Did you intend to intimidate me?" she asked in return. She knew he had. She knew he was playing games. But she made her living dealing with other people's mental games— mostly games they played with themselves, but the skills transferred.

"You know why I had to bring in demon hunters."

Again a statement. She didn't respond at all this time. The idea that he thought he'd "brought in" the demon hunters was laughable, though. No one brought demon hunters to help. Demon hunters showed up where there were demons about to break loose. The human summoning those demons was usually just a side issue for the hunters.

"You don't think I care for my daughter, so why would I worry about her privacy," Grant continued.

She still didn't comment. He was right. There was no need to say more.

"I do care for her," he said. "No matter what you or Sebastian or the other woman think. I do love her."

Angie assumed the other woman was a reference to Aidan. Aidan would be amused by being referred to that way instead of insulted, so Angie took insult on her behalf. She continued to hold her silence, though. At the moment, Grant's daughter Mara was all that mattered. Grant's excuses and justifications be damned.

"You don't believe me?" he asked.

This time it was a question. "My belief or disbelief doesn't have anything to do with me doing my job," she said. "Any more than your belief in my skills does."

"But I want you to believe me," Grant said.

"I know you do. That still doesn't matter to me."

His mouth ticked at one side. She couldn't tell if it was the beginnings of a snarl or a smile. He controlled the gesture too quickly to reveal more. But she'd hit a nerve, one way or another.

Sebastian remained silent during the exchange. At Grant's faint facial tic, though, Seb took a single step closer to her. She wondered if that was a protective move or if he thought he might have to intervene between them.

Could go either way, she thought, contemplating Grant's expression.

Grant turned his attention to Sebastian. "All that matters is getting my daughter back. Do what you have to do. I won't interfere."

Angie bit her tongue on her response to that last sentence. The demon hunters wouldn't let him interfere in their efforts to prevent a demon escape. Sebastian would stop it, and there wasn't a damned thing Grant could do about it, no matter what deal he'd made with his particular demon.

Demon deals were always tricky things. Demons were tricky things. Which was why she'd rather stick to her little psychic niche and leave the demon work to the hunters.

Sebastian ignored Grant's insinuation that he had much say in this matter, and said, "We'll get on with it then." He motioned Angie toward the door.

What he didn't do was thank Grant for his time, or ask permission to leave, or do any of the polite please-and-thank-you dance that Grant obviously expected. Because the man's eyes narrowed and his jaw tightened. Angie could feel the animosity pumping from him.

She should have attempted to shake his hand in parting, to get a reading on him. That was one of the things Sebastian had brought her here to do. But every part of her rebelled at the thought of touching Grant. She'd apologize to Sebastian later. She just couldn't touch Grant. Something about him… Those long fingers.

No, even the idea of getting that close to him made her skin crawled.

Whatever Grant might be, he wasn't a man to be underestimated. He was playing a game with them. Not just the obvious one of wanting his daughter back to finish his deal with the demon. There was more to the man than they knew.

And she'd be happy to leave whatever that *more* was to Sebastian.

Once they ensured Mara Grant was safe from the threat that was her own father.

CHAPTER FOUR

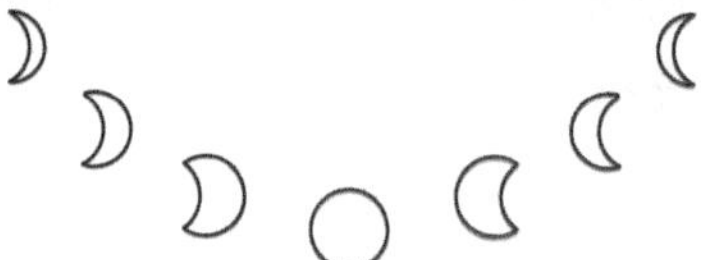

Carmen met them in the hall, reappearing from the stairs she'd disappeared down as if someone had called her. And perhaps Grant had. Angie hadn't seen a way to do that, but in the dark room she hadn't really been looking.

Light spilling in from the hallway window seemed overly bright after the dim study. She blinked a few times to adjust to the glare. Outside of Grant's presence, she felt like she could breathe again and gulped in a large lungful of the neutrally-scented air to cleanse her senses.

"We need to see Mara's room," Sebastian said. "Thank you, Carmen."

Angie didn't miss how much more polite and friendly he was with Carmen than he was with Grant.

Carmen glanced at the closed study door once before

saying, "This way, Mr. Sebastian." She glanced at Angie and said, "I'm sorry I didn't get your name earlier."

Angie waved away the apology. "It's a difficult time. I'm Angela Jordan. But please, call me Angie."

"Ms. Angie. Thank you for your help." She flicked a glance at the closed door again. Then gestured back toward the front of the house and the main staircase they'd passed earlier.

Carmen led them up two flights, the stairs switching back on themselves so that each landing gave Angie a brief view of that floor. Nothing she saw gave any more personal impression of the home occupants than the downstairs hallway had. There were only neutral landscape paintings on the walls—some she suspected might be quite valuable, though she didn't know anything about art—tables topped with single pieces of *object d'art*, but no personal photos or knickknacks, pale green walls, rug-covered hardwood floors. Spotless and nearly empty.

Either Carmen was the best housekeeper on the planet, or Grant allowed no signs of people actually living here in any place visitors might happen to see.

It was one thing to keep a neutral first floor, but the rest of the house?

On the third floor, Carmen turned to the back of the townhouse. There were two doors on this level, one facing the front, one the back. The one at the back opened onto a largish room and for the first time, Angie saw signs of a real person living here. The room was cluttered with clothes and toys—most of which were too young for a twelve-year-old, but at least it was something—and all the paraphernalia one might expect in a preteen girl's bedroom.

There were posters on the pale yellow walls, boy bands Angie didn't know. The rugs here were orange and fluffy. The large bed had a white headboard and the duvet topping the big mattress was a mix of burnt orange, yellows, and reds. A huge window bracketed by wispy white curtains took up most of the back wall, giving great views of the surrounding townhouses and letting in lots of light.

An overlarge dresser sat against one wall, and double doors stood open on a walk-in closet next to the dresser. Against the opposite wall, another open door led into a bathroom.

Angie wandered to the dresser, covered with scattered makeup cases, a hair brush, some hair clips, and a collection of stuffed animals lined against the wall. There wasn't a large mirror on the dresser, but a smallish makeup mirror had been turned face down on one side of the dresser top. The drawers were all neatly closed but for one which had some t-shirts falling over the side.

The floor inside the walk-in closet was choked with dropped clothing—mostly t-shirts and jeans, though there were a few skirts and pretty, girly dresses hanging on the circling rails, and a collection of sneakers any shoe connoisseur would envy.

The room smelled faintly of something citrusy, and while it wasn't perfectly tidy, there was no dust, no empty food cartons, no rug stains. The bathroom was clean, and the bed linens looked fresh. Clean—but mussed and lived in.

The place felt like a haven of reality and realness in the otherwise museum of a home. This was where someone actually lived.

Angie was careful not to touch anything, keeping one hand wrapped around her purse strap where it crossed her chest, as she took in a visual of the room first, wanting to glean what she could of Mara before moving to a deeper psychic reading. What she got was the impression of a girl on the cusp of being a teenager, yet still clinging to some of her childhood loves. A girl wanting to grow up and yet not quite ready to give up being a child.

There were books stacked on the small bedside table, but no bookshelf in the room. She wandered close to read titles. The top one had a funny cover featuring a large, bald cartoon man in his underwear and a red cape, with two young boys standing next to him looking bemused.

Under that, though, the titles got a lot more adult. One was a college level genetics textbook. Another was a book on curses. The three under that seemed to be about demonology, but she'd have to move the top books to see the titles better. All of them had library labels on the binding.

Angie very deliberately didn't touch the books. She'd save them for last.

Under the watchful gaze of Sebastian and Carmen, she finally reached out to make physical contact with her surroundings. She started at the dresser, with the disorderly makeup.

Opening her psychic senses, she pulled in a deep breath, let it out slowly, rested her hand on the pile of makeup…

She got the impression of a young girl, but a sense of someone older than she looked. Not that she was older than twelve, but that she had more understanding of the world and reality than a typical twelve-year-old. Angie felt longing, too. A wisp of wishing for less of that understanding.

There was a deep sense of…loneliness. Yes. Loneliness. Isolation.

Angie picked up the makeup mirror and carefully looked into the reflective glass on the side that showed things as they are, not the magnified side that would distort the image. The girl who looked back was quite pretty, though at an awkward age. Her nose was just a little bit big for her face, but her cheekbones were cut high, her chin and jaw curved down into a gentle point, creating a lovely heart-shape. Her straight brown hair was pulled back into a messy ponytail, with stray strands brushing her pale temple. Her eyes were a deep blue and fringed by dark lashes. Her lips were pursed as she practiced applying lipstick. Her mouth seemed a bit large for her face, like her nose, but all features she'd grow in to.

Mara Grant was a charmingly lovely child. A child who had seen and knew too much, and would prefer to just be a child.

Angie sighed, trying not to tear up. She'd had a great childhood—despite the demons and some early issues with controlling her magic—and a close family who'd gone out of their way to keep her safe and get her the teachers she'd needed to control all of her gifts, even though everyone but her mother was mundane. They'd looked after her, and ensured she had as normal a life as possible. Even her rotten brothers. They'd had a typical sibling relationship with a lot of love and lots of fighting and lots of annoyance, all wrapped up in a familial hug.

Her heart ached for the lonely child in the mirror, practicing makeup on her own, trying to pretend she didn't know too much for her age.

"Where's her mother?" Angie asked quietly. Because she was deep into her psychic senses, her normally deep voice had dropped even lower. She hoped Carmen had heard her.

Sebastian, to her surprise, answered. "According to Grant, she died when Mara was a year old. In a car accident."

Angie closed her eyes and concentrated on that thought. Did Mara remember any impressions of her mother? She'd been a baby, so she wouldn't remember her directly, but maybe she had a sense of her.

The impression Angie got made her gasp. Frowning, she opened her eyes and stared at the mirror. She saw her own reflection now, not Mara's. She was too deep in thought to concentrate.

Had she really felt…?

"Mara's mother has been dead for eleven years?" she asked, just to be sure.

"According to Grant, yes," Sebastian said. There was a note in his voice. A question that wasn't obvious to anyone who didn't know him.

He must have heard something in her voice, too.

She kept it to herself. She'd discuss this with him after they'd left the house. Instead, she moved on to the closet.

Mara might be lonely, but she was not without a substantial wardrobe. Here, Angie picked up a sense of urgency. A feeling that time had run out as Mara scrambled through her belongings. Angie had a flash of clothes being stuffed into a backpack, but not a traveling bag, a school bag. Books and folders scattered across the floor of the closet as small hands pushed t-shirts and jeans down to the bottom of the black backpack. Angie blinked away the image and looked for the school books but didn't see them anywhere.

She came out of the closet and surveyed the room. The bed gave her images of restless sleep. She couldn't tell how many nights, whether it was one night of restlessness or many, but Mara hadn't slept well here before she disappeared. Angie searched inside the bedside table, still careful not to touch the books on top of it.

"Does Mara have a cellphone?" she asked. Her voice was still too deep, but the sound at least seemed to carry better with this question.

"She does," Carmen said. "But it's turned off. We've called. It goes right to voicemail. We leave messages."

"But you haven't heard back from her," Angie guessed.

The cellphone wasn't in the bedroom anywhere that she could see. Unless Mara had hidden it in a drawer. Angie went back to the dresser to search the drawer that had been left open with t-shirts falling out. No signs of the phone.

She tried the bathroom. No phone. No more information about where Mara had gone.

One thing was clear, though. Mara had known something bad was happening. She'd felt a sense of impending danger. And the image from the closet left Angie certain the girl had at least planned to run away. Whether she'd succeeded before meeting with a demon was still unclear.

Although, if what Angie had picked up about Mara's mother was right…

Finally, Angie returned to the bed and stared at the pile of library books.

The books would be tricky. Many hands, many impressions. And while Angie had a great deal of control over her psychic gifts, an object that had passed through so many hands and lives was always a complicated thing to tease out. She might not get anything useful if too many others had possessed the books recently, only a headache for her trouble. But the titles under the middle school novel were not typical twelve-year-old reading. She had to at least try.

She pulled in a deep breath to settle her senses, letting her gaze soften as she picked up the kid's book. There was a riot of amusement and laughter and fun associated with that book, from a lot of different children. And more of that sense of longing, very distinctly from Mara.

Angie set the book on the bed and reached for the second in the pile. The genetics book. Here she got mostly interest and curiosity from a number of individuals. One very excited reader—not Mara. A few very uninterested readers. After a few moments, she found Mara's impression of the book.

Curiosity. A touch of…satisfaction? Interest and desire to know more but… Angie shook her head and set the book aside. Whatever Mara had encountered in the genetics text, it wasn't what she'd been looking for. She'd spent only a little time with it and there weren't any big, jolting emotions associated with what she'd learned.

The book on curses proved impossible for Angie to sort out Mara's presence from all the other people who'd handled the book. There was a *lot* of emotional overlay on that one, mostly anger or bitterness, a lot of revenge-minded individuals.

Angie set it aside with a sigh. As a witch, she believed deeply in what a lot of modern lore called the "rule of three," the idea that what you sent out came back to you threefold. She didn't necessarily believe in the "three" part, but she did believe things like curses could backfire on a person, especially a witch, because of this rule.

In fact, she'd recently been learning and practicing a spell that was a practical application of this idea, a mirror spell that sent back whatever someone else sent out. It was one of those neutral spells that could be a blessing or a curse, depending on the initial person's intent. Angie liked those kinds of spells.

She didn't mess with curses. But from a philosophical standpoint, she liked the idea of someone "getting back what they gave out."

The next book in the pile was a hardback encased in one of the plastic cover protectors libraries used to keep books in good shape for longer periods of time. The cover itself was simple enough, a dark brown with a gold leaf title in the middle of a fancy golden scroll frame.

An Encyclopedia of Demonic Rituals.

Angie shook her head. How the hell a public library had gotten a copy of this book was beyond her. Maybe they thought it was a fantasy, a fiction book designed to seem like non-fiction. Like the *Encyclopedia of Things that Never Where* or the *Encyclopedia of Faeries* or the dragon version with a similar title. Books designed to be fun and amusing. Not *actual* recitations of real things that existed in the real world.

The library had gotten that very wrong with this book.

She carefully lifted the volume, wondering if Sebastian had spotted it before now. It was the kind of book demon hunters looked out for so they could get it off the street and safely ensconced in The Bookstore—a magical bookshop that bought and sold just this kind of thing. But they were careful to whom they sold the dangerous books. The proprietor had a good sense of who should and should not possess a book on demonic rituals.

A twelve-year-old human child who seemed to have no magic powers or signs of an otherworldly nature was *not* someone who should possess this book.

Angie carefully leafed through the pages, letting her gaze go soft and blurred at the edges. She'd read this book before, years ago, when she'd initially gotten involved with the demon hunters. Before she'd tried to pull back and insisted Sebastian and the others leave her in peace. She didn't need to know the information in the book, the various ceremonies it described, the paraphernalia it outlined as requirements for summoning demons. Even the author of the book understood what was really involved in calling, controlling, and fighting off demons. And it wasn't all the *stuff*.

It was will. Pure and simple. The will to do it.

And if a person's will wasn't as strong as the demon's…

The demon won.

CHAPTER FIVE

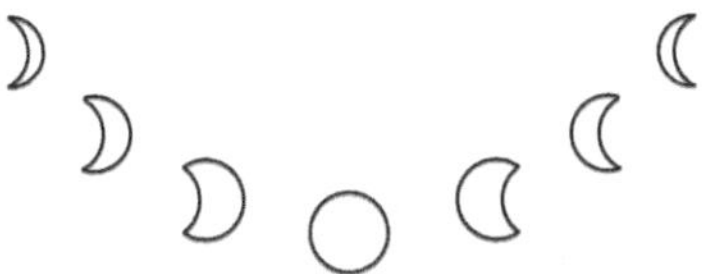

The paragraphs of text, the images printed on the page, all of it blurred together as Angie looked to a deeper level, trying to see what Mara had wanted—or used —this book for. Had she been calling a demon of her own to counter her father's sick plot?

Without conscious thought, Angie stopped on a page, and a sense of Mara's agitation filled her. Setting her fingers against the image on that page without looking at it, Angie let the sense of Mara fill her. Shock and hurt. But not surprise? Fear. A lot of fear. But also determination. And…

Angie pulled in a breath, let it out slowly, trying to understand what she was feeling. A sense of expectation maybe. Like Mara knew, before she'd found this image, what was happening? Angie couldn't be certain. There were a lot of emotions tied into this moment for Mara, and parsing them out proved complicated.

An image sprang up from the sensory feel. An image of an altar in a dark room. An altar topped with an animal skull of some small mammal with horns, a copper plate, a scattering of rune tiles too blurred for her to read the runes, a lantern that appeared to be made from bone, though she couldn't tell if it was real bone or not, and a few burning candles. A pentagram carved into the wood of the altar and filled in with gold leaf. An open book beside the copper plate. Some dried herbs behind the animal skull. A black robe tossed on the floor near the altar.

The image panned out and Angie saw clearly the circle traced in chalk on a wooden floor. The four cardinal points were marked with additional drawings of pentagrams and skulls and red candles set inside the images.

It was an elaborate set up. A blend of ordinary witchy paraphernalia mixed with the Christian conceptions of the devil. A relatively ordinary type of set up for someone attempting to summon a demon, especially if they believed the demon they called was the devil of Christian lore. The demon hunters saw set ups like this a lot because most humans, in the U.S. in particular, thought all this was needed to summon demons. They mixed their knowledge and myths together and came up with this.

Which was why the image was also in the book. An example of a typical set up for summoning demons.

Angie let her gaze sharpen on the 2-D picture beneath her fingertips. It was, down to the placement of the skull at the precise angle and the way the black robe was tossed to one side, a reproduction of what Mara had seen in real life. The only odd point was the bone lantern. That wasn't in the image, but it had been something Mara saw on the altar.

Angie frowned. Grant hadn't struck her as the clichéd summoner of demons. Well, in some ways he was, but maybe she was giving him more credit than he deserved. She'd assumed he'd have enough knowledge to set up his summoning space to his own tastes, not copy them so precisely from a book. But Mara had seen almost this exact image recreated in a dark room. And she'd realized what her father was up to.

Poor kid.

Something still felt off about it all, but Angie couldn't put her finger on what was bothering her. Not precisely enough to put it into words yet. She'd have to think about this a bit more.

Something to do with stage setting…? The lantern?

She finished flipping through the book, but she knew Mara had stopped on that image and not gone further. Setting the Encyclopedia aside, she moved to the next book down. A fictional listing of different demons. This was the kind of thing writers and artists used for inspiration, not anything that reflected real life. As Angie flipped through the pages, she sensed Mara had realized that about halfway through and put the book down.

The final book in the pile, however, was not a fictious listing of demon types. Somehow, the library had gotten another book that should not be in the hands of ordinary humans.

Where the hell was this library? She'd better send

Sebastian to check their stacks for any more of these dangerous volumes.

She studied the cover before picking it up. The title read simply *Demon*. It was an illustrated listing of the different demon species and the realms the writer had been aware of.

This particular book was an impressive collection of knowledge, as complete as almost anything available. The author had missed only two demon realms in her research, and had only minor mistakes in the lineages. But overall, the book was an excellent reference guide to demons, their realms, and their tactics for escape.

This was a rare book. Only about two dozen copies existed in the world. The one she'd seen at The Bookstore wasn't even for sale. An interested party could rent it for a short period of study, but unlike a library borrow, they couldn't remove the book from The Bookstore premises. They had to read and study it in the store. It was too rare and valuable.

And real.

Angie sealed her senses off from the book before touching it. She needed to brace for its impact. She'd handled the version kept in The Bookstore, but the first time had been a dramatic learning experience. She'd nearly passed out after being swamped by too many sensory images—impressions from the blood used as ink, from the sacrifices made to create the book, from the author, from the demon who'd aided the author's research… So much input it had overwhelmed Angie's psychic senses and fried her synapses for a good week.

She'd been much more careful picking the book up the second time.

She was equally careful now. Even the cover had the potential to carry a deep psychic imprint. Angie didn't want to pull in everything. She needed specifics and that meant focus. She put up a mental protection circle around her psychic senses, not unlike the kind of circle she'd draw to keep her safe while working certain kinds of magic. She'd learned that trick in her late teens from a very powerful witch, the bruja who'd been her first real teacher, and it had saved her sanity more than once over the years.

Carefully, she nudged the book around, touching it as little as possible as she angled the cover to show it to Sebastian. He nodded, his expression hooded and difficult to read. Carmen frowned and looked between them without comment. She folded her hands in front of her, her knuckles white as she clenched her fingers together.

Angie returned her focus to the book. The pale leather cover felt strange against her fingers, conflicting with the visual impression of it. Slick and slimy despite appearing dry and cracked. An odd disconnect that made her instincts balk. She nearly pulled her hand away. The covers for each copy of the book had been made from the skin of a sacrifice—rumored human, but Angie got the sense of something more mundane like lamb or goat for this particular copy—and the title had been branded into the leather with a hot iron rather than etched in with inks or leafing. The faint stink of the blood used for ink made her nose twitch even before she opened the book.

The library tag on the spine looked completely anachronistic against that strange cover.

Angie slowly cracked the stiff spine, keeping the book mostly on the bedside table as she braced it open and began flipping through the pages. She focused on the images, letting her instincts guide her while her psychic senses were controlled. Still, the book was difficult to look at, difficult to touch. More so this time than it had been in The Bookstore, she realized. Either The Bookstore's magic kept the thing better controlled, or Angie didn't have as solid a lock on her psychic senses as she'd assumed before opening the thing.

She double checked the mental circle she'd constructed. Still in place and protecting her.

Strange.

She touched the book as little as possible as she continued to turn pages. The images of individual demons were beautifully, horribly well-rendered. The artist so skilled the demons looked like they might come off the page. There was a strange 3-D effect that made the demons appear to move as the pages were turned, too, and that added to the sense that they might reach through the page and grab the reader.

How the hell had Mara looked at this book and not completely freaked out? If Angie had been a normal twelve-year-old this would have given her nightmares.

Though, by the time she was twelve, Angie had seen much worse and in real life, not just a book, so she didn't have the same reference point as other twelve-year-olds.

The text surrounding the images was mostly in Latin with

sections translated into English and French. Angie knew enough Latin to read the book if needs be, but she'd read most of it before. She didn't focus on the text too closely. And she tried not to focus on the drawings too closely either. She slowly turned pages and waited for something to strike her as important.

When it did, she gasped.

With her psychic senses shut down, she hadn't actually expected such a strong reaction, but she hit an image and everything in her froze. For a full ten seconds, she couldn't move even to take her hand from the page.

The image was of a Molder demon, one of the more powerful from a realm full of powerful entities. Anything that wasn't powerful in this realm—called Belhasten by the author of the book—got eaten.

Molder demons were large, and slim, almost willowy. Some looked skeletal, but with skin stretched over their bones. Their limbs were too long in proportion to their bodies. They were pale, light gray most of the time, though some shaded closer to charcoal. Their fingers were tipped with ferocious, long claws. Their toes similarly tipped. And while they didn't have venom in their claws like some demons, they could still tear a being apart with ease.

The image in the book had black eyes with a red pupil and was drawn smiling so that the rows of sharp teeth were easy to see. Around its narrow head hung long, tentacle-like hair. And unlike many demons, it actually had rags of clothe hanging around its body and head like clothing. The tattered garments in the drawing were shaded dark and hung on the demon like a cloak or a monk's robe.

Almost against her will, she reached toward the image and some weird trick of the drawing made it look like the demon was reaching back for her. Its smile seemed to grow, and its teeth looked like they elongated as she watched.

Whoa. That wasn't really happening. It had to be a trick. The very same image in the book she'd looked through before hadn't done that.

Her heart hammered so hard she thought Sebastian might hear it. Blood rushed through her veins, and her adrenaline spiked. A faint whisper of sound moved across her inner ear like nails on a chalkboard. She shivered and winced in response, trying to block the sound.

"Angie?"

Sebastian's quiet voice cut off the strange whisper, giving her some relief from its irritating grate.

"Fine," she murmured. She sensed him moving closer and raised a hand to stop him. "Give me a minute." If he got too close right now, her senses would short circuit. She knew him too well to cut him out of her sensory perception. And right now, anything added to her sensory intake risked overwhelming her.

She studied the image, staring at it. Why this picture? This demon? Had this been the demon Mara stopped at? The one she either recognized or had been looking for?

Without opening her psychic senses, Angie couldn't be sure. Her mundane instincts were on high alert but the adrenaline coursing through her system was fear, fueling a flight instinct she had trouble ignoring. She couldn't concentrate around that drive to run away, couldn't pinpoint why this image had stopped her.

She fisted her hands, then reached under her jacket sleeve and gripped the pentagram dangling from her bracelet. Rubbing her fingers around the small circle, she focused on it, on its power, its protective spells, letting that sense of power move through her.

She had to open her psychic senses if she was going to find out why this image had called to her. But everything in her balked at the idea.

Bracing her legs and gripping the pentagram tight, she mentally cut a line through the protection circle in her mind, releasing it and opening her psychic senses once more.

The demon on the page lunged up at her, screaming in triumph.

CHAPTER SIX

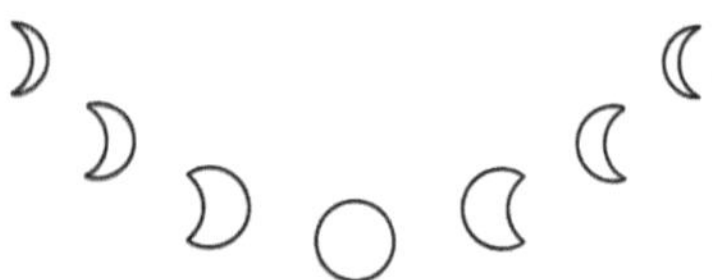

$\mathcal{A}$ngie screeched and stumbled back from the book as claw-tipped hands reached from the page toward her.

Not possible. Not possible.

The chant moved through her even as her visual senses belied it. But demons couldn't get into this world through a book. They couldn't rip from the page and come into this realm.

Unless she'd triggered a spell…

Images bombarded her then, overwhelming her flight instinct, her own self-preservation instincts. Images of blood and death. The stench of rotting flesh mingling with burning meat. Heat and the glass sharp cuts of lava rock. Screams of pain and torment echoed through her head so loud she couldn't hear above them.

And then the chittering started, that horrid chittering of approaching demons…

She pressed her hands to her ears but that didn't stop the noise. The demon from the page rose up in front of her inner vision, laughing, its sharp teeth sounding like knives scraping against each other.

"Coming for you," it said, staring at her. "Angela."

She screamed. And stumbled away from the vision, coming up hard against something solid and warm.

"I've got you," Sebastian said, his arms coming around her, his deep voice breaking through the cacophony in her head.

She let him hold her upright and turned all her focus and concentration toward cutting off the vision and locking the demon out. Slow breaths scraped over her raw throat. Her fingers pressed so tight against the pentagram charm she was sure she was leaving a bruise of the charm in her skin. She rebuilt the circle, calling up power, beseeching the elements as she focused on drawing that line between her and the danger. She kept her eyes closed, visualizing the blue light as she drew the circle clockwise around her extra-sensory perceptions.

She heard the demon screaming, screeching, knew instinctively it was reaching for her, trying to get to her before the circle closed. She almost wavered, almost lost concentration and dropped the circle.

A will stronger than her own seemed to reinforce her focus. She grabbed onto that will, used it to maintain her concentration. She brought the line around and connected it with the starting point, forming a complete shape. A flare of blue light rose in her mind's eyes as the circle closed.

And the chaos cut off abruptly, the vision gone.

She kept her eyes closed as she concentrated on slowing her pulse, regulating her breathing. Sebastian's heat surrounding her, the faint scent of his aftershave, gave her a solid hold on reality to cling to as she pulled herself together.

Carefully, she opened her eyes and looked at the book. The image of the demon was still in view, though she was several feet away now. She realized with a start the drawing no longer depicted the Molder demon as smiling. It was snarling, its claws raised as if it was scraping at something.

She shuddered.

"You okay," Sebastian said against her ear.

His voice was pitched so low she was sure only she could hear him. "I'll explain later," she murmured back.

"Got the gist," he said. Then over his shoulder. "No need to worry, Carmen. Happens sometimes."

"You're a bruja?" Carmen murmured.

"Witch," Angie agreed. "Not technically a bruja."

There were differences in the types of magic real brujas used. Though the word meant witch in Spanish, it referred to a particular type of witch in the witchy community, and Angie liked to ensure that distinction was noted, especially since her earliest mentor had been a bruja. She felt disloyal to her teacher if she didn't make it clear she wasn't one.

"Are you okay, Ms. Angie?"

"I'm fine, Carmen. Sorry if I scared you."

"You aren't the scary thing in this house."

Angie snorted at the understatement.

"Can you stand on your own?" Sebastian asked, again quietly against her ear.

She hadn't realized how much she was relying on him to support her weight until that moment. Embarrassed, she lifted away from him. "Thanks. And sorry if I scared you."

"Not the first time," he said, a rueful note in his voice. "Stay back. I'll sort the book."

"Take both." She didn't have to explain which ones to him. "They don't belong in a public library."

"Couldn't agree more," he said, though his tone was distant now.

He approached the volumes slowly, keeping the full force of his focus on them. After a moment of staring, he reached out and closed the still open *Demon*. Very faintly, Angie swore she heard a roar of protest. Or maybe that was just her imagination. She didn't dare open her psychic senses to find out.

With equal care, he picked up both books and looked around the room. After a moment, he went into the bathroom and came out with the books inside a plastic garbage bag, the small type that went into little bathroom garbage cans.

"Mind if I take this, Carmen?" he asked, holding up the bag.

"Take what you need, Mr. Sebastian."

Angie frowned at the woman for a long moment. "Carmen…" She tried to choose her words carefully. "Do you have somewhere you might go for an extended vacation?

Maybe for a couple of weeks? Can you take that much time off?"

This wasn't a safe house and with only Carmen and Grant here, after what she'd just experienced, Angie was a lot more worried for Carmen.

"I have been considering it," Carmen said. She glanced down the hall, toward the staircase. "My sister lives in Connecticut. I could go visit her for a few weeks. She's had some health issues. I'm sure Mr. Grant won't object. He prefers to be alone right now anyway."

Carmen met Angie's gaze. There was a lot of unspoken meaning in that look. Angie understood. Given the coziness of Mara's bedroom compared to the starkness of the rest of the house, Mara had to have had a friend here and Angie didn't have to guess that friend—that family—was Carmen. But if Carmen and Mara were close, Carmen was a potential tool for Grant to get to Mara.

Angie wondered why Grant hadn't used Carmen already in his quest to find his daughter. Maybe because Sebastian had gotten here before the man could.

"I think a visit with your sister sounds a lovely idea," Sebastian said. "Difficult times. Family is always good."

Carmen nodded. "Yes. I'll make the arrangements today. Thank you." She turned out of the room, waiting for them to follow.

But not before Angie caught the wetness of tears in her dark eyes.

"You okay now?" Sebastian asked quietly. "Good to leave?"

"We have things to discuss, so yeah, this is a good time to leave."

He nodded and motioned her to proceed him to the door. On the way out, though, she swung past the dresser and pocketed one of the lipsticks scattered there. At Sebastian's questioning frown, she put a finger to her lips and then mouthed later.

They didn't see Grant before they left, which surprised her. She'd have assumed he'd come out and demand information, insist on a detailed account of what they'd found.

Carmen solved that mystery when she nodded back toward the study and said, "He had to take a phone call from one of his political associates right after we went upstairs. But I am sure he'll be in touch."

As far as Angie knew, Grant didn't have a way to "be in touch" with Sebastian. Hunters didn't just hand out their cellphone numbers to everyone they met. In fact, they were extremely picky about who could contact them. But since Sebastian's hunt was ongoing—he'd have to deal with this demon Grant had summoned sooner rather than later—she assumed he'd just show back up at Grant's door when he was ready.

The fact that Grant wouldn't set aside a business phone call to learn what they'd found out about his daughter struck Angie as cold. But also sort of in character for the man she'd met that afternoon. His daughter was a pawn in a plan, not an actual person he cared about. Of course some power broker was more important.

Back out on the street, Angie took several deep breaths and let the evening air cleanse her shaking spirit. The temperature had dropped, putting a bite in the coolness that was a refreshing jolt after the nothingness of the house and her encounter with the demon book. She still carried a sense of Mara's loneliness and her fear with her, emotions she'd carry with her for a while. But the fresh air and the normal sounds of the city helped distract her from holding onto the girl's emotions.

Hazards of the job.

She pulled in another deep breath, let it out slowly, then faced Sebastian. "Thanks for your help in there."

"You going to explain?"

"When we're somewhere safe."

"Where?"

One of the safest places in New York City. For her kind anyway.

"Dana's Cauldron."

CHAPTER SEVEN

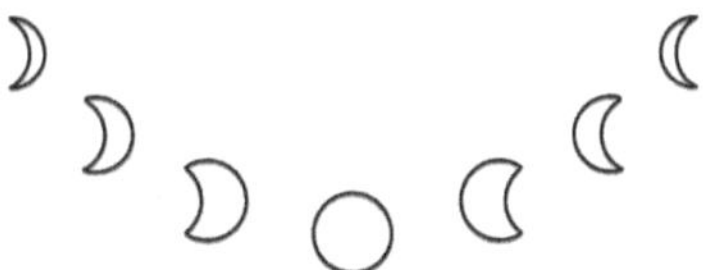

 ana's Cauldron wasn't just Angie's place of work. The three-level brick storefront in the Village, dedicated to all things witchy and pagan, was her favorite place in the world outside of her family home in New Mexico.

Walking through the door, the inevitable scent of patchouli hit her like a welcome home. Although, she never burned patchouli in her home. She didn't really have much of the supposed witch paraphernalia in her apartment. She had a small altar she used for the occasional commune with the Goddess—she was a pagan theologically as well as being a witch—but as far as home décor went, she preferred the southwestern styles she'd grown up with and that was reflected in her personal space.

Dana's Cauldron, on the other hand, was an ode to all things stereotypically pagan. At least on the first level.

The darker lighting was designed to simulate muted candlelight—though not so dark it hid the shelves of purchasable wears. The hardwood floor creaked a little when customers walked over it. The walls were hung with colorful swaths of material and posters of various gods and goddesses from around the world. The wooden shelves and tables were stacked with candles, crystals, incense, and the other necessaries a pagan might require. More shelves were filled with books on various spiritual pursuits and histories of the different pagan religions, along with some more supernatural fair that dealt with ghosts and psychics and all manner of otherworldly topics—and all of it fun. On this level, there were no dangerous books.

Decorative wrought iron tree stands with silver and beaded jewelry hanging from the branches stood on glass cases near the cashier's desk, cases which were crowded with more jewelry and some of the rarer Tarot decks. Another glass case held athames and various crystal and stick wands alongside a few realistic crystal balls. Small copper scrying bowls stacked against decorative pewter goblets. And little fountains scattered throughout the space filled in the soothing swoosh of moving water between the sounds of soft world music playing over the speakers.

It was a cacophony of pagan joy. And Angie loved it.

She stepped through the front door, the little wooden wind chimes overhead clonking their announcement that a new person had entered. The woman behind the counter spotted Angie immediately and waved.

"You're not working tonight," Laura said. "What brings you in?"

Laura Fuentes was an older pagan who'd been working at Dana's since it opened in the late sixties. She had let her more extreme hippy apparel go sometime in the early eighties —according to her—but she still favored bellbottom jeans and embroidered poet shirts. She kept her steel gray hair in two long, thick braids that hung over her still-strong shoulders. And she always wore a choker with a pentagram embossed in the brown leather and a small shark's tooth hanging from the band.

The choker itself was a present from her friends when she'd come out as trans back in the early seventies. She'd transitioned since then, but she kept the choker as a reminder of her coming out and the support she'd had. The shark's tooth was a more recent addition to the choker. She'd once claimed to a customer that she'd gotten it from a shark she'd communed with in the Pacific Ocean who'd offered it to her as a gift. Angie knew for a fact it had come from a cheap jewelry store a few blocks away.

"I need to do a little personal work," Angie said, stopping at the counter to give Laura a hug. "Is there a room free?"

The psychics who worked at Dana's Cauldron shared a series of rooms on the third floor where they conducted private readings for clients. Each room was covered with either a beaded curtain or a velvet drape which presented both privacy and a sense of not being completely cut off from the outside world. The semi-open rooms were to ensure both the customer and the psychic's safety. There were small, innocuous cameras throughout the level, monitored from the manager's office on the second floor, as an additional layer of security.

Dana's Cauldron was a safe space, and the owners and managers went out of their way to ensure that safety for everyone who entered.

"Room three is open." Laura glanced around Angie to Sebastian.

He hovered close to a nearby shelf, studying the glass statues of faeries and wizards as he tried to look innocuous. Angie realized he must be using some of his will to keep up that appearance because he *did* come across as significantly less imposing than usual. There were three women near where he stood and none of them seemed to take note of him. Given how gorgeous he was, and how large and imposing he could seem, and how many looks he drew when he wasn't trying, the fact that those near him didn't even appear to notice him was a telling sign.

"New client?" Laura asked. She narrowed her eyes as she studied Sebastian, then gasped. "Wow. That's some aura. I wouldn't have realized if I hadn't taken a deeper look." She frowned. Then her eyebrows shot up. "Oh. I see." She blinked at Angie. "I thought you didn't...do that work anymore."

"I don't," Angie said firmly. "This is a special case."

"You know I've heard that before, right?"

Angie opened her mouth to protest but Laura raised her hands, palms up.

"Not my place to comment. Take room three. Signal me if you need help. We'll be up to support you in a blink."

Angie's heart tightened. She gave Laura another hug. "Thank you," she murmured before pulling back. "I'm fine. But thank you."

She motioned to Sebastian and led him up the wooden stairs at the rear of the store.

When they hit the second-floor landing, the lovely scents of brewing tea and various cakes and pastries hit, making Angie's stomach growl.

Sebastian chuckled. "I'll feed you after we're finished here," he promised.

Angie rolled her eyes. She'd never made any attempt to disguise her appetite and the amount of food she ate, and for some reason, Sebastian found her appreciation of food amusing.

She cast a longing glance toward the little café that took up half this floor. She could use a cup of tea. Maybe with a shot of Tequila in it.

First business, then food and tea. And possibly Tequila.

On the third-floor landing, they met another one of the psychics who worked at Dana's. Bianca Martin was a curvy, bouncy blonde with a personality to match. She'd wrapped herself in her "uniform"—a black flowing skirt decorated with stars and moons, a black poet's blouse and a black leather corset that showed off her magnificent curves and creamy pale skin. Her blond hair was piled on top of her head in a loose, sexy bun. Her makeup was, as always, a work of art—tonight a smoky eye with muted lips—and she wore enough jewelry to jingle as she approached.

"Ang!" she greeted. "Didn't know you were working tonight, lovely."

"Just a bit of private business," Angie said, exchanging a hug with Bianca. "How're the readings going?"

"Fabulously!" Bianca threw her arms wide. "The spirits are in a fine mood, and so am I."

"Who's the new boyfriend?" Angie grinned. Bianca went through men with the *joie de vive* of a French widow.

"Patrick," she said. "A man with appetites almost as big as my own." She glanced at Sebastian and her grin grew. "Although, I could be persuaded to move on."

Sebastian raised his brows, a slight, befuddled smile curving his lips.

Angie shook her head. "This one is complicated. I'd stick with Patrick if I were you."

Bianca glanced between them. "Is he taken?"

"He is," Sebastian said, sounding amused rather than annoyed that they were talking about him as if he weren't there.

Angie cut him a look. "You are?"

His brows rose higher. "You have to ask?"

Her cheeks heated and she hurriedly looked away.

Bianca nodded in a knowing way that made Angie's cheeks even warmer. "I see," Bianca said. "Complicated."

Angie wanted to protest. She hadn't even seen Sebastian in over a year. But it was too…well… Complicated.

Bianca hugged her again and kissed her on both cheeks, a

move that required Angie to duck down a little. In her ear, Bianca whispered, "Complicated can be a good thing. Also, in this case, a gorgeous thing."

She patted Angie's shoulders with both hands, then moved toward the stairs. "Have fun you two beautiful people." She winked at Sebastian on the way past, which brought out his most charming grin. Bianca fanned herself on the way down the stairs.

"Hmm," Angie commented.

"Indeed," Sebastian said, his gaze softening on her.

She turned away. She couldn't think about all this right now. She had a missing girl to find.

The long hall was bracketed by seven rooms the various psychics and mediums could use with clients, with an eighth room near the back they used as a huge storage closet, personal locker space, and the occasional changing room if someone had to come to work in street clothes and had to "psychic up" their appearance. The corridor was lit by wall sconces at night, to give it a more eerie feel. During the day, the light from the far, uncovered window brightened the place up a lot. The wooden floor was polished and the walls were decorated with more pictures of beautiful gods and goddesses and mythical beings. The air was thick with the scents of various incenses and the soft murmurs of people from behind most of the covered doorways.

Angie went directly to the last room on the right, next to the storage closet, one of the smaller rooms with a picture of a moon goddess outside. A deep blue velvet curtain decorated with intricate silver Celtic knots covered the entrance. Angie pushed it aside and motioned Sebastian to proceed her into the room. He stood to the side as she followed him in and flipped a switch on the wall, turning the lights on. She adjusted the knob until the room was a comfortable level, bright enough to see and not have it feel too intimate, low enough she'd be able to scry without light interference.

"Will the lipstick be enough of a personal item?" Sebastian asked. He'd seen her scry before.

"Should be," she said as she pulled out a large copper bowl from under a wooden side table. "I got a strong sense of Mara from it, and a full image of her using it."

She carried the bowl in two hands to the large circular table in the center of the room, then pulled out a decorative silver flask from under the cabinet. She'd tell a client these were sacred waters, extracted from a holy place in the East, or perhaps from South America, depending on the client, but in reality, it was just ordinary distilled water bought from the local grocery store.

She emptied enough water into the copper bowl to ensure it was half filled, then capped the flask and return it to the side table. Next, she set a paper map of the city beside the bowl. It was possible Mara wasn't in New York anymore, but this was a place to start. She retrieved a large crystal hanging from a silver chain from her overlarge purse, setting the crystal on top of the map.

Finally, she pulled the pilfered lipstick out of her jacket pocket and set it next to the bowl, opposite side from the map and crystal. She took the strap of her purse over her head and set it to one side on an unused chair, then removed her jacket and draped it over the purse. There was a coat hanger near the entrance, for customer coats and bags, but Angie wasn't staying long enough for that much formality.

She kept her gaze on the scrying bowl as she settled her senses, letting the familiar feel of her surroundings sink into her subconscious, the deeply ingrained incense scents, the hardwood floor under foot, the soft murmur of voices from other rooms. The setting gave her the sense of safety and protection that she needed after her day.

Between accidentally breaching a demon realm in the Botanical Garden and then the demonic attack from the book, she was more shaken than she was prepared to admit to Sebastian. A part of her wanted to run away and hide in her apartment with a bottle of something alcoholic, a big bag of tortilla chips and guacamole, and a steady stream of innocuous cooking shows on the TV.

The thought of opening her psychic senses again gave her a pain in her stomach.

She unconsciously rubbed the pentagram hanging from her bracelet, letting the familiar charm settle her nerves. She was safe here in Dana's Cauldron. Every year on All Soul's Day, the witches who owned the place reset a protective circle around it, adding renewed strength and energy to the spell. It was a spell designed to welcome in those who meant no harm and chase away those who intended mischief—including demons and other dangerous preternatural creatures.

In the two years Angie had been working here, she'd never once had cause to feel scared or threatened by anything or anyone. Dana's Cauldron was as safe an establishment as it could possibly be, as safe as any place in New York. It was Angie's second home. And her sense of security here finally helped her release all the tension and terror of the day.

With a final cleansing breath, she dropped the protective circle keeping her psychic senses contained and stepped up to the scrying bowl.

Time to find Mara.

CHAPTER EIGHT

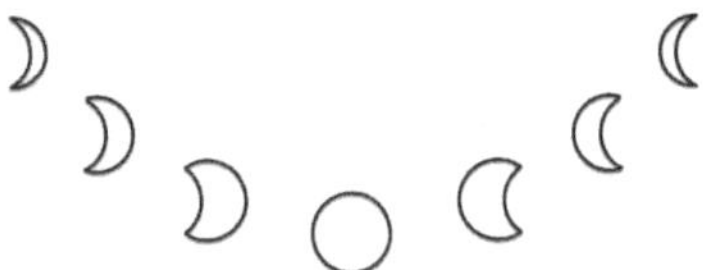

*A*ngie wrapped her hands around the outside edges of the bowl, let her gaze soften, and stared into the dark water. She angled the bowl a few times to ensure she wasn't distracted by any reflective lights, then let her mind fall into the depths.

When she felt settled, she lifted up the lipstick with her right hand and focused on Mara's face, visualizing the girl. She let the sense of Mara's spirit fill her as she concentrated on *seeing* her as she was in that moment.

At first, and for a long minute, the waters stayed clear, showing only the beaten metal at the base of the pot. Then the image darkened, the water going opaque. She let the image unfold, concentrated but not rushing the process, continued to let her sense of Mara's spirit dominate her conscious mind. Under her breath, she murmured a short incantation, an inquiry spell, requesting an answer.

The opaque water cleared again, revealing an image of Mara. The image was softened at the edges by the water but was clearly the girl in whose room Angie had been earlier. She watched, keeping her mind as still as she was able by chanting the short spell again, a kind of focus point to keep her conscious distracted so she could watch the vision before her play out.

Mara was talking urgently to someone Angie couldn't see, gesturing widely and motioning behind her. The girl shook her head hard and stomped her foot, a gesture so full of frustration, so much a sign of her youth, Angie's heart tightened. She ignored the empathetic reaction, keeping her gaze soft as she watched.

The image froze as the background came into clearer view, like a movie on pause. Mara was caught mid-action, her hands out in a sort of beseeching gesture, her gaze turned over her shoulder. Her blue eyes were wide and panicked. Behind her, a large red brick apartment building, the lobby door a solid metal with a metal wire-crossed window giving a glimpse inside. The interior of the lobby looked dark, despite the fact that it was night.

Maybe not a front door, Angie though vaguely. A back door? A door into a basement?

There was a small security light next to the door, but otherwise, the surroundings seemed dimly lit, too dark to see much beyond the building.

Without taking her gaze from the image, Angie lifted the chain attacked to the crystal on her left. She held the crystal up over the map and let it spin and move of its own accord, keeping her concentration on the image of Mara and letting the flow of magic move through her without consciously getting in its way.

She stopped chanting the spell she'd used to hold her concentration and murmured, very quietly, "Where are you, Mara?"

The crystal dropped suddenly onto the map. Angie blinked and straightened away from the copper bowl, pulling in a deep breath. The image inside dissolved back into crystal clear water with an unimpeded view of the beaten metal at the base.

A faint scent of something she couldn't immediately identify lingered even after the image had vanished. A strange reaction given scrying didn't often give her anything but visuals.

She held the scent long enough to ensure she'd recognize it if she encountered it again, then let that last bit of the vision go and looked at the map.

Sebastian came up to study where the crystal had landed as soon as she'd stepped away from the bowl. He was frowning at the location.

She moved the crystal just enough to see what it had landed on. A part of the upper west side of Manhattan, near Inwood. She took note of the cross streets, then leveled a look at Sebastian.

"Why are you frowning?" she asked.

He glanced up. In the dim light, the very faint hint of red in the depths of his brown eyes was easier to see, harder to dismiss as an illusion. All demon hunters, after a time, developed that spark of red in their eyes, a side effect of spending so much time in contact with demons and demon realms. The hunters with brown eyes could hide the effect easier. Most humans convinced themselves the red was just a weird trick of the light against the otherwise ordinary brown. The hunters with lighter eyes had a trickier job of disguising that tell-tale flash of red.

"This—" he pointed to the map, "—is the location of a previous demon fight I had. Maybe…twelve years ago."

Angie didn't miss the relationship to Mara's age. "You think the two are related?"

"Either that, or this building has bad luck built into the bricks."

Angie shivered. There *were* buildings like that in New York, old buildings with nefarious auras. Bad things had happened there, and the very foundations of those buildings had taken in the negative energy. There was a reason ghost tours of New York were so popular.

"I got the impression Mara was urging someone to leave the building with her. She won't be there for long. We should go tonight." So much for her hoped for cup of tea. And Tequila.

And being done with all this after locating Mara.

"We?" Sebastian said.

She sighed. "Until I know she's safe, I can't just walk away. You knew that from the beginning. Bastard," she added, not trying to hide her annoyance and resentment.

His lips lifted in a faint smile and her heartbeat picked up.

He always had that effect on her. Which only motivated her to call him a bastard again.

"Guess dinner will have to wait," he said.

Not that he would eat if he had to fight a demon tonight. Hunters tried not to. The smells could cause involuntary gagging and choke reactions. It was always better to have an empty stomach. They couldn't throw up what wasn't there.

Angie, on the other hand, hated to skip meals. Especially after working magic. Her stomach tightened in protest at the thought of not eating. "I'm stopping in the café on the way out. I need a sandwich at least."

"I'll buy," Sebastian said. "Least I can do."

"Yeah it is," she said with a snort.

She cleaned up her work space, ensuring the used water was poured into a disposal bucket. Since she hadn't needed to include any herbs or salt, the water would be reused to water the plants that filled in most of the second-floor recesses. If she'd used herbs or salt, that leftover water would be used in the fountains on the first floor. The owners of Dana's Cauldron preferred as little waste as possible, and Angie liked that approach to witchcraft. It had the feeling of balance to it that was all things in her world.

She realized as she slipped back into her jacket and put her purse strap over hear head, angling it across her chest, that demon hunting had an innate sense of balance to it too. The balance was tipped, broken, when a human tried to summon a demon into this world. The only way to restore that balance was to send the demon packing back to its realm of origin.

Sebastian's life was dedicated to maintaining this balance, a fact that might have been part of her attraction to him.

He held up the plastic bag he still held, the bag with the dangerous demon books in it that she'd somehow managed to forgot about.

"I need to store these," he said. "Not a good idea to bring them into a hunt."

She shivered. She had no idea what a demon might want or do with these books, but Sebastian was right, better not to tempt fate. "We can store them in my locker here," she said, gesturing vaguely to the storage room across the hall. "But only until tomorrow. I don't want that energy in this place for long."

Dana's Cauldron didn't deal in much demon-centered stuff, and what they did have here was mostly esoteric, related to creation myths, or fictitious and therefore harmless. The owners well knew that demons existed. They just didn't want real demon stuff in their witch store. That was yet another reason Angie loved this place.

Sebastian held back the curtain for her as she proceeded him from the room, and his scent wrapped around her, a deep spice of masculinity that was part aftershave and part earthy male. And all Sebastian.

She sighed. Balance wasn't the only thing that had attracted her to the man. His scent alone could keep her ensorcelled for a lifetime.

If it hadn't done already.

CHAPTER NINE

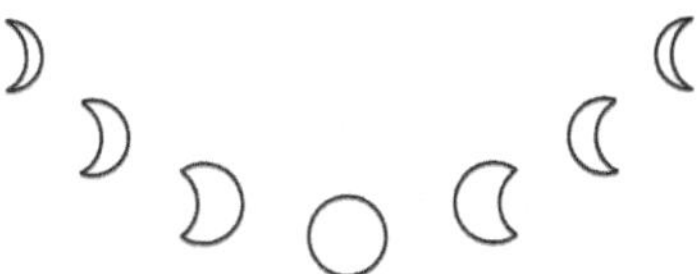

The apartment building was one of five, each maybe fifteen stories high, all surrounding an inner courtyard of cracked sidewalks crossing between sections of dirt that had probably been intended for grass or landscaping. In between two of the buildings was a surprisingly well-maintained little playground for kids, with a tall metal fence separating it from its surroundings to keep the kids inside safe and from running out into traffic. The complex was surrounded by a circular driveway that accessed all the buildings from the outside, and led back out to a busy cross street.

There were a few lamps with soft yellow lights illuminating the courtyard, but the ones with unbroken bulbs were scattered far enough apart to leave a lot of the area in dark shadows.

A cold autumn breeze brought with it the faint scent of

uncollected garbage, though Angie couldn't see where that garbage was stored. Her nose twitched as she caught the even fainter scent of tobacco smoke. She studied her surroundings, and the doorways into the buildings. She couldn't see anyone standing around smoking, so she assumed she was catching the smell of someone's leftover butt.

In fact, the area was incredibly quiet. Lights were on in windows throughout the complex, and from nearby she could just hear someone's television through their closed window, but other than that sign of life, the complex felt eerily still.

A skittering sound to her right made her pause. She glanced in the direction of the noise. If it was a rat, she didn't want to know. She wasn't a rat person. Her brothers made fun of her for it, but rats and mice creeped her out. Given she could see into demon realms, her brothers found this fact pretty hilarious.

Memories of her brothers, and their familial teasing, actually settled her jumping nerves more than she would have expected. She was probably due a visit home soon. Except everything that had happened, all the reasons she'd moved to New York, all of that had happened in New Mexico. Going home brought it up even as being with her family settled her soul.

It was a terrible, tricky dichotomy.

"Any idea where we should start?" she murmured to Sebastian. There was no one around to overhear them that she could see or sense, but the strangely quiet night seemed to call for quiet voices.

"This way," he said.

A strange note in his voice made her look more closely at him. He was focused on a building across the courtyard. She studied it as they moved through the open space toward its metal front door. The image of that door, the window with wire cross-hatching… It was similar to her vision, though all the doors looked alike so it was impossible to tell if *that* was the door she'd seen Mara in front of.

Sebastian went directly to that door, though, without looking around, without studying his surroundings. Like he'd been there before.

"You haven't told me something," she said, worry crawling into her stomach.

"I told you I had a hunt here," he answered without looking away from the door.

His voice was even deeper than normal but distant, his concentration elsewhere.

"You didn't tell me what happened," she said.

He didn't comment.

"Did you win or lose that fight?"

"I'm alive."

She supposed that was an answer. Rare for a hunter to lose a fight with a demon and survive. Losing typically meant death. Almost always in fact.

"This particular location, not a coincidence," she said.

"Not a coincidence I think."

"Is there a demon coming now?" She reached under her jacket sleeve to grip the silver pentagram charm.

When he didn't answer, her heartbeat jumped. She wasn't here to fight demons. She was here to find a child. But, as usual, whenever she got involved with the demon hunters, accomplishing one goal would mean doing the thing she wasn't here to do.

She really hated this world.

Sebastian paused a hundred yards from the door, then turned slightly to the left. Angie followed his gaze and realized there was another door there, at the bottom of a ramp, a door into the basement. Without a word, Sebastian headed that direction.

Angie hesitated, her grip on the pentagram imprinting it into her fingers. The cold breeze shifted through her hair, making her moon earrings tinkle. Her heart hammered so hard all she could hear for a moment was the blood rushing through her body. Adrenaline slammed into her, overwhelming her. And her flight instinct kicked in hard. She wanted to run, fast and far.

Sebastian reached the basement door, another solid metal barrier with a smaller window reinforced with wire cross-hatching. She glanced to her right, into the lobby. It was dark but for a single security light at the back of the large, open space. Inside, there was a wall of mailboxes to the right and two elevators to the left. The stairs at the back of the lobby got most of the light from the single bulb, but the space under the stairs was shadowed and impenetrable.

Another skittering sound behind her had her spinning, searching for the source. She was both disgusted and a little relieved to see the dark beady eyes of a rat as it glanced at her before scurrying off around the building.

Shivering, she pulled in a deep breath, and made her

choice. She followed Sebastian down the ramp to the basement door.

He had his hand on the knob, turning. She'd have expected the door to be locked, and it might well have been, but locks weren't an issue to hunters. At least not conventional locks. He paused before pushing the door inward, waiting and listening. Angie listened too, but her nerves were too jumpy, and she couldn't seem to hear beyond her own heartbeat.

Damn it, she wasn't going to do anyone any good this way. She made an attempt to settle her pulse and focused on the feel of the pentagram pressing against her fingers. She mentally started a shielding spell.

Most of her magic work consisted of spells, some potions, and occasionally working with charms. She didn't actually do much work in setting charms—the pentagram had been a gift from her earliest mentor—but she could manage it in a pinch. She was best with actual spell work. And spell work took time, and concentration. Say a word wrong, use the wrong hand gesture, and the unpredictable results could get someone killed.

The shielding spell was one she knew so well at this point, she almost didn't have to think about it. She could run through the words in one part of her mind and initiate the shield while another part of her mind was panicking or just moving too slowly to react to a situation. But given what they might be walking into, she didn't want to take chances. Initiating the spell, getting it started and built to a point where all she'd need to do is say one last word and combine it with the appropriate hand gesture, would ensure she could react fast and not get sucked into a demon realm.

She hated when that happened.

Sebastian finally pushed the basement door inward. It was pitch dark inside. Too dark to see into the interior even though her night vision was pretty good. Sebastian went in first. She checked behind them, watching for movement, or signs of someone coming from that direction to trap them. No one was around.

She followed Sebastian into the basement, her heart still hammering so hard she was nearly panting.

This was the worst part. The not knowing what they would face, what horror they'd encounter. Until the very moment when the awfulness unfolded in front of her, she had to imagine what it might be. And Angie had a very very good imagination.

She allowed the door to click closed behind her. In the silence, the noise of the settling door was loud, and it echoed. So much for any element of surprise they might have had.

"Do you mind light?" she murmured close to Sebastian's ear. He was only a few inches in front of her, staying close enough she didn't panic. But the darkness, the solid wall of it, was more than her jumping nerves could take.

"I think the motion sensor lights are broken," he said.

"That wasn't the kind of light I was thinking about." She reached into her purse and pulled out a small flask.

"Magic?" he murmured.

"This is Tequila." She took a gulp and handed the flask to him. Then she pulled out a small flashlight and clicked it on.

The little beam was just enough to illuminate the corridor before them out to about three feet. "I come prepared," she said.

She caught his grin from the corner of her eyes. He sipped the Tequila—not much but a sip—and handed the flask back to her. She slipped it into her purse with one hand while sweeping her little flashlight around the corridor with the other.

She actually could make a little ball of light from magic. It was a simple spell that required no extras, just the words and a very specific hand gesture. But it took magic and that wasn't an unlimited resource for any witch. Once depleted, it took time to build up again. Like muscle strength. Even the strongest people could only push their muscles so far before they had to rest and let their bodies recover. Magic took practice, training, proper fuel, and rest. And every use drained a little bit away that had to be replaced.

Since she didn't know what they were getting into, she wanted to reserve as much power as possible. Just in case.

The corridor they stood in was all concrete, the stone floors painted blue, the walls she was pretty sure were white. There was a line of lights overhead, but either the bulbs were out or they'd been removed. She couldn't tell through the light covers. A series of white pipes ran the length of the ceiling as well, making the space feel a little shorter than it actually was.

There was a closed door to the left a few feet ahead, the metal sign at eye height proclaiming it the compactor. Farther ahead and to the left, another door stood open, the interior dark. Beyond that door, the corridor turned to the right and disappeared into more darkness.

"You lead," she murmured to Sebastian.

He didn't argue with her.

She kept her beam of light on the ground in front of them a few feet ahead and they moved slowly toward the opened door. The compactor made a noise as they moved past it, a chunk and crunch that made Angie jump. She cursed at her own edginess. Sebastian reached back and squeezed her wrist once, then released his hold so they'd both have their hands free.

Beyond the compactor, the corridor was an echo of silence, the only noise their breathing and soft footsteps. Weirdly silent, actually. Most buildings made a lot of noise. Pipes clunking, elevators moving, things settling or turning on. It wasn't so late at night that there wouldn't be any people about. Yet it felt like three in the morning and even the building itself had gone to sleep.

The air was warm, the pipes overhead issuing more than enough heat. Almost too much. She was sweating under her jacket now. Although, that could have been anxiety.

A faint scent reached her. One she hated. One she recognized.

The very faint rotten egg smell of sulfur.

"I smell it," Sebastian said even before Angie could comment.

"You ready?"

"Always."

He wasn't boasting, Angie knew. Demon hunters had to

be ready for a hunt at every moment. If he let his guard drop, if he let his will to overcome any demon lapse for even a moment, he would die.

They edged forward, toward the open room. Angie pointed her flashlight through the door. Silence and stillness greeted them.

Several rows of washing machines lined the wall to the left, dryers lined the back wall. There was a table for folding clothes and a small card machine for adding money to the cards the washers and dryers took. Scuff marks on the card machine gave evidence to its abuse. Four metal laundry carts on wheels lined up next to the row of washers. Nothing obviously moved. None of the machines were in use. No shuffling sounds. No cockroaches skittered out of the light.

The space behind the row of dryers was big enough to hide a person, though, which made Angie distrust the quiet.

The scent of sulfur was stronger now, but as she took a single step into the laundry room, the scents of soap and dryer sheets overpowered the sulfur.

"Not here," Sebastian murmured.

She nodded. This wasn't what they were looking for. As soon as she turned back to the corridor, the smell of sulfur hit her again. The dark corner that veered to the right. The scent was coming from that direction.

On instinct, she cut the light from her flashlight. They were plunged into darkness. She expected Sebastian to protest, but he held perfectly still next to her and didn't say a word. He stood close enough for her to feel his presence in the dark, though, and that was very reassuring.

A primitive part of her nearly panicked without any light, her finger tapping the flashlight button without hitting it hard enough to turn it back on. Holding off that inner panic long enough for her eyes to adjust to the darkness took effort.

Finally, her eyes adapted, and a red glow emerged from the dark, just around the bend in the corridor.

"Mm hmm," Sebastian murmured.

A new kind of panic gripped her. She'd known what they were walking into. She'd known what they were going to face. Still, with the evidence in front of her, the red glow, the sulfur… Her heart hammered so hard she had to blink back spots. She hated this. *Hated* it. It was partly why she'd moved, why she'd given up so much. Why she kept trying to give it all up.

Sebastian took hold of her free hand. "You don't have to go," he murmured. "This part is my job, not yours."

"None of this is my job," she muttered, mostly because annoyance and anger were easier than the fear.

He sighed, audibly. "I know."

"Don't apologize," she warned. "Not now. Not yet. We'll talk later."

"Still willing to talk to me later? A good sign."

"Don't count on it." She was too scared to be nice.

It didn't matter how often she'd had to face demons and the demon realms in the past. She'd never gotten completely used to it, never shaken that fear. Give her wizards and shapeshifters and vampires. She could deal with those. But her innate ability to see into the demon realms had only made her more terrified of demons, not less.

She'd never been intended for the life of a hunter.

They slowly approached the bend in the corridor, the red glow guiding them now. Angie wanted to flick her flashlight on again, but if they still had any element of surprise at this stage, the light would end that.

She couldn't imagine whoever was back there hadn't heard them approaching. They'd been quiet but not silent this whole time. Still, no one was attacking them so that might, *might*, be a good sign.

She hoped.

As they reached the corner, Sebastian eased her behind him and they both leaned against the wall so he could look around the corner. He didn't react at all to what he saw. No fast, indrawn breath, no grunt, no gasp. He looked and then he leaned back against the wall and faced her, frowning slightly.

"What?" she mouthed. Now that they were this close, any noise seemed a bad idea.

His lips flattened in a scowl and he shook his head. Then, without warning her, he stepped around the corner. Instinctively, she reached for him but he was already gone.

Damn him.

She squeezed her eyes shut for a beat, completed the spell that put a shield in front of her, and followed him around the corner.

CHAPTER TEN

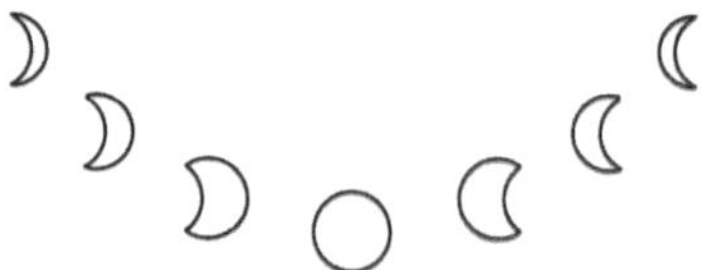

ngie blinked into the red and yellow light, brighter now that she faced it fully. It took a moment for the scene to resolve itself. And when it did, she gasped.

The corridor opened up into a larger room, like a recreation room or meeting room, but without anything in it. At the far side of the room were two elevators, but the doors were obscured by the flames rising from the circle of fire in the center of the room.

Inside the flame circle, an Anchor demon stood, looking out with eyes white with heat. The demon itself looked like a skeleton encased in flames, just the barest of structure for the racing fire to adhere to. The skeleton was mostly human-shaped, though larger and thicker, but the skull was the skeletal shape of a bull, complete with thick horns coming out of its head and a snout shaped of fire where the nose would be. Its feet were hooves. Its bone hands were human-like though with only three fingers and a thumb. Still the kind of hand that could grasp and hold.

Angie's heartbeat hammered. Not the same beast. But from the same realm as the Fire demon…

The demon's full focus was on someone much smaller than it standing just outside the circle. The girl was about five-foot tall, her light brown hair loose down her back. She wore jeans and a sweatshirt that had to be sweltering in the heat created by the Anchor demon and the circle containing it. She had her arms raised and was chanting something difficult to hear over the sounds of the rushing flames.

Angie didn't have to see her face to know who the girl was.

She opened her mouth to call Mara's name, but stopped herself just in time. Interrupting someone controlling a demon could be a disaster. Especially if their control over that demon wasn't very strong.

Though, as Angie moved slowly closer, she realized the Anchor demon looked well contained. The circle held.

The scent of sulfur was stronger here, making her want to gag. It blended with a kind of burnt scent that was a little too close to roasting meat for Angie's peace of mind. She'd be off meat for a month after this, and she loved a good steak.

She looked around for Sebastian, but she didn't see him anywhere. She'd expected to see him closer to Mara, but… Nothing.

Where the hell was he?

There was nowhere to go. Except the elevators. And the lights over the doors indicated they were on much higher levels. He wouldn't have left the room anyway. Not with a demon right there. He might be a bastard sometimes, but he was an excellent hunter.

She narrowed her eyes and searched the area with a sense outside her normal five, a sense she didn't call on often. She couldn't see auras well or consistently the way her workmate Laura could, but she could…sense things if she concentrated.

The roar of flames broke her focus, the sound like a living thing, all its own.

"I will help you, child," the demon said. "If you meet my bargain."

"You'll kill him? Before he can take me? Before the other demon is called again? You'll kill him?"

"I will." The demon leaned forward with that promise, getting as close to eye level with Mara as it could while still inside the circle.

Angie opened her mouth to shout a warning to Mara. This was the moment, the worst moment. If the bargain was made, things got a *lot* more complicated.

But before she could utter a sound, Sebastian seemed to materialize out of the air right next to the girl, facing the demon.

The demon reared back to its full height and a sound like the screeching of a flock of eagles escaped it.

"You have no place here, hunter," it said.

"I beg to differ," Sebastian said. He moved to put Mara behind him. "No bargain, beast. You will not enter this world this day."

"The child has made her choice."

"Not yet. And I intend to talk her out of it."

The Anchor demon laughed. "Her father will kill her, sacrifice her to the other one. Their deal is set. The bargain made long ago. You cannot change that."

"Won't have to," Sebastian said. "And unless you want a full fight and want to test your will against mine, I'd recommend leaving."

"You think your will can overcome mine?" the demon growled, lowering its head to put its face close to Sebastian's this time.

Sebastian leaned closer as well, close enough only the column of fire from the flame circle separated them. "You'd like to test me? I've nothing better to do right now. Your choice."

The glowing white eyes flared briefly inside the skull head. The bone area where a bull's snout would be, that hole in the front of its face, released a stream of steam, almost like the demon was letting out a breath.

As they stared at each other, the hairs on Angie's arms rose. The demon was testing Sebastian, a silent clash of wills, and while she couldn't see or hear anything of the fight, her instincts jumped and her nerves tingled with awareness of it. A staring contest might seem innocuous to most. But with a demon, it carried a whole level of danger the observer couldn't comprehend.

It was the strangest thing, sometimes, watching the demon hunters work. Will, and the act of wielding it against a monster, was... She didn't have the word for it. Just strange.

Finally, the demon straightened away, towering up over

Sebastian's head. Sebastian leaned back slowly without taking his gaze from the creature's face.

The demon looked away first but pointed a finger at Sebastian. "This isn't done between us, hunter. The child will call me again. And when I'm free, I will come for you."

"Looking forward to it," Sebastian said quietly.

The demon made that screeching sound again, loud enough Angie had to cover her ears.

"I'll be back," it snarled.

"Right you are, Arnie."

The white glow of the demon's eyes flickered, as if it blinked at being called Arnie. Then it let out the screech again and vanished in a cloud of steam and a column of flames.

The flame circle remained. But the center was empty.

"Best cut the circle now," Sebastian said as he turned to face Mara. "Wouldn't want him sneaking back."

"What have you done?" Mara wailed up at Sebastian. "Why did you do that?"

"To keep you from making a mistake," Sebastian said gently. "Because no matter what your father has done, this isn't the answer."

"How the hell do you know? How can you possibly know?"

"It's my job," he said, still quiet and gentle.

"What job is that?" Mara spit. There were tears streaking down her cheeks. She swiped at them angrily.

"Demon hunter."

That brought Mara up, her shoulders straightening. "What?"

"I hunt demons."

"Why haven't you stopped my father?"

"I'm working on it."

Angie saw the faint twitch in the muscles along his jaw in the light from the still-burning circle. Something about all this was more significant to Seb than just an ordinary hunt. What had gone wrong the last time he'd been here?

"You can't," Mara said, attempting to fall back on her earlier anger.

But some of the heat had leeched away. She sounded very young. And very scared. And Angie wanted to pull her into a hug and assure her everything would be all right. She didn't move from her spot. She didn't dare touch the girl just then, when her own senses were so heightened. But the desire to comfort choked her up.

"I will," Sebastian said. "I will stop your father, and I will keep you safe."

"I'm not the one he's really after," she said, loudly, then slapped her hand over her mouth.

Sebastian's eyes narrowed.

Angie stared at the side of Mara's face for a long time as some of her earlier impressions and the jigsaw puzzle of suspicions settled into place.

"Your mother," she finally said, stepping fully into the room so Mara could see her. "She's not actually dead, is she?"

CHAPTER ELEVEN

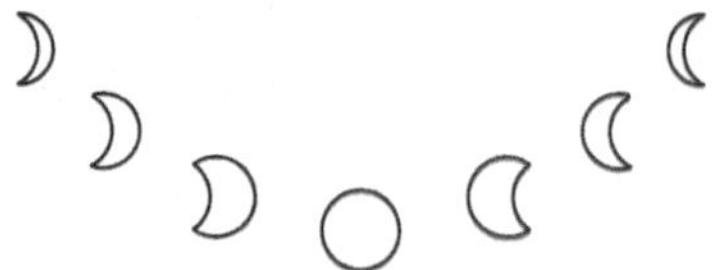

Mara started and faced Angie. "Who are you?" she demanded. The flame circle still burned brightly behind her, obscuring the elevators behind it. But the flames were lower now that the demon was no longer contained inside the circle.

Angie made an effort to appear as harmless as possible as she introduced herself. "Angie Jordan. A friend of Sebastian's. And a witch," she added, just to be fully upfront. The girl had been through enough betrayals. Secrecy wouldn't win Angie any points.

"What kind of witch?"

"I refer to myself as a green witch. Gets out of those black and white dichotomies. That part's mostly theological, though. Practically speaking, I'm a touch psychic, and I can work magic through spells."

Mara blinked at her a few times. "I don't believe you."

Angie smiled. "You were just trying to bargain with an honest-to-goddess demon and you don't believe in witches?"

"How did you find me?"

Angie held out the lipstick she'd kept in her jacket pocket. "Sebastian was…called to your house because of the demon issue. Your father asked him to find you. Sebastian brought me in to help. I got this from your room to help scry for you. But that was after I'd touched a few things and tried to see if I could…pick up your location." She paused as Mara's face squinched up into a scowl of anger. "I'm sorry we invaded your privacy. Carmen was there with us. We didn't damage anything. We wanted to find you and make sure…" When Mara narrowed her eyes, Angie shrugged. "We wanted to make sure you weren't dead or taken by the demon your father summoned."

"He's horrible."

"The demon or your father? Because I'm afraid I agree with both."

Mara's mouth twitched. "He's not really my father, you know."

"That would explain a lot."

"You're not surprised? Did you psychic that out?"

Angie's turn to nearly smile. "No."

"Why aren't you surprised?"

"Not a lot surprises me."

"You're not scared?"

"That's something different. I'm afraid of a lot of things. Just not often surprised. Not by people anyway." She shrugged again. "Occupational hazard for a psychic."

Mara looked between her and Sebastian. "I can't trust anyone."

"Fair enough," Sebastian said. "You don't know us from Adam. No reason to trust us. And given your own father was going to sacrifice you to a demon, I imagine your trust is in short supply."

The blunt assessment of her situation seemed to settle Mara somewhat. Like being able to just talk about it and not dance around the subject took a weight off her shoulders.

"I was just a…a bonus sacrifice," Mara said quietly. "He's really after my mother."

"I think there's a lot of story here," Sebastian said. "If you're willing to tell us, it'll make protecting you, and your mother, easier. It's not necessary, though. If you'd rather keep your secrets, they're yours to keep. I'll stop the demons either way."

"You sound very sure," Mara said.

"I am sure."

Sebastian had to be, Angie thought. Any sense of unease, any doubt, would impact the strength of his will. A deadly outcome. Absolute confidence in their skills was as necessary to the life of a demon hunter as breathing.

Yet another reason she'd refused that life—or kept trying to. Over and over again. Fear and doubt when it came to the demon world haunted her. They had from the very beginning, but that had only gotten worse when she had, for a brief period, embraced Sebastian's life. Because she wanted to be with him. She'd made mistakes. She'd almost been killed, more than once. She'd very nearly gotten stuck in a demon realm with demons surrounding her and trying to kill her…

She suppressed a shudder. No, she wasn't cut out to be a hunter. She didn't have the will.

"He tells everyone my mother is dead," Mara said, circling back to her father. "That she was killed in a car accident." She looked at the ground. "I believed him for a long time. Too long."

"I'm very sorry," Sebastian said.

"You didn't do it," Mara said with a very teenager shrug. But tears still leaked onto her cheeks. She rubbed them off with her sweatshirt sleeve.

Angie glanced at Sebastian, then at the still burning circle. An active circle meant a demon could overhear them. If Mara was willing to talk about all this, it was better they didn't have a demonic eavesdropper.

"Mara," Sebastian said, "would you please cut the circle? It's safer for everyone. Then we can talk more."

Mara blinked and looked up at him, then at the circle as if she'd forgotten it was there. "I… Sorry. I know I'm not supposed to leave it like this. That's…" She shook her head, as if shaking off the comment.

She bent down and picked up a small athame off the ground at her feet. Angie finally noticed the collection of stuff that Mara had used in her ritual to call the demon. A thick yellow candle burned on a glass candle stand next to a little package of matches. A bowl with salt, a thick stick of sidewalk chalk, a bowl of water, and the small ritual knife—a plane silver athame with no obvious designs or etchings on the blade and very simple Celtic scroll work on the hilt—were all set in a semicircle in front of Mara.

Beside it all, a small book sat open but with its pages fluttering in the breeze created by the fire.

One of the books she hadn't left behind in her bedroom, obviously. Although, given what she'd left behind, Angie was afraid to think what the book at her feet contained.

Using the small knife, Mara cut a line in the air down the front of the flames jumping around her circle and murmured a dismissal. The fire collapsed instantly, leaving a charred black circle in the cement and smoke billowing into the air. Without the firelight, the room plunged into a solid darkness. Angie flicked on her flashlight. The beam landed on the smoking circle.

A physical line through the blackened remains of the containment circle had appeared at Mara's feet. Angie considered that. When most demon circles collapsed, the "cut" in them wasn't so visible because that break happened on the magical plane.

She looked a little closer at Mara. She hadn't sensed magic in her when inspecting her room, but that didn't mean it wasn't there. Mara was at the age where it might only just now be manifesting. Some magic showed up from birth, and was always a part of a person—Angie's had been like that. Some magic appeared early and then grew, taking a leap at puberty. And still other times, magic didn't present at all until the hormonal shift of puberty.

If Mara was coming into magic, that might explain why Grant wanted to use her as a demonic sacrifice.

After the circle had stopped smoking, Mara moved around the outside of it in a clockwise direction sprinkling water over the top. Not enough water that it would have extinguished any flames, just a sprinkle to seal and end the ritual. It was a final step not all people took when summoning demons, but it was the safest way to ensure they didn't sneak back into an improperly broken circle. Mara had done her research.

Once finished, she dumped the rest of the water down a drain at one end of the big room, a drain Angie hadn't noticed in the dark. Then she collected all her demon-calling equipment and shoved it back into a plain black backpack which had been tossed against the wall. The last thing she put into the backpack was the book. She handled it with a great deal of care. Angie tried to catch the title, but she'd have had to shine her flashlight directly onto the cover to see it, and she didn't want to make her efforts that obvious.

"We need to go upstairs," Mara said. "It'll be safer to talk there."

"Is your mother here?" Sebastian asked.

Angie noticed a strange note in his voice. Still gentle and quiet to put Mara at ease, but there was definitely more going on here.

Something to do with the last time he'd come here to hunt a demon…

Mara didn't answer his question. She just walked to the elevator, not waiting to see if they'd follow or not.

On the way past the circle, Angie rubbed her foot over the line of remaining soot, smudging the edge, just to further disrupt it. An image jumped up and stopped her in her tracks, of another circle, another demon. A bargain unfulfilled. An argument between a woman and a man.

Sebastian.

The images came in pieces, not a nice easy-to-interpret vision. Not a full scene. Flashes of feelings and snippets of conversation. Fear. A lot of fear. Panic. Desperation. A lot like the feelings she'd picked up in Mara's room but…older. These things had happened a while ago.

And Sebastian had been here for that incident too.

Angie blinked as the images dropped away. Spots danced in front of her eyes, as if she'd been looking into the flashlight beam and now stared into darkness. She kept her gaze on the wall for a few breaths to let her eyesight clear.

Sebastian had stopped when she had and was frowning at her. She gave a very faint head shake. She didn't want to talk about this in front of Mara, not until she'd worked out what she'd just seen.

But she stared at the remains of the circle as the elevator doors closed on the three of them and wondered what had happened here the last time a demon had been called.

CHAPTER TWELVE

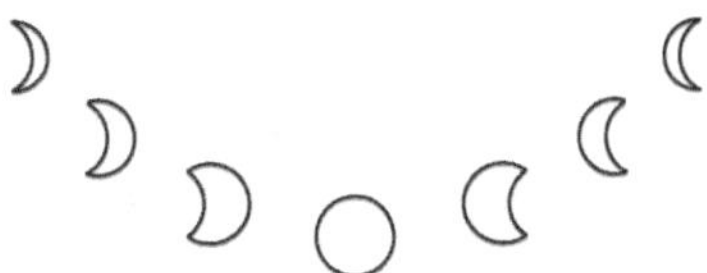

They rode up to the fourteenth floor, just two from the top of the building. The corridor was comfortably lit, unlike the darkness in the basement, and there was noise coming from the surrounding apartments. The flooring was a solid black marble that would be easy to clean. The walls were freshly painted a pale yellow-cream color. The doors were all uniformly black with little brass peepholes at eye level.

Mara led them to the far end of the hall, near the emergency exit door, to apartment 14-12.

She didn't knock but used a key to let them all inside.

A part of Angie was relieved she'd had a safe place to be this whole time, not living on the streets or anything. But given what they'd disrupted down in the basement, calling this environment "safe" might be a stretch.

As they stepped into the small, neat apartment, a woman came around the corner from another room. She looked at Mara, at the two adults with her, and her eyes narrowed. "What's happened? What's wrong? The laundry machines aren't broken, are they?" Then her gaze settled more fully on Sebastian. "You!"

The woman charged forward, fists raised. And to Angie's horror, Sebastian just stood there.

She stepped between the angry woman and Sebastian and raised her own hands, palms out. "Whoa whoa. We're not starting this meeting with punches thrown."

Angie had moved between angry brothers more than once in her life—and to be fair, had had a brother step between her and another brother once or twice, too; probably more than twice—so she wasn't afraid of taking an accidental punch. Her jaw could take it. But it wasn't exactly the way she'd like them all to start.

The woman skidded to a halt, her fist still up as she glared at Sebastian. "What are you doing here?"

Sebastian sighed. "Your daughter was summoning a demon."

The woman blinked. Angie finally took a moment to realize how much she looked like Mara. Both had the same shape and color eyes, blue with dark lashes fringing them. Where Mara's hair was a light brown, her mother's was a pale blond threaded with enough gray to give it a silvery sheen. The color was lovely and complimented her rose-toned complexion. There were deep lines between the mother's eyebrows, and some around her eyes and mouth.

She was a handsome woman, the kind who had presence more than any kind of standard beauty. The sort of woman you looked twice at on the street because she demanded it.

And she looked very out of place in the tiny apartment, dressed in sweat pants and an overlarge t-shirt.

"Maybe we should introduce ourselves and have a seat?" Angie said, before Mara's mother could respond to Sebastian's comment. "I think we have a lot to talk about."

"I'm not talking with *him*," the mother spat.

"Grant is the reason I'm here," Sebastian said. "He's hunting for Mara."

"And you led him right to her!" Panic filled the woman's face. She motioned Mara toward a door. "Go pack. We're leaving."

"No." Angie raised a hand again. "He doesn't know where we are."

"He'll have had you followed, you idiot," the woman hissed.

Angie sighed and glanced at Sebastian. "Were we followed?"

"No," he said. "I ensured we weren't."

"There," Angie said. "We weren't followed."

"How can you *ensure* anything?"

"He's a demon hunter," Angie said. "It's what he does. Now, can we please calm down. Introductions and a conversation are in order. I'll start. I'm Angela Jordan. Everyone calls me Angie. I'm a witch. You've obviously already met Sebastian. There's a story there." She cut a look at Sebastian.

He nodded faintly but his attention was on Mara's mother. And instead of worry, or offense, or any of the emotions Angie might have expected, the only thing she read in his expression was curiosity. She suspected that if she touched him now, and let her senses open to a reading, she'd pick up a lot of the story since it was so near the surface.

She wouldn't invade his privacy that way. Not on purpose. And if he didn't want her to pick up the history, he wouldn't let her—willing her to sense only a blankness, a move he'd done to her before. But her curiosity was starting to overwhelm her at this stage.

Mara glanced between her mother and Sebastian, her eyes narrowed. "What happened between you two?"

Thank you, Mara!

"It's a long story," Mara's mother said, not meeting her daughter's gaze.

"Mom," Mara said, letting out a long breath. "Enough. There's been too many secrets already. I can't take anymore."

Her mother's shoulders dropped and she pulled Mara into a hug. "I'm sorry, baby. You're right." She looked at Sebastian again, then settled her attention on Angie. "Let's sit. This will take some time. Do you want coffee? Tea?"

"No thank you," Angie said before Sebastian could ask for tea. He was so English sometimes with his tea drinking. When they weren't in the middle of a demon hunt, she found it funny and endearing.

That brought up memories she preferred to ignore, though. To bury the memories, she made herself take stock of the apartment.

Her first impression of small and neat held on closer inspection. The main area was a living room with a couch, a triangular wooden stand with a small flatscreen TV on it pushed into the corner, a basic green rug covering the hardwood floor, and a small glass coffee table under which piles of magazines were stacked. Angie could only see a few of the top magazines. They all seemed to be fashion or architecture focused. A pillow and a blanket were folded up on the edge of the couch.

Three large windows, all with the thick, green curtains pulled closed against the night, took up most of one wall. There were no hanging or framed pictures around the room, not even a generic landscape or kitschy poster. No knickknacks on shelves. No real shelves, she realized. Only the area under the TV stand, filled with a cable box and a DVD player. There wasn't really anything personal in the space outside of the magazines.

The door Mara's mother had come through led to an enclosed kitchen. Another closed door likely led to a bedroom or bathroom. She couldn't tell if this was a studio or one-bedroom apartment with that door closed, but what she could see wasn't a large space. Just big enough for one person. And her daughter on visits.

There weren't any extra chairs, just the single couch, which left them very little room to sit.

Sebastian didn't bother. He moved to the windows and stood leaning against the wall between two of them, his hands tucked into his pockets as he attempted to appear harmless. He did a pretty good job of it, all things considered.

But Mara's mother continued to throw suspicious glances his direction as she settled on the couch with Mara.

After a glance at the remaining space on the couch—which wasn't much and would crowd Mara—Angie decided to settle on the floor. She didn't want to hover over them by standing because she didn't have Sebastian's knack for slouching and looking innocuous. And frankly, she didn't want to touch anyone or anything that might have memories just yet. She could keep the readings at bay, she hoped, but she didn't want to take the chance yet.

Mara's mother raised her brows as Angie settled cross-legged on the rug. "You can sit on the couch."

"I'm good." At Mara's mom's skeptical look, Angie said, "I got used to living with little to no furniture in college."

Which was mostly true. She'd shared a small apartment with two other women for two years during college. They'd had a futon for a couch and no other furniture because they couldn't afford it, so they'd ended up sitting on the floor a lot. She had furniture in her apartment now, but most of her rituals were performed on the hardwood floor with only a pillow to sit on, so she really was used to this.

"Shall we begin with the last few introductions?" Angie said, pointedly.

They still hadn't gotten Mara's mother's name. Although, Sebastian might know it. And Angie could glean if from a quick peek at the magazine address labels if she wanted to bypass the formalities. But Angie always found it settled people if she didn't address them by name before they'd actually said their name aloud.

Mara's mother stared at Angie for a long moment, her eyes narrowed. "You're working for Bart."

Angie didn't raise her brows at the nickname for Bartholomew but she did wonder if the controlled, dangerous man she'd met earlier that day would like being called Bart. It didn't seem to fit the image he was trying to project.

"I'm not working for anyone," Angie reiterated. "I'm just helping a friend save a child."

"I'm not a child," Mara protested.

"You are," her mother said firmly. "And I warned you about trying to use that book."

"You used it," Mara said, in perfect pre-teen pout voice.

So much for not being a child.

The detail about Mara's mother calling a demon wasn't lost on Angie, though. She'd guessed as much, but it was good to have the suspicion confirmed. "Did you summon the demon to counter something Grant was doing?" she asked.

"How…?" The older woman shook her head. "You're psychic?"

"Well, it is one of my skills," Angie said. "But this was pretty obvious given all the glares you're throwing at Sebastian and what Mara just said."

"How old are you?" the woman asked.

Angie blinked only once at the non sequitur. "Twenty-seven."

"Young."

"Old enough."

Mara's mother snorted. "I thought I was old enough too at twenty-seven. I had Mara at that age."

Angie nodded, waiting for her to continue, knowing the woman would talk more, given the chance, because she'd been holding on to a lot of secrets for years and she was ready to let them go. Angie didn't need to be psychic to see that, anymore than she'd needed to be psychic to guess the woman had summoned a demon all those years ago.

"I was still a baby," the woman said. "But I thought I was so wise."

"Most young people do," Angie confirmed.

"You're young. Do you think you're wise?"

"Not at the moment." She cast Sebastian a look. He smiled back. The look was personal, and intimate, and nothing she could handle just then. "But I have been around the block a few times, you might say. Maybe a little more aware than many my age. I wouldn't call it wisdom."

"You sound smarter than I was just by admitting that," the woman said with a soft grunt. She hugged an arm around Mara, pulling her close. "I don't regret any of it, though."

"Then it wasn't unwise," Angie said.

"My name is Ellen, by the way."

"It's a pleasure to meet you, Ellen."

Ellen laughed, but it wasn't a happy sound. "We'll see if you feel that way by the time this is all over."

"If we're all alive, then I will feel great about having met you."

Ellen blinked at that. "You're sure you're twenty-seven?"

Angie just smiled.

"Do you have children?"

"No." She didn't want children. She loved them. But she

had no interest in procreating herself. She'd leave that to her brothers. Especially since her older brother was already working on the effort with his new wife. Being the witchy aunt who could spoil her nieces and nephews and then return to a quiet home while her siblings handled the hard parts of child rearing appealed to her a lot.

She might get a dog one day, though.

"It changes you, having kids," Ellen said.

Angie nodded.

"You do things you never thought you'd do."

"Like summon a demon?"

Ellen looked away. "I was in love with Bart when we married. I thought he was the most handsome, wonderful man I'd ever met. I was only twenty. Much too young to look past the exterior, the sophisticated style, the deep conversations. He's ten years older than I am, and I found that very glamourous at the time. My father tried to warm me that Bart was a gold digger. I didn't listen." She glanced at Mara. "Daughters can be willful."

Mara rolled her eyes.

"I married Bart despite my parents' objections, and because they loved me, they gave in and accepted him into the family. They bought us a house, arranged for Bart to meet with influential people in the financial industry so that he could get good work, did everything to ensure we had a good start."

"What went wrong?" Angie could guess, but again it was better for Ellen to tell the story on her own, out loud. There was relief in finally telling someone your secrets. Angie saw it all the time in her work.

"At first, I didn't…I didn't really understand *why* things went wrong. We weren't getting pregnant, despite trying for years. I was disappointed and upset about it. I really wanted kids. Bart just got angry. The more time passed, the angrier he got. He said it was my fault, and I was ruining everything." Her mouth tightened into a thin line as she paused, staring at the glass coffee table.

With a deep breath, she continued, "I believed him at first and went to a doctor to see what was wrong. But it wasn't me. When I told him, he got angry enough he nearly hit me. Raised his hand to, then pulled back at the last minute." She met Angie's gaze. "That was the first moment, the first realization that I was with someone I didn't know as well as I thought I did."

Angie tried not to picture the situation, but a hazard of her job was that she could "see" people's stories very clearly, even when she wasn't reading them psychically. And she could picture the scene between Ellen and Grant all too clearly.

"What did you do?" she asked Ellen, holding her gaze.

"I started looking more deeply into the man I'd married. I went through his things, his files, his desk while he was at work. I searched through his belongings, his drawers. I hunted the entire house to see if I could find out *why* he was so angry." She blinked a few times and looked away. "I wasn't prepared for what I found."

"You expected something more mundane," Angie said.

"I expected something that made sense. Something real. Not..." She shook her head. "Not demon worship and magic and evil."

Angie considered correcting Ellen's assumption that magic was evil, because it was something she often found herself having to emphasize with people who didn't understand the magical world. But she supposed the magic Grant had been messing with was evil, so she let the issue go. She didn't want to distract Ellen.

"It took me a few months of study and research and more snooping before I pieced it all together," Ellen said. "What he'd been doing. In our basement. Right under my nose." Her fist clenched in her lap and her arm tightened on Mara.

Ellen glanced at Sebastian. "And you didn't stop him. You stopped me. But not him."

"I wasn't called to him," Sebastian said, not sounding upset at the accusation. "My job isn't an exact science, unfortunately. And I wasn't the hunter sent to stop Grant."

"Someone else was?" she asked. "Because I never saw them."

Sebastian didn't answer. He just held Ellen's gaze, his expression soft.

Angie wondered at that. If another hunter had gone to stop Grant, wouldn't Sebastian have known? The hunters kept a history. The community was small and they all knew each other. If someone had died fighting off a demon Grant had summoned because it was about to escape, the hunters would know. Shouldn't Sebastian have known who Grant was before all this?

Or had he, and he'd left that out of what he'd told her about the situation?

"If they'd stopped him," Ellen went on, "none of this would have happened." She flicked a glance at Mara and frowned. "I wouldn't have had to give up my daughter just to survive and keep her safe."

"He still offered me to the demon," Mara said. "None of it worked."

Ellen's expression collapsed then, and tears leaked down her face. She hugged Mara closer, tucking her daughter's head under her chin. "I'm so sorry. I'm so so sorry. I never meant for any of this to happen."

Angie sat quietly for a few moments, giving the mother and daughter time to settled their emotions. Then she prompted Ellen to continue. "What did you do after you found out Grant was summoning a demon?"

"I didn't know what to do," Ellen said, still clinging to her daughter. "I spent another week just considering my options. I didn't really understand the demon stuff and at first tried to convince myself he was just crazy, worshipping something that didn't exist. Finally, I fell back on research. I figured the more I knew and understood, the better able I'd be to make a decision."

"Why didn't you leave?" Angie asked quietly. It was a question that had to be asked. "You had a supportive family that would have taken you in."

And in this case, Ellen had also been the one with the money. She wasn't beholden to or dependent on Grant, not the way so many abused women ended up. But emotions and emotional abuse were a lot more complicated than just having money and a support system to turn to. Angie wanted to understand what made Ellen stay long enough to have a child. Knowing who Mara's father was might also clear up some of the story.

Ellen didn't meet her gaze when she said, "I was ashamed. I'd gotten myself into the mess with Bart. I didn't want to go to my parents and admit I couldn't handle the situation. That I'd been so very wrong." She shrugged. "And I was afraid my father would have him killed."

Angie blinked. She'd said that so bluntly, as if it wasn't just a euphemism.

Ellen said, "I was their only child and they were always very protective. If they thought there was even a hint of someone abusing me, they wouldn't rest until he suffered for it. Neither of them. But my mother would have been more… merciless. My father would have just had him quietly murdered." Ellen shook her head. "I didn't want that. Not on my parents' souls just because I'd made a mistake. And, though I can't believe it now, looking back, a part of me still loved him. I suppose I maybe thought I could save him? I don't know. It's been so long. I don't remember what I was thinking. But I knew I had to handle the situation on my own."

She glanced at Mara, then ducked her chin. "I made mistakes there, too."

"Mara said she isn't Grant's daughter," Angie prompted.

"She's not." Ellen confirmed. "He can't have kids as it turns out. He tried with other women after… After we didn't succeed. But it's something wrong with him." She chuckled, a very unpleasant sound. "There's something cosmically perfect about that."

"Why?"

"Because the asshole sold his firstborn child to a demon for money and power."

CHAPTER THIRTEEN

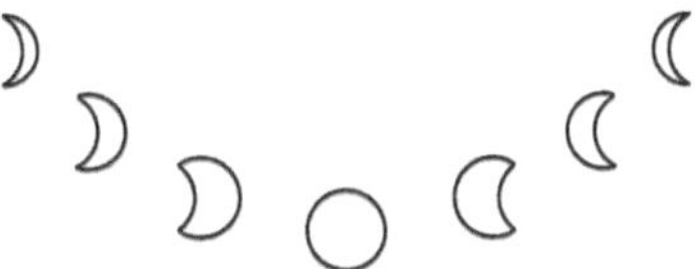

Silence followed Ellen's statement. Angie stared at her as all the pieces started to fall into place and the threads started coming together. Especially Grant's anger when Ellen couldn't get pregnant.

Ellen shivered hard, a rough jerk of her shoulders as if tossing off a bad feeling, and said again, more quietly, "He'd promised his firstborn to an evil entity and then couldn't produce a child of his own."

"Did he marry you specifically for creating a baby he could give to the demon?" Angie asked.

Ellen winced but didn't shy away from Angie's bluntness. "Yes. I was supposedly his 'reward' from the demon. His way of accessing the money and power he wanted, and of conveniently producing a child he could sacrifice. From the beginning, I was a means to an end for him. Never love. Never any feelings at all." She pressed her lips together hard enough the skin around them turned white. It took her several deep breaths before she relaxed enough to continue. "I've never been sure what hurt the most. His betrayal, or knowing just how stupid I was at that time."

"We all make mistakes when it comes to love," Angie said. She was thinking of her clients, but her gaze jumped to Sebastian and she had to look away. No one was immune to mistakes when it came to love.

To his credit, Sebastian didn't react to her comment in any way. Not even with a muscle twitch in his jaw. If he'd taken offense, or viewed her comment as a personal jab at him, he kept that to himself.

"Ellen," Angie continued when silence descended for too long. "I have to ask. If you knew what Grant was trying to do, why did you have a child?"

Ellen stared at Mara. "I really wanted a baby," she said. "I knew I couldn't take chances on having one with Grant, though. But my research led me to some interesting information." She met Angie's gaze. "Did you know, if a human offers up a child not of their own blood as sacrifice to a demon they've made a blood deal with, the demon will consider that a breach of the agreement and kill the human who's summoned it?"

Angie did know that, but she didn't do more than nod. The fact that Ellen had known before having Mara meant Ellen wanted to arrange Grant's death. She was admitting, essentially, to planning a murder. Or, maybe more accurately, a suicide. If looked at from a certain angle.

"It took me a long time to decide if I really wanted Bart

dead or not," Ellen said. "I knew I didn't want my parents to have anything to do with it, but after a time, I wasn't as opposed to having that stain on my soul."

"Things got worse in your relationship with him?"

Ellen gave a brief nod. "We fought a lot. I didn't ever admit I'd found his altar, but I did quietly go on the pill so I wouldn't get pregnant. He got increasingly angry about the lack of a child, and we fought over that often. Then we fought about other things. I finally decided he'd earned whatever came his way when he hit me the first time."

"First time?"

"The only time until… Until much later. He'd lifted his hand and stopped himself a few times before that, especially when we fought over not getting pregnant. But I guess he finally couldn't resist anymore, and he punched me. In the gut. Stole my breath and knocked me to my knees for a few minutes. He got in my face and said things would go worse for me if I couldn't give him the child he'd asked for, the only thing I was supposedly good for in our marriage."

Angie worked not to fist her hands in her lap. She wasn't new to stories of abuse. It came up in her work. She'd studied some of this in college, too, as her degree was in psychology. But still, she had trouble containing her rage. Grant was a monster, as much as the demon he'd summoned, and Angie wanted to curse him so badly, she had to concentrate hard not to issue one.

From her, that curse would be real. And it would have repercussions. A witch learned early on to be careful of such things. They could backfire. And they could come back to haunt the witch in unpredictable ways. Angie didn't do curses. Ever.

But this was one of those times she would have considered making an exception.

She silently swallowed her anger and let Ellen continue without interrupting her.

"I made a decision then," Ellen said quietly. "One I don't regret because I have Mara, but…" She shook her head. "I went to a sperm bank. Well, I went off the pill first and then avoided Bart's bed for a couple of weeks, feigning illness. I'd gotten good at timing my cycles before I learned what my husband really wanted, so I fell back into that rhythm easily. This time, I ensured I was sick or otherwise engaged during my fertile periods. I had to use a day-after pill once, when he…he surprised me."

"Rape?"

"No. I always went along with the sex because I didn't want him to get suspicious. He never had to force me. I didn't let it get to that point. But I didn't have an excuse lined up, and he caught me just at the end of my ovulation cycle so I went for the backup just in case." She shrugged. "I only had to do this for a couple of months before I was ready for the artificial insemination, though. And I got pregnant immediately." Her chuff of laughter was full of bitterness. "I got pregnant easily," she said, "without Bart's bad sperm getting in the way."

"So you don't know who Mara's father is?"

"Just a number and a medical background. Some physical

details. I hoped she'd at least vaguely resemble me and Bart. I didn't want him suspicious right away."

"What happened when he found out you were pregnant?"

"Everything in our relationship changed. He became the most loving, devoted husband. You'd think he'd been replaced with another man." She dropped her gaze to her lap. "And you know…for a few months, I almost believed the change. I almost believed that all his anger had really been about *just* desperately wanting a baby. I started to talk myself into believing he hadn't ever really intended to sacrifice anything to a demon. That I'd somehow misinterpreted what I'd found, what I'd learned in my research. That it was all in my imagination. I almost…almost fell for his lies all over again."

She shuddered and fell silent. Angie didn't push, though she wanted to hear the rest. The puzzle was coming together. She could just about see the picture now and she imagined she knew what happened next. But she wanted Ellen to tell them in her own time.

Finally, Ellen let out a deep breath. "After Mara was born, I was… I was in pretty bad shape for a few weeks. Exhausted all the time. I might have had a little post-partum depression, but I never talked to anyone about it, so I'm not sure. I found myself bursting into tears while I was nursing for no good reason. And Mara was a hungry baby so she ate a lot."

Mara rolled her eyes at her mother over this, and Ellen gave her a found smile. The moment of lightness vanished quickly from Ellen's expression.

"One night, about six weeks after Mara was born, when I was really really worn out and just needed to sleep, Bart offered to look after her for a few hours. Give me a chance to shower and nap, maybe even eat without a baby in my lap—which was a luxury because Mara didn't like being put down, so I had to carry her a lot. Anyway, I was so tired at this stage I agreed. I'd… I don't know. I guess I forgot all about the demon threat because I was so happy to have Mara but so exhausted from the new experience of having a baby. And Bart had been kind and loving and the best of husbands for almost a year. It felt like our troubles were well behind us."

She met Angie's gaze, avoiding Sebastian's when she said, "I took a shower and a nap, while he took my baby, my beloved, sweet, innocent baby, into the basement to sacrifice her to a demon."

The starkness in Ellen's expression made Angie want to weep and pull her into a hug. She didn't dare touch her. Not with all those memories and emotions so close to the surface. It would take more control than Angie thought she had to *not* see that past or feel Ellen's guilt. She could feel that guilt from a distance. Touch would be overwhelming.

Tears leaked down Ellen's cheeks as she said, "He woke me from a sound sleep by tossing Mara at me. Tossed her. She was just a baby! And he threw her onto the bed like a sack. She was crying so hard. I was disoriented. I grabbed and held her instinctively, trying to sooth her. I was distracted by her crying and didn't at first understand why Bart was yelling or what he was saying. Then it sank in."

She closed her eyes as she said, "He accused me of

having an affair, that he knew the baby wasn't his, and he called me all sorts of awful names. The usual whore, cunt… worse. He said I'd betrayed him by giving birth to a bastard."

"When did you realize what had happened?" Angie asked quietly.

"I don't remember for sure. Sometime during his rant, while I was trying to sooth Mara. It hit me that he had tried to sacrifice our…*my* daughter. That of course she'd been rejected because she wasn't of his blood, wasn't what he'd promised his demon. Which had been my original plan, even though I'd lost sight of that. I was still too disoriented for much of this to sink in. Eventually, he slammed out of the room, claiming he was going to divorce me." She met Angie's gaze. "He would lose everything my parents had given him if he divorced me, but at that moment, I didn't realize that either."

She hugged Mara closer again, and Mara showed no signs of objecting. The girl's expression was carefully closed off, at least as much as was possible for a guarded twelve-year-old, but her jaw was tight and her bottom lip trembled slightly. She leaned into her mother's embrace and kept her gaze focused on the coffee table.

"I didn't sleep the rest of that night," Ellen continued. "I held Mara as she finally slept and thought about what had happened, about my options. What I would have to do. The demon hadn't killed him like I thought it would, since he'd offered a baby not of his own blood. Since he wasn't dead, I assumed he'd talked his way out of it. He'd somehow talked the demon into an alternative deal. A deal I didn't know."

"Which meant you couldn't anticipate what he would do next," Angie said.

"Exactly. I didn't know if he intended to kill us, or... Well, I didn't know what he intended, couldn't even guess. I just knew I had to protect Mara no matter what it took. I looked into her little face, knowing I'd almost let that bastard murder her, and I could never allow that again."

How the hell did she end up living with him, then? Angie thought, but didn't ask aloud. She'd derail the story if she did, she was sure. But in all this, the fact that Mara had ended up living with a man who'd tried to sacrifice her to a demon when she was just a baby was the part that most baffle Angie. The rest, she understood in its way. The rest she could sort of find the flawed logical thread. But why not run away with Mara? Why not go into hiding from Grant and keep Mara protected?

Why the hell had Mara spent the last twelve years with a murderer when her mother was still alive?

CHAPTER FOURTEEN

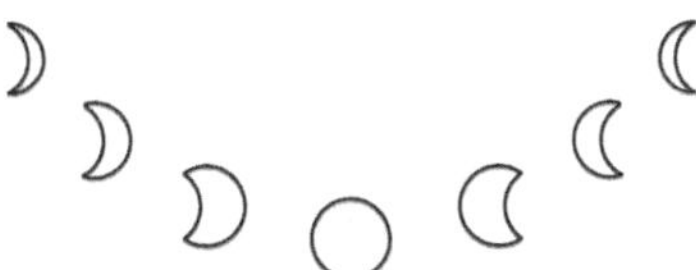

*A*ngie's cellphone broke through the heavy atmosphere just as she opened her mouth to ask another question. She winced. "Sorry."

She dug the phone out of her bag, intending to turn the ringer off, but when she saw the caller ID on the screen, she paused. She frowned up at Sebastian. "It's work."

"They shouldn't be calling you?" he asked and stated at the same time.

"Not on my night off after they've already seen me once. Anything they had to tell me, they could have while I was there." She answered the call.

"Ang? Laura here. Am I interrupting anything?"

"What's wrong, Laura? Did I forget something when I was in earlier?" She couldn't tell Laura she was interrupting a discussion of demons. Well, actually, Laura would understand. But the information wasn't hers to tell so unless it was vital, she'd keep Ellen and Mara's confidences.

"I didn't think this could wait," Laura said sounding hesitant. "There was a…a man in here earlier. He was asking about you. Real pushy. Kept trying to insist I tell him where you were, if you were in the store… This guy's aura was super dirty, Ang. He gave me the willies. So I thought I'd better warn you someone like that was looking for you."

"Did he leave a message? Give you his name?" She held Sebastian's gaze as she talked. He couldn't hear what Laura was saying, she knew, but he'd be able to tell from her expression this was something serious.

"No name, but he did leave a card with a number on it and said you should call him immediately."

"What did he look like? Besides his aura," she added, because if she didn't that was what Laura would lead with.

"Short, rail thin, dark brown hair, brown eyes, very very pale skin. Like if not for the brown hair and eyes he'd have looked like he didn't have any pigment at all. His features were kind of skeletal, the cheekbones and jaw line very prominent. His eyes seemed a little sunken. And he didn't have eyebrows which was a startling look given his dark hair. I might not have noticed that if his hair had been blond."

Angie frowned. That didn't sound like Grant. But maybe one of Grant's associates? She'd been living a quiet life until that afternoon, at least for the last year and a half. She doubted this had anything to do with her specifically. The man wasn't one of her clients or Laura would recognize him —and Angie didn't work with people who had auras Laura claimed were that "dirty" anyway. This had to be something to do with Grant and the demons.

"Thanks for the call," she said to Laura. "If he comes back, don't let him know you've talked to me."

"You know who this is?"

"Not sure."

"Does he have something to do with that hunky hunter you were in here with earlier?"

"Maybe." She was still staring at Sebastian as she spoke. He stared back, his expression carefully neutral so she couldn't read what he might be thinking.

"Stay safe, babe," Laura said. "If you need any help, let me know. We've got your back."

"Thanks, Laura. I appreciate that. I'll call if I need you."

When she'd hung up, she remained silent for another few moments, not sure how much to say in front of Ellen.

"Emergency?" Sebastian asked.

"No. Just someone looking for me at Dana's."

He tilted his head a little, a slight, almost imperceptible nod toward Ellen and Mara. To someone who didn't know him, it would look like he was moving his head in consideration of what she'd just said. But Sebastian didn't do things, even slight gestures, without a reason. She returned his gesture with a very faint one of her own, a shrug of uncertainty. He'd recognize it, but she hoped neither Ellen nor Mara would pick up on it. She wasn't as good at this as he was.

"I can deal with it later," she finished. "We need to finish here first."

Ellen stared between them with narrowed eyes. "Is it Bart? Has he found you?"

"It wasn't Grant," Angie said with complete honesty. Unless Grant was able to change his look that dramatically…

And while the hair and eyes were easy to disguise, and maybe even the eyebrows, the rail thin physique and short stature would have been obvious even with Grant sitting during their entire meeting. The skeletal look of the man's face didn't fit Grant either. She would have noticed the shadows in that kind of facial structure even in Grant's darkened study. The only similarity was the pale skin, but even then, Grant hadn't been on the edge of no pigment in his skin tone.

No, it wasn't likely the man himself. Maybe one of his employees, or a hired thug, but not Grant.

Her sincerity must have come through clearly to Ellen because the woman let the topic go.

"I suppose you want to know how Mara ended up living with Bart after everything?" Ellen asked, returning to the topic, and going directly to the question Angie had wanted an answer to but hadn't dared asked.

"That has crossed my mind," Angie said as neutrally as possible.

"I ran away with her at first. I left the next night. I didn't see Bart that entire day or evening. According to our housekeeper, he'd left the house and wasn't expected back for another day or so."

The fact that the housekeeper knew the man's schedule but his own wife didn't would have been an infuriating and terribly sad point in any other story. In the midst of this story, Angie wasn't even surprised.

"So I packed a bag and took Mara to a hotel in New Jersey, someplace I didn't think he'd look for us, but also someplace I could get to without a car since I didn't have one at the time. I didn't go to my parents because he'd look there, and I didn't want to drag them into this. At least not yet. Not until I figured out how to handle it all." She stared at Mara, her chin down. "Don't you ever do what I did. You can always come to me, no matter what. Don't dare try to handle things just to keep me safe."

Mara made a face and looked away from her mother even as she leaned closer into her. Her cheeks had flushed a deep, splotchy red. Since Mara had been in the basement earlier trying to do exactly what her mother was warning her not to do, Angie thought the admonishment might have hit the girl a little close to home.

Ellen shook off whatever thoughts she'd fallen into in that moment, and said, "To make an already long story short, I tried to bargain with a demon myself. I used all that research I'd done and summoned one and asked it to kill my husband."

"What did you offer it in return?" Angie asked quietly, making an effort to hold Ellen's gaze and not flick a glance at Sebastian.

"My soul of course. What else did I have to give?"

"When?"

"When I was old and ready to die. I wanted to be around for Mara, to raise her, so I made that a part of the deal. That

I'd go willingly but only after Mara had grown up and I was old."

"What went wrong?" Because when dealing with a demon, something *always* went wrong. Angie knew that from firsthand experience.

"We set the deal. It agreed to the bargain. Even the part about waiting to collect my soul. We were about to finalize things, and then… Then it got pulled out of the circle I'd confined it to. I wasn't even sure what happened exactly. I only found out later."

"Another demon," Sebastian said quietly. "A stronger one prevented the bargain."

Ellen nodded. "You're the one who told me that."

"What happened here? Between you and Sebastian?" Angie watched them both staring at each other. Sebastian's expression was closed. Ellen's hostile.

"Because I didn't understand what had happened the first time," Ellen said, "I thought I'd done something wrong. I wanted to strike the deal, so I tried again on another night. I read some more, did some more research. And decided I needed a better setting."

"Here?" Angie asked.

"Believe it or not, this particular apartment complex was originally built by an architect who worshipped demons. He aligned the buildings to form a sort of outer circle within which the setting of a protective circle to summon a demon was easier. Most of the people who live here don't know anything about that. They wouldn't live here if they did. It's also why the rent is super cheap for a Manhattan apartment, even all the way up here. You won't find rents like this anywhere else on the island."

Angie wondered if that explained the visible cut in the circle in the basement—she'd considered maybe Mara was coming into magic of her own and that's why something that usually manifested in the magic realm like the cut in a containment circle had appeared in this one. But if the whole complex was designed to make summoning demons easier, that might be a better explanation.

"So, you...moved here?" Angie asked.

"Not at first. At first, I just snuck into the area late at night, set up my circle and called a demon. I tried to summon the same one I had already dealt with, but it didn't show. Another appeared. This one was... Scary."

"Aren't all demons scary?" Angie had always thought so, and she was as used to them as a person who wasn't a hunter could get. No matter how often she faced them, she always found them terrifying.

"Yes, but there was something a lot more challenging about this one. Holding it was harder. It tested the circle, and I wasn't prepared for that. It was sly and calculating, and I had expected that, but maybe not as well as I thought because I was way out of my depths."

"And Sebastian came and fought the demon off," Angie guessed.

"It was a Molder demon," Sebastian said.

Angie blinked at him a few times. The same demon who'd tried to grab her from the book in Mara's room. A demon who haunted nightmares and stole souls in torturous ways. A demon who ate those souls after roasting the husks of the humans who'd carried them.

"Why did you call a Molder demon?" Angie asked, her voice quiet.

"I didn't on purpose," Ellen said, sharply. "I was attempting to call something else. It just…showed up."

"What happened then?"

Ellen flicked a glance at Sebastian. "I told him about my husband trying to kill me and my child. He said if my husband was calling a demon, he'd be taken care of. But he wasn't." This last she threw at Sebastian.

He didn't flinch except for a slight tightening around his eyes. There was more to this story from his perspective, too, but Angie didn't want to ask in front of Ellen. If he wasn't volunteering the information now, she knew it was either something he didn't want to discuss and she'd have to wring it out of him later, or something he *couldn't* discuss with strangers and she'd have to ask in private.

He caught her gaze, held it for a split second before looking back at Ellen. She knew it was something he *couldn't* discuss then. She'd have to bide her time.

"In the fight with the Molder demon," Angie said slowly, "was any deal made?"

"No," Ellen said. "There wasn't time, and I was a lot more scared with that one. I hesitated longer."

"You're lucky," Angie said simply.

"I didn't feel like it after," Ellen said.

"Believe me, whatever happened next, you're still lucky

you didn't make a deal with a Molder demon." Torture was too light a word for what they did to their captured victims.

Humans thought when they "sold their souls" to a demon that the demon took that non-physical part of them and they died. They considered that their souls might suffer, but they didn't understand it, not on a physical level, because they didn't think their physical bodies would be involved. Those with a religious background that involved a conception of Hell were more prone to thinking the sale of their soul would be a bad thing, but the rest… They never understood.

Giving a demon your "soul" gave them everything. It gave them the physical body as well as anything that was "you," and what the demon did with its conquests was often much much worse than simply killing and eating them.

A Molder demon didn't just want freed of its realm and turned loose in this one—that was the end game for a lot of the demons that heeded the call of humans. They wanted to be freed here in this realm, even if it meant having to sacrifice some of the power they held in their own realms. Each demon had its own reason. Some weren't particularly powerful and just wanted to escape and live here quietly away from the torture of stronger demons. Some wanted to live the high life here, ruling over minions. Some…

Well, some wanted to murder and torture and kill as many humans as possible. When those escaped into this realm, they almost always made the news in some form or another, at least in this modern era—be that the war they created, the bodies they piled up, whatever it was, they always came to the public eye. And that always brought the demon hunters.

That kind didn't last long because of that. The ones humans really had to worry about were the smart ones, the demons who knew how to hide their atrocities. The ones who enjoyed the torture but knew how to keep their activities away from public scrutiny. They were the worst.

A Molder demon was that kind of demon.

Had the demon escaped Ellen's hold, it would have been a disaster for everyone, including her baby. It would have abided the deal it made, but that deal would have had loopholes and ways out that Ellen wouldn't have even recognized until too late. And the demon would have been able to do whatever it wanted while still "abiding" by its deal.

Angie realized, with a growing horror, that because Mara had stopped on that image in her book, she might have seen one of those demons before. Angie stared up at Sebastian as that sank in.

"He's been dealing with a Molder demon," she said, her voice quiet.

Sebastian's eyes narrowed enough she knew he'd come to the same conclusion.

"Oh, shit," Angie muttered. "It's free, isn't it?"

CHAPTER FIFTEEN

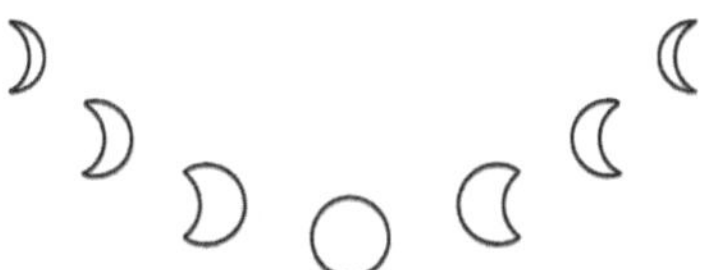

A freed demon. That would explain a lot. A demon couldn't come out of a book and reach for her if it wasn't freed in this realm. Yes, she could see into demon realms. Yes, she could rip a hole into a demon realm without meaning to and let loose demons onto her world if she wasn't careful.

But she couldn't do that through a book. She couldn't just randomly contact a demon. She needed the specific instance of a naturally occurring "V" in a tree trunk. Not even every tree caused issues. They had to be very specific designs. Shapes mattered in magic and preternatural happenings. Shapes always mattered.

The demon being able to attack her through a book had been a horrifying oddity. And she should have realized the implications a lot sooner.

There were only so many ways a demon could get loose in the human realm. The most common way, the way the hunters spent most of their time trying to prevent, happened when a deal with a human went bad and the human lost control of the demon they were trying to contain. Once the demon broke out of that containment, whatever it was, they were free to rampage through this realm with only the hunters standing between them and disaster.

But there were other ways as well.

"Ellen," she said, trying to keep some of the urgency from her voice, "what happened with Grant after you called the Molder demon? Why was Mara living with him?" There was no more time for niceties. Angie had to know. Because if there was a freed Molder demon in her adopted city, it had to be stopped.

"After Sebastian left, when I knew summoning a demon of my own wouldn't work because either he'd come back and stop me again or the demon would escape my control, I panicked. I didn't know what to do. I knew I had to keep Bart from killing Mara, but how?"

"Your parents?"

She hung her head. "I was so ashamed to go to them. They were people of faith and would have been horrified to discover I'd dealt with a demon." She looked away. "I might have gone at that point, though. I was desperate enough. But they died suddenly. A car accident." She didn't meet Angie's gaze. "I've never been sure if it was an accident or not. The police said it was, but..."

She closed her eyes, let out a long breath. "That cut off

my last option, my last real support system. I'd been too late…" Choking on a sob, she pressed her hand to her mouth.

"What did you do?" Angie asked.

"I went to Bart to negotiate. It was my only option. I wasn't just dealing with an abusive husband I could hide from. I was dealing with a man who could call demons to hunt me down. Demons that would find me no matter where I went. I didn't stand a chance against that and I no longer thought I could summon a demon of my own to counter him because I knew someone would stop me." She threw another glare at Sebastian.

"I told Bart he could have the money," she continued, "the status, everything. I'd even give him my inheritance. And I'd leave. So long as he didn't kill Mara. She wasn't to be sacrificed. He didn't need to if I gave him everything."

"He wasn't satisfied with that?"

"He said he didn't trust me to keep the deal. He knew I'd tried to call a demon of my own."

"He knew? How?"

"I don't know. He might have been guessing for all I know, but I gave myself away in my reaction. Stupid. So even if he'd been guessing, he knew he was right after that. He said there was no way to trust I'd hold to my part of the bargain. Unless I left Mara with him."

Angie straightened. "What?"

"He said, if I left Mara for him to raise, she would be his guarantee against me doing something to harm him. She would be a guarantee for us both."

"He held her as a hostage?"

Ellen pressed her lips together before answering. "This was the deal we struck. I would pretend to be dead so she wouldn't come looking for me. He would keep her safe and raise her well. If I tried to summon a demon to get revenge on him, he'd kill her. If he tried to sacrifice her or hurt her, I would kill him." She snorted, a bitter sound. "I don't think he believed I could kill him, but because I'd called a demon—two as a matter of fact—he wasn't entirely sure. At the time at least, he was worried I'd destroy him. If he hadn't been worried, he wouldn't have proposed the deal."

She looked at Mara, her eyes full of sadness. "I didn't know what else to do to keep her safe. I believed he could get to us, no matter what. And I knew—even if he didn't—that I wouldn't be able to control a demon to counter him. I thought the deal would keep him from hurting her. He was worried enough to make it. I thought it would keep her safe." She lifted her chin. "And it did. For twelve years. She was safe."

"What changed?"

"Honestly, I don't know," she said, frowning in confusion this time. "I stayed in New York, moved here because its cheap and close to Mara. I didn't let her know I was alive, of course, but I wanted to keep an eye on her, make sure she was safe. I didn't let Bart know where I was. I was careful. He didn't have a clue I lived here—I'm not sure it occurred to him that I'd lower myself to live in such a place." She shrugged. "I don't know if he knew about the architect of these buildings and that the area is good for demon contact. Maybe he did, and he did know I lived here. Maybe because I live where it's easier to summon demons, that's what ensured he kept our bargain."

"If he knew you were here, he would have come here to look for Mara, though, wouldn't he?" Angie asked.

She glanced at her daughter. "Maybe. Or maybe that's why he sent you here. Maybe he can't come. Maybe the demon he's dealing with can't reach us here?"

"Why would that be?" It was possible. Angie could think of several ways it could happen, but she wanted to know what Ellen knew. What Ellen thought.

"He was shaken when we talked, when we made our deal. He was scared, even if he didn't want to admit it. Something had changed for him as well. I left him with the resources to find me if he'd been determined to hunt me down. He never tried."

"Did you give him your inheritance?"

"I kept some of it, but most of it I let him have. Willed it to him so he'd receive it after I 'died' in an accident. But I kept some so I could live without needing to find on-the-books type work. Not enough to have hidden from him indefinitely, though. If he really wanted to track me down, I think he could have. He didn't come looking for me. And now, when he wants to find Mara, if he knew I was here this whole time, he'd have come here to check. Or sent someone to find us. If he was able. Right? So maybe he isn't able."

Maybe he isn't Grant anymore, Angie thought in an instinctive flash. Maybe the demon Grant had originally bargained with had finally taken him, and that's what had changed.

While the most common way for a demon to escape into this realm was for it to break out of its summoner's control, they lost power when they did that. The only way to enter this realm and still maintain their full power was to "possess" a human host. But that wasn't as easy as people thought. It took a very powerful demon, a lot of blood sacrifice, a lot of time, and in the end, the human didn't survive hosting a demon for very long. Possession wasn't a plan for a demon to get loose into this realm for more than a few days at most.

But it was possible. And a Molder demon was powerful enough to have turned Grant into a host.

With the realization, everything that was happening suddenly got a lot lot worse. A demon couldn't occupy Grant's body for long periods without killing him. But it *could* take over his body if there'd been enough time, preparation, and the deal they'd made had allowed for it. And if it was inside Grant's body, it could walk around free in this realm.

"We need to go," Angie said, rising from the floor in a rush. "Sebastian, we have to check in at Dana's Cauldron. Now."

He nodded and moved away from the windows.

Ellen launched off the couch. "Wait. What will happen to us? To Mara? If he comes here for us, if the demon comes here, we don't have any protection."

"Stay here, in this building. In this complex. Don't leave," Angie said firmly.

"And don't call any demons of your own," Sebastian

warned. "That will only make matters worse. I promise you that."

Mara hung her head. "I can't let him kill her," she muttered. "He took her from me once. I won't let him do it again."

"But a demon isn't the answer," Sebastian said gently. "Stay here and safe. We'll deal with Grant."

Angie didn't miss how he didn't call the man Mara's father anymore. Which was a kindness to her as well as the truth. Grant might have raised Mara and pretended to be her father, but he'd never been a real one to her. Not in any way that counted. Blood or no blood, Grant had held her as a hostage. He hadn't been a dad.

"And if he kills you both?" Ellen said. "What then?"

"Another demon hunter will come," Sebastian said, without flinching. "My mentor will ensure you're safe."

"Who's your mentor?"

"A legend," Sebastian said. "And she trained me well. Don't worry. We'll stop Grant. No matter what it takes. We'll stop him."

"Why didn't you before?" Ellen asked the million-dollar question. Again.

Angie watched Sebastian carefully. His expression didn't betray any of his inner thoughts. But the faint red in his dark brown eyes was more prominent just then.

He looked from Ellen to Angie and said, "Because Grant's demon killed the last hunter who went after Grant."

Her chest tightened. She'd been afraid of that. But

hearing her worst fears confirmed made her gut hurt. If the demon had already killed one hunter…

It could kill another.

"What makes you think that won't happen again?" Ellen snapped. "To you."

"I have a stronger will than it does," Sebastian said, holding Angie's gaze.

For a demon hunter, that was all that mattered.

CHAPTER SIXTEEN

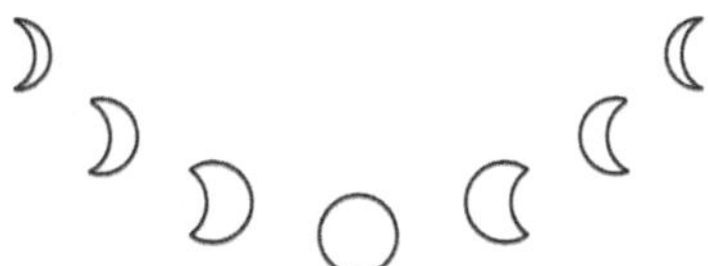

$\mathcal{A}$ngie was nearly jumping out of her skin by the time they reached Dana's Cauldron. It was well past midnight at that stage, and the shop closed at ten, but she'd been given a key a few months ago and the code to the security system.

No one was inside. At least, it didn't appear to be occupied from the outside. Sometimes the psychics worked late or had private clients in during afterwork hours. The trusted psychics, like Angie, were given the key and security code for this reason. But if someone was inside after hours, they pulled down a purple shade over the front display window to let the other employees know.

The shade wasn't pulled tonight.

Angie let out a deep breath, relief making her weak.

"You okay?" Sebastian asked. He'd been quiet all the

way here. There wasn't much they could have said on the subway anyway.

"I'm not sure. I'm happier knowing the place is closed up and no one is here, but…"

"We'll go inside," he said. "You can make sure."

"Thank you." She unlocked the door and raised the inner security screen.

Most of the surrounding businesses had outer metal screens they pulled down to cover windows and doors at the end of the work day. But that system gave away when someone was inside late at night, so the owners had moved the protective screen system to an interior design. It meant the occasional broken window to fix. But since anyone who knew what Dana's Cauldron was usually worried the "witches" might curse them, the store went mostly unmolested.

She punched in the security code on the panel just inside the door. Then closed and locked up behind her, including pulling down the security screen again. The interior of the store was dark, with only some faint light from a few working lava lamps and one of the small water fountains bubbling away near the front of the store. Angie didn't need light in Dana's to know where she was going, though, so she left the overheads off, preferring to keep her night vision.

Sebastian didn't question the choice. He had excellent night vision.

She started at the counter, where she knew the man who'd come looking for her would have stopped to talk to

Laura. For a long moment, she stared down at the counter top, afraid to touch it. If the man with the dirty aura had actually been a demon, Angie wasn't sure she wanted to sense him.

"I've got your back," Sebastian said quietly. "I'll pull you away if you get overwhelmed."

"I hate that you know me so well still," she murmured.

"Two years isn't long enough to forget."

She closed her eyes, briefly, the truth of his statement a sharp jab to the gut. "I haven't forgotten anything either. Despite my best efforts."

"I'll be pleased with that later. Sorry, but I will."

She rolled her eyes. Too many memories. It was so easy to fall back into a comfortable rhythm with him. Too easy for all the old feelings to come crashing in.

"Don't touch me unless I really need your help," she said so she didn't have to deal with the deeper undercurrents.

He grunted yes and stayed a few feet away, ready to move but far enough to keep from distracting her.

She let out a long breath, opening up her inner senses, letting her vision blur. She stepped closer to the counter and gently touched the glass surface. A cacophony of different impressions rose up at first, all the customers, queriers, all the employees that had been moving over this spot for the last days. She let the onslaught roll over her, breathing calmly through it, watching but not following any of the impressions as they streamed past her inner eye.

One unexpected impression made her pause a moment—a

newer employee of Dana's Cauldron was pregnant. They'd have to celebrate as soon as Zadie told everyone. Though to be fair, trying to keep that a secret in a store filled with psychics, aura readers, and assorted witches seemed a waste of time. Still, it was Zadie's information to give out. Angie let the good news go and went back to sifting through the images for the one she needed.

Her breath caught when she finally hit it. The sense of Laura's discomfort grabbed Angie first. Laura had seen and been through a lot in her years at Dana's. She didn't waver or worry over every character that walked in. This was New York after all, filled with Characters and Interesting People. And Dana's Cauldron attracted a lot of those types. But Laura had very very good instincts about people.

And when the pale man walked up to the counter, Laura raised an inner psychic shield. Angie actually felt that shield go up. Which meant Laura hadn't read the man's aura the minute he'd stepped close. It wasn't his "dirty" aura that had caused the reaction. Laura had shielded against him first. Instinctively.

That was telling.

Angie breathed slowly through her nose, trying to let the images play out without hiding from them or flinching from Laura's fear. And there was a lot of fear there, along with confusion. Laura didn't know why she was afraid. But she was too smart to ignore the instinct, thankfully.

A full-blown scene unfolded for Angie with bits of the actually dialogue rising up. A vision so clear and detailed, it was like watching a movie.

Laura greeting the man with a forced, professional smile.

The man leaning on the counter near where Angie's hands were now, lowering his voice. A deep voice with a slightly sibilant sound in it. Not Grant's voice. At least, not the voice Grant had used in his study. But there was something vaguely familiar about it.

"You have an Angela Jordan working here," the man said. "I need to speak to her."

"Is there anything I can help you with? You need a psychic reading? Or perhaps you'd like your Taro cards interpreted? We have some lovely candles that just arrived yesterday if you need clarity."

Laura neither confirmed nor denied that Angie was an employee. Clever and something all the people on the main floor were taught to do. While Dana's Cauldron got mostly harmless clientele, there were the occasional stalkers everyone had to watch out for.

"I need to speak with Angela Jordan."

"Do you have a card? Contact information perhaps?"

"Is she here or not?"

"I can ask one of the managers to help you if you need something more specific?"

Since Laura was a manager, Angie knew this was a sign of distress and Laura would be calling in the Calvary soon if the man didn't stop badgering her.

The man fell silent for a moment and narrowed his eyes at Laura. "This is important," he said quietly. "It's a matter of life or death that I speak to her."

Laura hesitated, just a moment—to open her senses

finally and take in the man's aura. Angie wouldn't have recognized what she was doing in that beat of hesitance if she hadn't known Laura. The pause was subtle, and to an outsider would look like she was considering what the man had just said.

Laura's gaze sharpened again, and she stared at the man's cheek. Not his eyes. She was very carefully not looking him in the eyes, Angie realized. Laura had been doing that on instinct since the beginning. The sense of her fear spiked again, but there was an undercurrent now, not just fear, but determination. A swirl of stubborn determination.

"Would you like to leave contact information for our staff? Someone is sure to get back to you. The owners like to take care of their people." Again, words that sounded polite and gave very little away. But the last line was pointed and spoken very clearly.

We protect our own and you won't be getting any answers here, demon.

Angie blinked a few times as that last bit settled in. The "demon" had been a part of what Laura was feeling in that moment. Laura recognized that "dirty" aura as belonging to a demon. She hadn't said as much on the phone, but she'd known what Sebastian was after reading his aura—or trying to. Angie wasn't sure if Sebastian had allowed that or not, but even her inability to read his aura would have tipped Laura off. She knew demons and hunters existed. And she obviously knew the man-demon was dangerous enough she didn't even want to refer to him as one out loud.

But he wasn't Grant. At least, not as far as Angie could

discern. The question was, did he work for or with Grant? Was he the freed Molder demon shifted into a human disguise? Or was that demon living in Grant's body—as she'd worried earlier—and this was something else entirely?

Too coincidental for a demon to come looking for her now, after eighteen months of not dealing with their kind in any way. This was something to do with Sebastian returning to her life. Something directly linked with Grant and Mara and Ellen. She just couldn't tell how it connected.

Angie tried to shift her focus on the vision away from Laura and her overwhelming sense of fear to the pale man and what he was thinking and feeling in that moment. But she came up against a granite wall of silence when she did that. The demon's psyche was impenetrable. Most were. She might know them at a touch. She might be very familiar with the demon realms—much more than she'd ever wanted to be —but reading them was usually impossible.

Worth a try, though.

She tried to shift her attention back to Laura, to see how the rest of the interaction played out, but the image wavered and turned fuzzy, her sense of the exchange fading at the edges. She concentrated, trying to keep her focus on the scene.

Everything cleared again, the image snapping back into focus.

And the demon turned to face *her*. Looked right at her even though she was supposedly just touching a memory impression. The pale man smiled, revealing rows of sharp teeth, his eyes black now, with a hint of red in the depth.

Behind him, Laura seemed frozen in the moment. Everything around her had frozen. Angie was no longer seeing a movie scene. She was looking at a still picture. Everything paused.

Except the demon.

The demon had moved out of the picture and was smiling at its audience of one.

"Angela," it said, the hiss in its voice stronger now. "I'll see you soon."

It reached toward her, long fingers tipped with sharp claws brushing against her arm.

Angie gasped, nearly screamed, and jumped away from contact with the counter. The image shattered around her like glass, falling down in sharp shards. She blinked hard to pull reality back together, to refocus on her surroundings as they were now.

Sebastian's hands steadied her, gentle on her shoulders, something to help her refocus. A part of her recognized that any sort of touch should have bothered her just then. But Sebastian's didn't. She always recognized it was him holding her, his touch keeping her grounded and steady, helping her return to the moment, without invading her psychic senses with his thoughts. He willed his touch to only comfort.

For a touch psychic, having a demon hunter for a partner had its advantages.

She shivered as the afterimage of the demon reaching for her rose up. She could still feel the brush of its claws against her skin.

Sometimes, having a demon hunter for a partner was *not* an advantage at all.

"What happened?" Sebastian asked.

He didn't release her, and for that she had to be grateful because she wasn't sure she could stay standing just then without his support.

"The man who came looking for me was a demon."

"A freed demon? In a human host or just disguised to appear human?"

"If it was riding a human host, I've never seen the man he was occupying before." She described the scene she'd seen, and the way the demon had talked to her, touched her after she'd tried to read it. "Should have known better," she muttered as she finally pulled away from Sebastian.

"You broke contact on your own this time," he said, quietly. "That must mean something. Was it a Molder demon?"

"Not sure. I broke contact too quickly. I wasn't expecting it to…notice me. I hate the way those fuckers twist space and time."

Sebastian's snort of agreement made her smile faintly. As the after images faded, she settled more and her pulse returned to a steady thump.

"Been one hell of a day," she muttered. "Twice had a demon reach through my psychic senses to get at me. Had to see a demon in this realm about to make a deal with a child. And nearly let one loose at the Botanical Garden because I'm out of practice avoiding the wrong kinds of trees." She shook her head.

He frowned a little. "What happened at the Garden?"

"One of the trees caught me. I didn't mean to look and I

found myself staring into the 'V' and breaking open that barrier. A demon tried to climb through. If a little girl hadn't distracted me and made me look away…" She let the sentence trail off. He knew what happened when she opened that barrier between their realm and a demon realm.

That's how they'd met.

"Why didn't you tell me this earlier?" His voice deepened and a touch of anger crept in.

She scowled. "I wasn't planning on getting involved with all this," she said, gesturing back at the counter. "I'm not supposed to be working with demons anymore. And I hadn't intended to spend the day with you after our meeting. I didn't think it was relevant."

Sebastian put his hands on his hips and lowered his chin, giving her a look. "You know nothing is ever irrelevant where demon hunting is concerned. It always ties together somehow."

"Don't you dare lecture me. I was only there because *you* asked me to meet you there."

"You could have said no."

"You could have chosen a different location." She mirrored him, putting her hands on her hips and staring him down. If he was hoping she'd meekly take criticism from him, he was sorely mistaken. Not in this moment. Not ever.

"You could have insisted we meet somewhere else. Or not at all. You still showed up."

"You said it was an emergency."

"You still could have stayed away." He leaned in close, his face in hers. "You made the choice to be there."

"You ensured I showed by playing on old feelings," she snapped.

"Those old feelings haven't gone away."

"Stop." She held up a hand and leaned away from him. She couldn't have *that* conversation now. Not when her nerves were still raw from the demon attack. "We agreed."

"I only agreed reluctantly." He leaned back too, but his gaze had darkened.

And there were emotions in his expression—hurt, anger, regret—all things she didn't want to see. "Because it was for the best," she said. "We both knew it. I don't belong in your world."

"You were made for this world or you wouldn't be able to open the realms."

An argument he'd made before. She snarled and pointed a finger at his chest. "I've only ever come back to this because of you. I would have avoided it. I wouldn't have almost let a demon out this afternoon, if it wasn't for you."

"Don't blame me. You're the one who isn't practicing."

"Because I haven't needed to," she said, her voice rising. "*You* brought me into this again. I was quietly living my life without any demon trouble at all. You're back for one day and it's all demons all the time again."

Her anger rose with her voice. There was a reason they hadn't spoken in so long, and it wasn't just because she didn't want to be part of the demon hunting world anymore. It was because they couldn't be together without fighting about it all. About the demons. About what she did and didn't tell him. About how she used her skills. Or didn't. About how she wanted to live and how he had to live.

They'd loved. But they'd fought. And Angie didn't want to spend her life fighting with the man she loved.

Unfortunately, since she was still in love with Sebastian, it looked like that might just be her fate.

CHAPTER SEVENTEEN

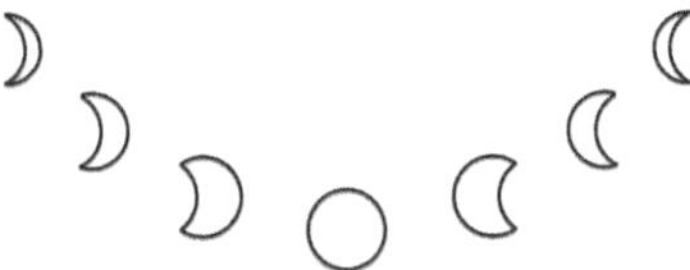

"You're only yelling at me now because you're scared," Sebastian said, his voice lowering even as hers had risen. "I won't be blamed for your fear."

"I wouldn't be experiencing this fear right now if it weren't for you."

Even the usually calming patchouli scent of Dana's and the gentle trickling sound of the water fountain couldn't calm Angie's anger. Not even the soothing darkness inside the closed store. She wanted to throw something, break something, smash her hands through the glass counter behind her until the fear and rage subsided. And because the urge was so strong, she stuffed her hands into the pockets of her jacket.

Sebastian opened his mouth to say more. She prepared to lash out at whatever he had to say…

And then her stomach growled.

The sound was loud and very obvious in the quiet store.

His lips twitched. She tried to keep scowling but his expression made her tension break, and she ended up rolling her eyes.

"It's been too long since I ate," she said, almost defensively. And even then, shoving a sandwich into her mouth on the subway uptown barely counted.

"And I promised to feed you and then didn't." He shook his head, a smile breaking over his gorgeous face and loosening all the tightness in his shoulders. "Ah, Ang. I've missed you so much."

Her heart tightened. "Even this? Even all the fighting."

"Everything." He raised his hand as if he'd touch her but stopped himself, fisting and relaxing his hand at his side instead. "But I've especially missed your appetite."

She snorted.

"You need food. And we need a break."

"There's still a demon on the loose."

"We'll track him down better if you aren't passing out from hunger."

"We?"

"We?" he asked as well.

She sighed. She was already in this time, and they both knew it. One way or the other, and despite her continued resistance. She was with him until this demon was stopped.

"If you feed me, I'll probably be less annoyed by all this," she said on a sigh.

"Not likely," he said, though he smiled when he did. "But

you'll be less likely to take my head off if you're not hungry."

"True enough."

"And maybe some tea? Or better yet…Tequila?"

She narrowed her eyes. "Stop showing off that you know me so well."

This time his smile made her pulse thump. He'd always done that to her and the bastard knew it.

"You're sure the demon can wait?" she asked, because she needed to look away from the heat simmering in his gaze.

He paused and she knew he was… Well, he called it listening. Aidan always called it sensing. They knew when they were needed, an instinct that came with the job. They knew when they were imminently required and when the fight could wait. The instinct came, and they went into a hunt. Sometimes, they had time to research their subjects, learn a bit about what the dumb bastard summoning the demons was up to. Sometimes, they had to jump right into the fight.

Sebastian couldn't explain the instinct exactly, any more than she could explain how she felt magic flowing, or the way her touch psychic sense worked in detail. She could get close with vague comparisons. So could he. But in the end, those explanations couldn't ever really convey the *feel*.

The fact that she *didn't* sense when a demon was about to break free had always been the confirmation for her that she wasn't meant to be part of the demon hunting world. She was no hunter.

His gaze refocused and he said, "Everything is safe. For

now." He gestured toward the door. "Let's go find you some food."

"This late, where?" she asked as she headed out.

"This is New York. Someplace will be open."

They found a late-night diner only a few blocks from Dana's.

The bright lights made Angie squint as a professionally stoic server showed them to a small booth at the back of the long, narrow restaurant. There were only two other people in the diner, each sitting by themselves in the small two person booths. One, a man reading the newspaper and picking at a plate of eggs. Another, a tired looking woman stirring a cup of coffee as her waffles went ignored. The scent of coffee and French fries made Angie's stomach rumble again.

She slipped out of her coat, hanging it on the tall hook next to her seat, tossed her purse onto the inside of the seat, and slipped into the booth with a sigh. She waved away the menu when offered and said, "Tea, very hot, please. A Spanish omelet. And a very large plate of fries."

The waiter didn't bat an eye at the order. "And for you, sir?" he asked Sebastian, who'd taken the menu.

"Tea as well. And a regular soda."

"Will that be all?"

"For now," Seb said, handing the menu back.

"Anticipating a fight later?" Angie asked once the waiter was out of ear shot. If he was, he wouldn't want to eat and risk having something in his stomach to throw up.

"In the next twenty-four hours," he said. "I can eat now.

I'm just deciding between a burger or something with pasta in it."

"I love New York diners," Angie said with a smile. And she did. The variety always made her happy.

Silence descended as the waiter returned with their heavy porcelain mugs of hot water and a small, rectangular metal carrier stuffed with tea bags. There was already a little pot on the table with sweeteners and a miniature jug of milk.

When the waiter left, Sebastian sighed as he pulled out one of the sealed tea bags. The particular brand wasn't to his taste. She grinned at his resigned dunking of the bag.

"You want better tea, you'll need to bring your own. Or go someplace that caters to your snobby British taste buds."

He chuckled. "I really should carry a few packets around with me, shouldn't I?"

"I've been telling you that for years." She stopped shortly and swallowed hard. She didn't want to talk about their past. She hadn't meant to bring it up.

He held her gaze. "You can stop now," he said. "Go home, go to sleep. Leave the rest to me. You've helped me with what I needed you for—finding Mara."

"And uncovered a lot more complicated situation than you thought it was," she reminded him. "Or did you know all along this would tie into a fight from your past?"

"I thought it was simply a matter of finding Mara and fighting off the demon Grant had summoned." He shrugged as he kept his gaze on his steadily darkening tea.

Angie noticed he didn't directly answer her question. She narrowed her eyes at him. "You knew Grant had killed the last hunter who'd come after him, though. You knew Grant was a problem."

"Aidan told me. After we'd come for Grant's demon. I didn't know ahead of time."

"Just coincidence then that you were in the area when instinct sent you to Grant?" Angie didn't believe in coincidences where the hunters were concerned. They worked off instincts—to find the fight, to know when it would happen, the actually fight itself—and will. Not coincidences.

He sighed. "You know there aren't any coincidences with us."

She tried not to roll her eyes or scowl that he'd echoed her thoughts so precisely.

"I felt the draw to New York, but I was in Kansas at the time. I assumed the others were busy elsewhere and I was the closest one free."

Well, that did happen. There just weren't enough hunters in the world to cover all areas, and sometimes the jolt that told them they had to be somewhere for a fight came while they were pretty far away. She remembered Sebastian once having to go directly from a fight in California all the way across the country to one in South Carolina because he'd been the only hunter available for it.

They went where the instincts told them to go.

"I didn't make the connection between Grant and Ellen until we were standing outside Ellen's apartment building," he said quietly. "Even then, until we saw her, I wasn't positive this linked to her, and that the ex-husband she'd told me about all those years ago was Grant." He pulled his tea bag out of his mug, concentrating on the moves instead of looking up at her as he murmured, "I wondered why Aidan joined me for this fight. And encouraged me to contact you."

"That was Aidan's idea? Of course, it was her idea. I owe her one for that." She didn't mean that in a good way.

Sebastian's lips lifted in a soft smile.

"How did she know there was a connection if you didn't?" Angie asked.

"Even after all these years, some of the things Aidan knows surprises me." He shrugged. "We all knew that a demon hunter had been killed in a fight here twelve years ago. It happened…" He paused. "Two days before I fought Ellen's demon."

Angie didn't comment. They lost hunters. That was part of the job. But there were few enough spread around the world that they knew pretty quickly when one of their own died. Most tried not to think about it—at least according to Sebastian. They had history keepers to record it, to disseminate the story. The hunters tried to learn what went wrong and ensure the mistakes weren't made again, but they didn't dwell on the death. It might weaken their will if they did.

"I didn't know that fight had involved Grant until Aidan told me a few days ago," he said quietly.

"Why didn't someone else go after Grant and his demon? Why was he left to just continue summoning demons for years if your people knew about him?" Angie couldn't blame Ellen for asking this, for blaming the hunters for this. She could have kept her daughter, ensured her safely, if the hunters had stopped Grant before now.

"We don't go in until the demon is about to break free," he reminded her. "There aren't enough of us to prevent stupid humans from summoning demons. The best we can do is intervene to prevent the demon from escaping. Or go after them once they do escape."

His tone had taken on that professorial lilt that made her teeth hurt—just a touch too much condescension for her. He was telling her things she knew, but telling her again because she'd asked a question she should have known the answer to. That didn't make his tone any less irritating.

"So you're telling me that even though a hunter died going after Grant's demon—who was obviously on the edge of escaping—" she threw him a look that said *did I get that right, professor?* He ignored her expression completely. "—that no one went after his escaped demon?"

"The demon didn't escape," Sebastian said bluntly.

She straightened. "But if the hunter died…" That's what happened. Hunter dies. Demon escapes… Demon usually kills the person who'd called it.

But Grant was still alive.

That was the strange part in all this. The timeline. Grant should have been killed twelve years ago. First, when he tried to offer a sacrifice that wasn't what he'd agreed to. Then when the hunter had gone in and been killed by the demon. The demon should have escaped at either of those times. The fact that Grant hadn't been killed during any of that was… Not normal.

Well, as normal as anything could be when dealing with demons.

It was possible the demon had occupied Grant's body, taken it over and moved through this realm inside the human host. But demons of any strength at all couldn't occupy a human for long without the process killing the human. That was the tricky bit for a demon wanting to hold onto its powers.

Breaking free of a confinement circle and the human who'd summoned it, breaking free into the human realm, cost a demon some of its strength and power. While inside the circle, they were still linked with their own realm, and therefore at full power. Once free of their realm, cut off from their origins, they lost something.

Many demons didn't care because either they weren't strong enough to begin with to worry about the sacrifice— they'd still be dangerous in this realm even weaker than they'd been in theirs—or they were desperate enough to get here to accept the loss. The stronger the demon, the more power they lost.

A demon might get around that by grooming and then taking over the body of a human host. They could keep most of their power that way, using the host to move through this realm at almost full strength. But the demons strong enough to do that were too strong for their hosts and the humans died pretty quickly.

Grant was still alive.

Twelve years later, he was still alive.

"I was told the demon didn't escape," Sebastian added, his frown deepening.

"None of this makes sense," Angie said. After removing her tea bag from the mug, she dumped enough sugar into her tea to make Sebastian wince. She ignored him and added some milk. "Grant should have been killed a long time ago. His demon is obviously one of the scary powerful ones. Strong enough to kill a hunter. But then it didn't bother to escape after that? And then, Grant waited out twelve years before looking to sacrifice Mara or figuring out where his ex-wife was to sacrifice her?"

"Demon timelines aren't the same as ours," he reminded her.

"The demon might be patient, but from everything we've learned, Grant is not. Why did *he* wait so long? And then why now? What's changed? You're here because Grant's demon has escaped or is on the verge of escaping again. Otherwise, none of the hunters would be here right now."

He didn't comment.

"The Molder demon got at me through my psychic senses. That shouldn't happen if it's in another realm. They can't attack me if I don't open a breach."

"You're sure?"

She paused. She wasn't absolutely certain. Mostly because… "It's never happened before."

"You haven't dealt with a Molder demon before."

He didn't have to ask. He knew almost all of her demon past. He'd been involved in some of it directly. She'd told him the rest. And anything she'd been too young to remember, or had purposefully blocked, she was certain Aidan had told him.

"But the demon walked into Dana's Cauldron and talked to Laura," she continued. "That wasn't just a psychic connection. She called, worried about it. It happened in this realm. The demon has to have escaped. And it has to be strong enough to get around the wards and protections erected around Dana's." The wards wouldn't have necessarily kept the demon out, but they would have made coming in extremely uncomfortable for it if its intent was harm.

And demons always intended harm.

"*A* demon went looking for you at Dana's," Sebastian said. "It wasn't necessarily the same Molder demon who attacked you through the book. For that matter, it didn't have to be a Molder demon in the book at all. We don't actually know what kind of demon we're facing. Not for sure."

That was a scary realization. Knowing what kind of demon they faced helped them know how to fight it. It wasn't absolutely necessary. The hunters didn't always know. But it helped.

She shook off the fear to return to her main point. "Whatever it is, it's free. And a freed demon looking for me right, after I get involved in a hunt again, is too coincidental. It's all connected. Whether it was a Molder demon or not, a freed one walked into my place of work. It wanted to find me badly enough, it found a way past the protective circle around the place that should have made going inside very difficult for it. A freed one *must* have been responsible for the attack through the book, because I can't breach realms without a living tree, and I didn't summon a demon in any other way."

They fell silent as the waiter brought her food. Sebastian looked at the fries and sighed, then ordered a burger and fries of his own.

"Can I have some of your burger?" she asked.

"If you share your eggs."

She grinned, but her pleasure in their old habits died fast.

"This situation is really wrong, Sebastian. Something isn't adding up."

"I know."

"We're missing something."

"We are."

"So what do we do about it?"

He held her gaze this time, silent for a long moment. Finally, he said, "We eat. Then you go home to sleep."

"And tomorrow?"

"Tomorrow, you'll go back to work. I'll…talk to some people. I'll stop the demon."

"I've already said I'm in this. I'm not leaving you to fight alone. Not like this."

"I didn't bring you back in to fight demons again, Ang. I really didn't."

She hadn't believed that earlier in the night. Now, though, she could read his sincerity. Oh, he could be fooling her. His will was strong enough to make her believe what he wanted her to believe. But he'd never used his will on her that way. She didn't think he was now, either. She believed him.

"I won't leave you to fight this demon on your own," she

repeated after a moment. "I know I should. It's not my job. Hasn't been for a while now."

"Until I pulled you back in. Again."

She ignored that because it just sparked her anger and she didn't want to argue again. "I may even distract you," she said instead.

"That's as good an excuse as any for you to tap out."

"But the demon, or demons, or whatever…they know me now. A demon came to my place of work looking for me by name. I can't walk away."

She moved her toast to her egg plate, cut her omelet in half, put a chunk of it onto her toast plate, then pushed the smaller plate over to Sebastian. He smiled down at the food.

"A demon knows how to find me," she said, pulling him back to the conversation. "That puts everyone I know in danger. I have to finish this."

With a very faint nod, he dug into the food, not arguing with her anymore.

They ate in silence, and when his burger arrived, he cut it in half and they shared that too—her with lots of spicy mustard added. He sinned against burgers by adding mayonnaise to his half.

When she was down to her last few French fries and her stomach finally felt satisfied, she spoke again. "What now?"

"Now, you need sleep or you won't be any good to me."

She made a face but didn't argue. She was exhausted. Though she often stayed up late into the night, the night that had been in it had drained her. Having a full belly wasn't helping.

"I'll make sure you get home without a demon following," he finished.

She narrowed her eyes. "Where are you staying?"

"Don't worry about me."

"You need sleep, too. I know you big bad demon hunters can do without if needs be, but you'll be better off if you sleep while you can."

"I'll be fine."

"You're not going hunting again tonight? Do you have to?"

"No. Everyone has settled for the night as far as I can tell."

Which meant his instincts weren't driving him to a specific location to prevent disaster. Nothing was about to break free onto this realm. Although, given the number of near misses today, she was starting to wonder about his instincts.

"You didn't know Mara was summoning a demon until we were at the apartment complex," she said, slowly, the realization finally sinking in. "Or you would have known where to find her without me scrying. Which meant her demon was under control. She's only twelve. That's some serious will. An Anchor demon is no small beast to manage."

He nodded. "I noticed."

"Did you notice the physical line in the circle after she'd cut it? The one that showed up in the ash of her containment circle?"

He raised his brows a little. "I missed it. What did you see?"

"When she cut the circle with her athame, and it died down, there was a blank line right through the circle with no ash or anything. A very very distinctive cut through the circle."

"That doesn't usually manifest in the physical world," he said.

"My thought exactly."

She worked with magic circles all the time. They were an important part of both her magic and her theology. And according to her first mentor back in Albuquerque, Angie had a significant amount of magic she still hadn't tapped—Angie suspected this was Esmerelda's way of nagging her into more training. But even with the training she had, and the magic, and the amount of time she'd spent setting and cutting magical circles, she'd never once had one show the cut in the physical world if she didn't *make* the cut in the physical world. A line she'd physically smudged through a circle of salt was one thing. The mystical cut…that didn't manifest anywhere but the mind of the person who set and broke the circle.

"Could she have physically drawn a line through the circle while you weren't looking?" Sebastian asked. "She was cautious in the way she broke the connection."

"A smudged line through ash shows…smudging," Angie said. "Smears of black and even the imprint of a shoe. The basement was dark, but I still saw a very clean, very non-smeared cut in the ash. She didn't just drag her foot over the line to make sure it was inactive."

"Like you did," he said.

"You saw that?" She'd thought she'd been more subtle about it.

"I like that you're cautious."

It was on the tip of her tongue to say, "Not cautious enough." Not where he was concerned. She'd never been cautious enough with him, and that had landed her into more trouble than she cared to think about.

She held her tongue by gulping down the rest of her lukewarm tea. She grimaced a little at the taste—too sweet and cool for her now. Sebastian didn't even try to hide his grin. He raised a finger and the waiter returned. She should go home and sleep. But instead of asking for the check, she ordered another cup of tea. So did Sebastian.

"What do you think it means that Mara's athame cut showed up in this realm?" he asked once they were alone again.

"I thought at first maybe she was coming into powers of her own. I didn't sense any magic in her in her room. But sometimes puberty brings these things on."

"At first?"

"After finding out the apartment complex was designed specifically to make summoning demons easier, I thought maybe that was the real reason. Something about the place makes setting and breaking the containment circles easier?"

He frowned a little and his gaze turned inward. She waited him out, sweetening her tea when the waiter returned with fresh mugs of hot water. The waiter cleared the table while he was there, leaving them with just the two mugs between them and the check discretely placed at the edge of the table with two soft mints on top of it. She plopped one of the soft mints into her mouth—she loved them enough to steal both if Sebastian ignored his for too long—and watched Sebastian think.

That was always fascinating. In fact, she enjoyed watching him do anything a little too much. She finally dropped her gaze, afraid she wouldn't be able to stop watching him if she didn't now.

He'd never answered her question about what he'd do once they left the diner. In those first few months, after she'd tried to leave, after she'd moved to New York to escape demon hunting and to put distance between her and Sebastian, when he'd come looking for her, drawing her back into the mix... In those months, she'd brought him back to her place. And she'd missed him too much to make him sleep on the couch.

She glanced up from beneath her lashes. Eighteen months hadn't changed that part at all. She still missed him too much to make him sleep on the couch. And that's what worried her.

She was a little worried she'd always miss him too much.

Over the months of peace and quiet, she'd wondered, more than once, if they could manage to be together while she stayed out of the demon hunting part of his life. When she'd left, she'd known better. A part of her still knew better. But lonely nights had her wondering, and plotting ways they could manage it.

Esmerelda would have told her to spend more time studying her witchcraft, less time brooding over a lost love.

She smiled a little and sipped her tea, hot enough to burn

the roof of her mouth. After the lukewarm gulp of her last cup, that was a significant improvement.

Sebastian finally looked up, blinking his way back into the present moment. "I'll do some research on the building complex tonight. I've never heard of what you described happening without the human summoner having magic of their own."

"Which means Mara might be coming into latent powers. Maybe that's what's changed? Why Grant and his demon are after her and Ellen now?"

"Maybe. Or maybe your other theory is correct and the complex makes these things simpler. I'll research, see if I can eliminate any possibilities."

"You need to sleep sometime," she reminded him.

"I'll sleep after I've looked into the building complex and its architect."

She lowered her chin and gave him a look.

He grinned. "I promise."

Oh, that grin. She sighed. "Fine. Where?" Time to be blunt. She couldn't invite him to her place this time. She couldn't. Because all the old feelings, all the old…habits would take over. Her heart thumped a little harder as she waited for his answer. Anticipation? Anxiety?

Fear?

"I'm not asking to come back to your place this time, Ang," he said quietly. "That always leads us…backward."

"I'm not inviting you to my place for the same reason. That doesn't stop me from worrying about you."

His fingers flexed against his tea mug. "I'll get a hotel room."

"Last minute? It'll be a dump."

He grinned again and her heart thumped harder again, and now it was her turn to hold her mug tighter so she didn't reach for him.

"I've slept in dumps before, but I may treat myself to something fancier this time. Being in New York and all. Maybe the Waldorf?" He wagged his eyebrows.

She tried to smirk and roll her eyes. What she really wanted to do was pull his face close and kiss him like there was no tomorrow.

"I'll be fine," he said. "And I'll be in touch tomorrow. What time are you done with work?"

"I see my last client at seven. I'll be done by eight."

"I'll meet you at Dana's at eight." His expression turned serious. "Stay safe until then. I know why I can't..." He pressed his lips together, cleared his throat, and said instead, "Ward your apartment. Since I won't be there to watch over you. There's a demon out there with your name on its lips."

She nodded. She always warded her apartment anyway—because working with a demon hunter had left her with a habit for cautiousness that she'd never dropped.

"Don't talk to strangers," he added. "And don't touch any strange books."

She snorted. "I know better how to take care of my psychic health than you do."

They swung past Dana's on the way to her apartment so

they could retrieve the demon library books they'd left in her locker. He stayed close to her the entire time, a warm hand on her lower back when she gave the counter where the demon had talked to Laura a wide berth. He even took the trash bag with the books out of her locker so she wouldn't have to touch it.

Then he walked her home, ensuring she was inside her building before leaving to finish his own last errands.

And despite all her talk, it took willpower she didn't know she had not to call him back.

Willpower to go upstairs to her quiet apartment alone.

CHAPTER EIGHTEEN

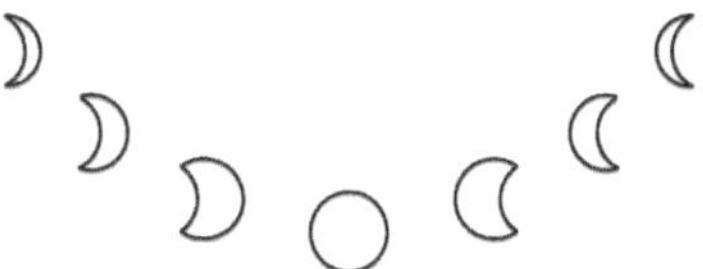

Sebastian was waiting for her on the first level of Dana's at exactly eight the next evening. She'd come down right after her client left, just to check. He leaned against the counter talking with Laura—and Laura looked utterly charmed.

"You haven't been waiting long?" Angie asked.

His gaze swept over her and he flashed that killer grin of his. "I find your witchy uniform very sexy, you know."

"That's because you're a bit of a pervert," she said, even as her tummy danced in delighted little loops of anticipation.

He laughed and those giddy tummy flips got worse. Goddess, he looked delicious. He must be doing that on purpose. Nothing a hunter did was on accident. And she should be mad at him for it. But she was too busy feeling all tingly and needy from the sound of his laugh.

"Are you going out tonight like that or do you need to

change?" He nodded to her flowing, black velvet skirt, speckled with stars and moons.

She actually loved wearing this skirt for work because the material was so soft. If she had to wear a uniform, there could be worse options. She jingled with the extra jewelry she wore at her ankles and around her neck. Her red peasant shirt hung a little low on her shoulders, the billowing sleeves bunching at her wrists so she hadn't added additional bracelets. And the sleeves hid the pentagram bracelet she never took off. She still wore her favorite moon earrings. And her hair was pulled back by two silver hair combs covered in Celtic knots.

She didn't feel particularly sexy in this uniform. She felt silly sometimes, dressing up like a "witch" for clients. She would never begrudge the pagans who loved this style their freedom to indulge it. But it wasn't her personal aesthetic.

The fact that Sebastian had always found this look sexy on her did, occasionally, have her rethinking her personal aesthetic, though.

"I'm going back up to change," she said defiantly. "Occupy yourself for a few more minutes. I won't be long."

Behind his back, Laura widened her eyes at Angie and fanned herself.

Angie ignored her.

But she did wonder why Sebastian was letting Laura see him as himself and not some innocuous guy just hanging out. Since he knew Laura saw auras, maybe he just wasn't bothered wasting his willpower on her—he could disguise his aura of course; it just took more effort. With a demon on the loose, appearing harmless and ordinary for Laura did seem like a waste of his will.

Angie was back downstairs in fifteen minutes, her overlarge purse slung over her shoulder, dressed in jeans and a t-shirt under her short jacket—her street clothes—with two cups of tea in to-go cups in hand. Sebastian stood to one side of the check out desk while Laura dealt with a customer.

He smiled at the cups. "If those are both for you, I'm going to be disappointed."

"I was tempted." She handed him one.

He lifted the lid and pulled in a deep breath, savoring the scent. She'd gotten him the good stuff and ensured it was just as he liked it, dark and with just a drop of milk.

"Thanks." He raised the cup in a little solute before taking a long sip.

She grinned and took a sip of her own brew, sweet and milky, before asking, "So now what?"

"Did you sleep?"

"Eventually." She'd stayed up for an hour after getting home, doing a little research of her own. Though she'd been determined to leave the demon world behind, she'd still managed to build up a small library of reference books— books she kept hidden in the bottom of a wooden trunk in the back of her closet in the vain hope that she'd never need them.

He held her gaze for a moment, then said, "Let's walk and talk."

"Where to?"

"Eventually, the Upper East Side and Grant's house."

She pulled in a breath. "Is he…doing something tonight?"

"Feels that way. We'll see. But we have time." He gestured her to proceed him out of the store.

She waved goodnight to Laura as she left. Laura winked before returning to her customer.

Outside, the autumn air was crisp and chilly. Angie buttoned her small jacket with one hand, adjusting her purse strap across her chest. "Which way?"

He motioned to the left. They wandered randomly through the Village's narrow, twisty streets, moving in a generally uptown direction.

"What did you learn?" he asked.

The fact that he knew she'd stayed up doing research, that he still knew her so well, was less surprising than it should have been. "I wanted to see if a demon could still attack me psychically across the realms, or if it would have to be in this one to accomplish that."

"And?"

"And it has to be in this realm, but it doesn't have to be a freed demon." She watched his expression as she spoke. He didn't give any hint of what he was thinking, so she continued. "If it's been blood bound with a human, it could ride their awareness while they're moving around, affecting this realm even though they're still technically in their own."

That wasn't something that happened often. Only a very few specific kinds of demons could "ride" a human's awareness that way. Not all of them. And their ability to affect this realm was limited when they did that. But riding a human's awareness was the option that kept the human alive the longest because the demon wasn't actually occupying the person's body. Just...riding along in the background of a human's mind.

Most demons preferred to escape and run free through the human realm. But some...they were patient. And their plans more twisted.

"Only certain demons can do that," Sebastian said.

"A Molder demon is one of those kinds."

"And there's a lot of blood bonding and blood sacrifice involved."

"We know whatever demon Grant has been dealing with is strong," she said. "It pulled away the demon about to make a deal with Ellen that first time. You had to fight it off the second time she tried a summoning. It was a Molder demon that time, right?"

"It was."

"This long term game, whatever it is, seems like just the kind of game a Molder demon would play."

Most demons were sadistic in their ways. All the blood and torture that appealed to them so much. But the Molder reached new heights and enjoyed psychological torture almost as much as it enjoyed blood and eating living beings.

The fact that it most enjoyed the souls and bodies of its victims to be alive while it ate was a particularly gross part of its process.

"It was about to break free of Ellen's control when I arrived," Sebastian said. "Which was why I showed up. I kept it from breaking free then. But it was going to. It wants into this realm physically, not just riding a human host."

"Long game. Because hunters do keep showing up."

"It killed one hunter already. And could have gotten out then."

She huffed. "I know. That's still bugging me. Twice it could have escaped, or was about to escape. With you, it was forced back, but with the other hunter, it could have gotten freed. What's keeping it confined to its own realm? It can't just be that it doesn't want to sacrifice its power to get here, because it's trying to get free."

"Maybe it's not," Sebastian murmured.

"What?"

"Maybe it's really not trying to break free." He frowned a little, stepping behind her to let a pedestrian pass before moving up beside her again. "Maybe the humans calling it aren't strong enough to contain it—which is why we hunters show up—but even if the human lost control, it wouldn't step into this realm. Maybe it's been riding human hosts on purpose, to tamper in this realm, but not enter it."

"But why?"

"Have to ask the Molder demon."

"Or its partner."

"The man who walked into Dana's? Two demons, then?"

"What else?"

"The Molder riding the human host. The man could just be another host. Like the book. Like…anyone. Which is why it could affect you in this realm."

"The Molder would be getting around a lot, then. And we still don't know why."

"We could go ask it."

She stopped in the street, facing him, forcing the other people coming up behind them to go around. "I thought you were joking about that."

"We'd get our answers."

"And you'd have to fight it again."

He shrugged. "Sooner rather than later."

"Is that why you want to go back to Grant's tonight?"

"I told him I'd find his daughter. I have. She's safe."

"You're not telling him where Mara is!"

He scowled. "You know me better than that."

She let her shoulders slouch and started walking again. "Sorry. I'm edgy. I have been all day."

"Did you have trouble with your readings?" He fell into step beside her.

"No. Well, I did get distracted during one. Poor man just needed to talk about his marriage, and I almost missed some of the crucial information he was telling me and gave him the wrong reading."

"Wrong reading?" Sebastian's mouth ticked up.

She shrugged. "What I do is as much counseling as anything else. I just have a little psychic leg up on most counselors. But I do have to pay attention to what my clients are telling me."

"Did you give him the right advice in the end?"

"We'll see when he comes back next week. He booked four sessions in all."

Sebastian considered her, his gaze on the side of her face. "You enjoy this work, don't you?"

"I do. I help people. It feels good. Grounding and solid."

She smiled a little. "I suppose its why I got my psychology degree in college, why I was leaning toward being a regular counselor. But I like my current office hours better."

His expression remained thoughtful, but he didn't smile at her attempt at a joke.

"What's wrong?" she asked.

"You helped people when we worked together, too."

"But I wasn't doing what I was meant to do. I'm…better at this. This is what I'm able for."

"You underestimate yourself. You always have."

"Now who's acting like a counselor."

"We've gotten off topic."

"Yes." She gestured toward a subway station half a block up. "Ride or taxi?"

"You're ready to face Grant? You could stay away."

"I need this demon to know it hasn't sent me into hiding." She didn't meet his gaze when she said, "Even if that's exactly what I want to do. No, we need to end this. If you have to fight a demon, I'll be there to have your back."

"What happened to this not being your job?"

She made a face. Then more seriously, "The thing, or things, or whatever it is, knows where I work and came looking for me. It can reach me through my psychic senses. And it won't just back off and leave me be if I go into hiding. It won't stop being a danger to my friends and colleagues. I will help you send it back into its realm in any way I can. Because I need to ensure my friends are safe."

"And then?"

"I'll worry about then…then."

He paused, his expression suddenly turning inward, which wasn't what she'd been expecting. She frowned at him. That was his *listening* expression.

Something was happening.

Her heartbeat kicked up. "What is it?"

"Change of plans," he murmured. "We need to get to Ellen and Mara. Now."

CHAPTER NINETEEN

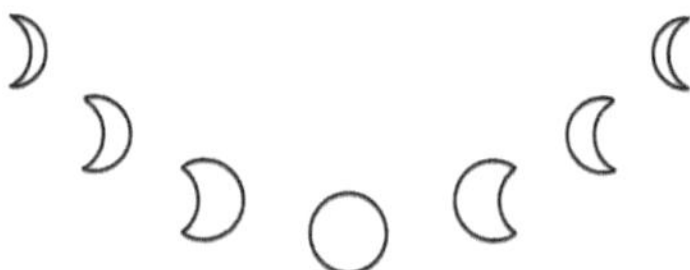

Sebastian put a hand out and a yellow cab pulled up to the curb immediately.

A result of his will because there was no way that happened otherwise.

Angie wanted desperately to ask what was happening. But the taxi driver was the chatty type and he kept tossing back questions through the plexiglass barrier. Tourists? Locals? Where you going?—that one they had to answer—Where're you front?—that one to Sebastian with his English accent. He added a recommendation for his favorite Cuban restaurant in the Bronx and a great Greek place in Queens.

Angie tried to be polite but her gut was a tangle of nerves, her own questions pummeling her—mostly worry for Mara and Ellen's safety.

She took her turn talking with the taxi driver whenever Sebastian got that faraway look in his eyes. And when he returned to his surroundings, she questioned him with her gaze. He could have told her more, willed the driver not to listen, but if there was a demon about to break loose into this realm, he was going to need that will for the fight. So she let his hand squeezing hers suffice as explanation for now.

But she'd never wanted to hurry traffic along so desperately before.

They reached the road leading up into the apartment complex and Sebastian had the driver let them off at the corner rather than taking them up into the complex. The trip uptown had taken more than forty-five minutes thanks to an accident on the West Side Highway.

Angie stared up the drive at the collection of buildings and rubbed the pentagram charm on her bracelet. There weren't any trees she could use to force a demon back into its realm here. Though that meant she couldn't accidentally let any more out either, which was always good.

She had a few prepared bottles in her bag, potions from friends and one or two of her own concoctions. She didn't do a lot of potions, but she did a few protective ones and kept them on hand. Old habits died hard.

Other than the potions, she was able to set protective binding circles, and do that pretty quickly because that was something she'd been practicing her whole life. And she had a few spells she could call down without having to think about them or worry about getting the words or gestures wrong and fucking up the end results. She'd added a few more of those to her repertoire since the time she'd almost gotten stuck in a demon realm and only had one of those ingrained spells at her fingertips when she'd panicked. She'd practice several more over the last two years, repeatedly so she could cast without having to think.

Outside of those spells and her few backup potions, though, she wasn't exactly a sword-wielding Amazon jumping into this fight. She wasn't the hunter here.

Sebastian ensured the taxi had disappeared around a corner before stalking up the drive into the complex. She followed without a word. He was in hunter mode now and his attention was on his inner voice, telling him where to go, where the danger was…

To her surprise, it wasn't at the building where Ellen and Mara lived.

He led her into the center of the complex, then turned right, moving toward the building two over from Ellen's. Angie frowned but followed, trusting Seb's instincts. The air was crisp and sharp, a biting edge of cold from a wind blowing in off the river. The faint scents of trash she'd gotten the last time she was here were gone. All she could smell now was the cold in the air, and barely that. She pulled her jacket tighter around her. She wasn't dressed for the temperature drop—the weather report hadn't predicted this.

They neared the building cautiously and Sebastian paused to study the lights inside the lobby, the windows overhead. Like the last time they'd been here, there were plenty of lights on inside, signs of life, faint noises from a few apartments, but the area outside was eerily quiet. From another building, Angie heard a dog bark.

She raised her brows at Sebastian, without speaking

because in the quiet any sound seemed too loud, and motioned toward the building. He shook his head, paused, then shook his head again.

Something was strange and wrong.

Finally, his expression cleared and he took off at a loping run around the building. She took her purse in one hand so it wouldn't slap against her leg and trotted after him. Behind the building was a surprising copse of trees—from inside the complex that bit of nature wasn't in view from any place they'd been. Although since they'd only been here at night so far, getting a good view of the place hadn't been possible.

The trees were oak, solid and tall.

But oaks could have split trunks.

She skidded to a halt, staring at the dark clump of trees, her heart pounding.

She shouldn't go in there. She shouldn't risk it. How could she risk it?

Sebastian didn't wait for her, or even check behind him to see if she was still following. He charged into the trees, the copse thick enough that he vanished inside the darkness under the branches.

Faintly, beyond those deep shadows, Angie saw a red glow.

She squeezed her eyes shut. She had to do this. It wasn't her job to fight the demon, but there was a human in there. Someone who might be desperate like Ellen had been. Or Mara. Someone who'd need her protection while Sebastian fought the demon.

Around her rapidly thumping heartbeat, she pulled in a

deep breath, opened her eyes, and kept her focus on the ground and base of the trees as she moved into the shadows.

Inside the clump of trees, darkness was almost complete. For a heartbeat, Angie could forget they were still in the middle of the city. None of the normal light pollution leaked into the blackness under the branch canopy, and she couldn't see but a few inches in front of her face.

When her night vision finally adjusted, darker shadows emerged from the background, separating into tree trunks against the night. She blinked a few times, ensuring she could see well enough not to knock herself out running into a tree, then followed the red glow deeper into the woods.

The clump of trees turned out to be larger than she'd assumed from the outside. She should have encountered a road after a few hundred yards. But the darkness and trees continued to spread out in front of her.

She made an effort not to look up too high, to keep her gaze at the base of the trees and only look up enough to follow the glowing red light. Even in the dark—especially in the dark—she could get caught by that natural tree shape that allowed her to open a portal into a demon realm.

Sometimes she wished her ordinary magic worked that easily. Her psychic senses had when she was younger and still in need of training. All she'd had to do was touch someone or something and all this information would come pouring in. She didn't have that often these days and it was a relief. But her other magic, the spells and castings, the occasional potion, she had to practice those, study and learn and train. Invest energy and effort to make things work the way she wanted them to. Magic didn't just fall out of her finger tips.

Or rip open a doorway into a demon realm when she wasn't ready.

There was something there… The ease of opening demon realms. The ease of her touch psychic skills. But the glow ahead of her intensified as she neared and she lost the tentative connection between the two ideas even as her heartbeat tripled.

She clung to a tree when she finally spotted the source of the glow.

Another circle, this one faintly white in the dark dirt, but not a circle of fire. This was almost a moon's luminescence, the glow of cleaned bones against a black background. The red light came from inside the circle, from the demon standing there engulfed in a red mist.

A Molder demon.

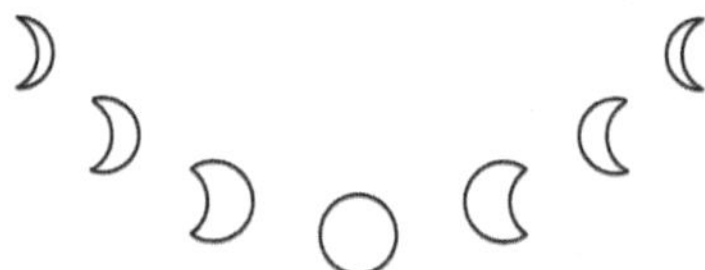

The Molder demon looked so much like the image from the book, Angie couldn't breathe. Long tentacle hair hanging limply against a skeletal gray face. Tattered clothes hanging off a bone frame. Black eyes with glowing red pupils. Sharp sharp teeth. And a smile to haunt nightmares. The overly long arms of the creature hung at its sides as it grinned at Sebastian.

"I'm glad you came, hunter," it said, the sibilant hiss in its voice like nails on a chalkboard in Angie's brain. It glanced up, its smile growing to grossly exaggerated proportions at odds with the size of its face. "And you brought the witch, I see. That's good, too."

No, Angie thought. No, it's not. Not even a little bit good.

"You should be more worried about yourself," Sebastian said.

His voice was deep, his will a living thing in the clearing.

"Why should I worry about you hunter? I've killed your kind before."

"You remember me. You didn't kill me."

"An oversight on my part."

Sebastian's chuckle showed no signs of the terror clutching at Angie's throat. She swallowed. This was the demon in the book. The one who'd come to Dana's Cauldron looking for her. She knew it. Knew it in her bones.

But it was contained! It was inside a circle. The red mist swirling around its body didn't disguise its physical shape. It was solid inside that mist, inside that circle. It was *not* fully in this realm.

"A failure, perhaps," Sebastian said. "You'll fail again."

The mist flickered around the demon, like a breeze had moved through it.

Angie hunted the surroundings for the person who'd called the demon, expecting to see Grant somewhere.

When she did spot the human who'd summoned the demon, laying in a crumpled heap beside the circle, she gasped.

"Carmen?" The housekeeper from Grant's home?

Sebastian started to chant in Spanish, though with an accent that made the language difficult for Angie to understand. Her Spanish was rudimentary, fed mostly by her knowledge of Latin and her Spanish-speaking friends growing up, but it was the Spanish of Mexico, Columbia, and Cuba. The words, the accent Sebastian used made her frown.

She'd have to concentrate hard to understand even a little of what he was saying.

But she could guess what he was doing. He was using whatever Carmen had used to call this demon. An old incantation from the feel of it.

A spell. With actual magic in it.

The Molder demon hissed and swatted in the direction of Sebastian. Sebastian leaned to one side a little before straightening to his full height again. He widened his stance, and the chant grew deeper, louder.

The demon charged the edge of the circle. "You can't stop me," it whispered, that grating noise piercing Angie again. It reached down into the mist tightening around its lower half. "I will have this world. And you won't stop me, hunter."

From the mist it pulled a shape that didn't at first make sense to Angie. It was an illusion of some sort, ephemeral, transparent, a shadow of a real thing. She had to stare at it for a long moment before…

Recognition made her gasp again.

The image of the altar Mara had seen in that dark room, the same image echoed inside one of her demon books. The stage set to look absolutely identical to the image in the book —but for one small detail. In the real-life setting, there'd been a lantern, similar in shape and size to a camping storm lantern, but the edges of the thing, the covering top, all looked like whitened bones.

The demon held that bone lantern in its clawed hand.

Or at least an illusion of that lantern. Not the real one.

From the corner of her eye, Angie spotted movement. Carmen was crouching, her gaze on Sebastian. In her hand, she also held a lantern just like the one the demon held. Only this one was a real, solid object. Not an illusion. She raised it a little. The light inside illuminated Carmen's face with strange, sinister shadows.

The woman smiled. The demon, still looking at Sebastian, also smiled.

Angie moved before she thought, before she knew what she was going to do. She didn't even take the time to shout Sebastian's name.

She wrapped her arms around Carmen, spun in a circle and hit the lantern away at the same time. Carmen lost her grip and the lantern went flying. She screamed something, but Angie ignored the curse and drew a magic circle around her and Carmen, a solid blue line forming in her head encompassing them, flaring brightly in her mind's eye as she connected the ends.

When she opened her eyes, Carmen was struggling against her grip. The woman was smaller than Angie, but strong as all hell, and she succeeded in breaking out of Angie's hold. She reared back to punch Angie in the face. Angie dropped to her knees, putting herself under the woman's lunge—she'd learned that trick from her oldest brother—and reached forward to set a hand against Carmen's thigh.

The shock spell was as innate as any spell she ever called

on because she'd used it a lot as a kid to get her brothers to back off when they were teasing her or picking on her. The intensity of the spell could vary, which made it very handy when she wanted to warn off a brother, or in this case, incapacitate a person who may or may not be in the control of a demon.

The flare of power she sent into the spell pulsed against Carmen's leg, and Carmen's muscles tightened beneath Angie's hand. Carmen gasped, then she dropped to the ground, her eyes rolled back in her head. Angie made sure her pulse was still beating—strong and steady—checked her eyes—no dilation—assuring herself Carmen was just knocked out.

Then she turned to face Sebastian and the demon, keeping Carmen within easy sight as she did. Turning her back on someone working with a demon was always a bad idea. Another lesson she'd learned a long time ago. The hard way.

The Molder demon howled. Angie winced. She stayed in a crouch so she could protect Carmen, or lay her out again, depending on what was called for. But it was very tempting to cover her ears.

Sebastian said something Angie couldn't hear over the demon's shriek, but the demon must have because it stopped yelling, the sound cut off with an unnatural abruptness that left Angie's ears ringing.

Sebastian continued chanting in Spanish under his breath, his English accent giving the words a unique twist and emphasis. This time, though, she understood the words better.

At least enough of them that the general meaning was clear. He was chanting a banishment spell, a reverse of the spell he must have suspected Carmen used to call the demon.

The beast snarled at him. "I will be back for you hunter. And your witch." It smiled at Angie, revealing its row of pointed teeth. "I will own you too, witch. Your mind is mine."

"No," Angie said. She didn't have a hunter's will, but she had a strong will nonetheless. One strong enough to command and control her own magic. And that was no little thing. She strengthened her protective circle and met the demon's gaze with the force of her own will as Sebastian continued to chant.

The mist swirling around the demon darkened, turning blacker around the edges of the red, and thickened into an almost solid mass.

Sebastian's voice rose, and he raised his hands revealing a knife Angie hadn't seen earlier. His or Carmen's? He slashed a pattern in the air with the knife, a glow following the movements, almost as if the knife were on fire. The glow wasn't enough for her to discern the pattern so she'd have to ask him afterward what he'd drawn. But whatever it was, it had the desired effect on the demon.

The demon rolled the ghostly illusion of the bone lantern in its clawed hand, and the lantern vanished like smoke. It snarled at Sebastian again. And when Sebastian slashed through the center of the image he'd drawn, the demon dropped its head back and screeched as it was engulfed completely in the now solid black mist. The mass of shadow and darkness swirled around the demon in a tightening storm, growing smaller and more dense, narrowing down to a basketball-sized sphere.

And when the sphere of black mist winked out…

The demon was gone.

CHAPTER TWENTY-ONE

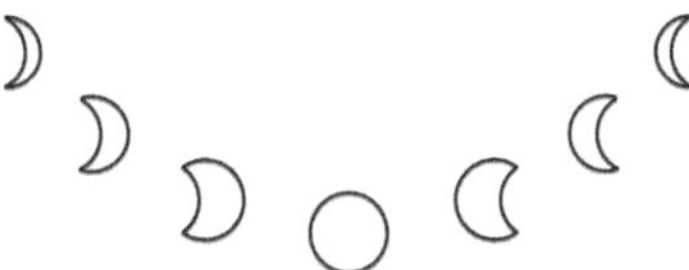

*A*ngie looked down at Carmen, still unconscious. She checked her pulse again, ready with the shock spell just in case.

"I think her lantern rolled that way," she said to Sebastian, gesturing into the trees at her right. "After you cut the circle, would you get that? I don't want to touch it yet."

Without a word, Sebastian did as she asked. He thoroughly cut and destroyed the containment circle first, smudging his foot across the salt and chalk used to draw it into the rough dirt.

Now that the fight was over, Angie could hear the traffic again, and some noise from the apartment complex. All the ordinary sounds of a New York night. She could even see the flash of car lights through the trees.

So, the copse wasn't as thick or isolated as she'd felt it to be just moments ago. That was interesting.

She kept her gaze on Carmen, watching for movement, twitches, changes in her breathing pattern. It served two purposes—ensuring Carmen didn't take her unawares, and keeping her gaze off the encircling trees.

When Sebastian stepped close, lantern in hand, Angie finally rose to her feet and stepped back from Carmen's prone body. She'd only created a very small protective circle, to keep the demon from reaching and using Carmen, so she didn't have much room to maneuver.

"Ready for me to cut this circle?" she asked Sebastian.

He nodded.

She mentally drew a line through the blue light, using her finger as the physical link to slash through the magic barrier. The blue light in her mind's eye winked out, and Angie felt the magic break apart, some of it spilling into the ground, some of it rushing back into her.

"Willing or not?" Sebastian asked.

She didn't need him to clarify. She kept her gaze on Carmen as she said, "I couldn't tell. I didn't open to her when I was touching her because I didn't want to open to the demon."

"Fair enough. Want to try now?"

"Nope," she said.

He didn't argue with her.

Carmen groaned and moved a hand to her forehead. Angie watched her closely, ready with a shield spell just in case. Carmen rolled to one side and pushed herself up to a sitting position, then her eyes widened as she took in her surroundings.

"Where am I? What's happened?" She looked up. "Ms. Angie? Mr. Sebastian? What's happening?"

Angie let Sebastian take the lead as she studied Carmen's reactions.

"How do you feel?" Sebastian said, his tone quiet.

"Sore. A tingling in my body. What happened, Mr. Sebastian?" Tears welled in her big brown eyes. She looked around again but didn't attempt to stand up.

"Do you remember anything?" Sebastian asked.

"No. I was packing to go to my sister in New Jersey." She put a hand to her head. "But I don't remember leaving."

"You have another sister?" Angie asked.

Carmen blinked up at her. "What, Ms. Angie?"

"You said you were going to your sister's house in Connecticut yesterday," Angie reminded. "Do you have more than one sister living in the area? Why did you change your mind about which one you were going to visit?"

"Did I say Connecticut? I don't have any family in Connecticut. My sister lives in New Jersey."

"Maybe you were just worried," Sebastian suggested. His grip tightened on the lantern he held.

"That must be it, yes." Her eyes narrowed slightly.

Angie sighed. "Carmen, why are you dealing with a Molder demon?"

Carmen's lower lip trembled. "A demon? Oh, Ms. Angie, I'm not summoning demons. That's Mr. Grant who does that. I would never do that." She crossed herself and said a few words of a Catholic prayer in Spanish.

Angie nodded. "We'll get to the bottom of it, Carmen,

don't worry." She reached out a hand. "Here, let's get out of here. Somewhere warmer, where we can talk better."

Carmen stared at Angie's hand for a heartbeat. She didn't reach up to take it when she pushed to her feet.

"That would be good, Ms. Angie. I'm very scared. What's happening?"

"Well, Carmen," Angie said, lowering her hand to her side, "one thing that's happening is a near Oscar-worthy acting performance. Though maybe all the 'Ms. Angie's' and 'Mr. Sebastian's' are a bit over the top cliché."

Carmen let her bottom lip tremble again. "I don't know what you mean." And now the tears flowed down her cheeks.

"Wow," Angie said. "I mean, really that's super impressive."

"What are you saying? I don't understand."

"If you're being honest with me, Carmen, why don't you just take my hand for a moment. That'll ensure we're all being honest." She reached out again. "A touch on my palm would be enough. I don't have to hold your hand or restrict you. So you feel safe." She infused her voice with her "reassuring psychic" tone, the one she used with skittish clients who'd paid for a reading but were actually terrified of anything paranormal.

She met Carmen's gaze as she held her hand, palm up, between them and waited.

Carmen let another tear drop roll down her cheek, she raised her hand to set her fingers into Angie's palm. A moment before she touched Angie's skin, she folded her fingers into a fist and pulled her hand back.

She let out a sigh and her entire demeanor changed. Her shoulders straightened, her baring relaxed. She made a face and rolled her eyes. "It was the Connecticut-New Jersey mistake that gave me away, wasn't it?"

Angie lowered her hand and shrugged. "That didn't help," she confirmed. "You keep changing your accent, too. Subtly, but enough to notice."

"Damn. I wasn't expecting a white chick to pick that up."

Angie didn't comment.

"Your boyfriend didn't." Carmen threw Sebastian a kiss.

He didn't comment either.

"Did you suspect all along?" Carmen said.

"No, no," Angie said. "You're very good. I assumed you were just what you wanted me to assume you were. Overworked and overburdened domestic help."

"Well, that's something I guess." She glanced between them. "What now? It's not like you can arrest me." Her grin turned sly. "Just practicing my religion. I'm free to do that in this country."

"What's the lamp for?" Sebastian asked, raising it slightly.

Carmen's gaze narrowed, and something like real worry moved through her expression. "Just part of the…process."

"So, if I touch it, I'll only pick up…process?" Angie said.

Carmen considered her. "Your choice. I wouldn't recommend it. For you."

"Why?"

"Why the lamp?"

"No, why all this? Why are you calling demons? Why sacrifice a child?"

"I would never," Carmen said with absolute outrage. "Who do you think helped that child all these years? And helped her escape her asshole father? Who do you think told her her mother was still alive so she'd go looking for her?"

Angie glanced at Sebastian. "But… That demon just now, that was Grant's demon. The demon he intended to sacrifice Mara to." At least she was pretty sure that was Grant's demon. She kept her uncertainty to herself, though. "How can you claim that wasn't your intent?"

Carmen pressed her lips together. "I'm not inclined to do the whole bad guy monologuing thing. It's none of your business."

"Actually," Sebastian said, "it is my business. It's my actual job to prevent humans from releasing demons in this world. And that demon of yours was about to break out, or I wouldn't be here."

"The last one of you who showed up didn't do so well against that particular beast," Carmen said, smiling slightly. "Though…it might have had help."

Angie growled. "You helped kill a hunter."

"The hunter should have kept his nose out of my business," Carmen said with no signs of regret. Not even a little twinge.

"So, your basically evil, then," Angie said.

"Only evil to those on my bad side," Carmen said.

"You killed a hunter trying to prevent a demon from

wreaking havoc on this world," Angie hissed. "You fall well and truly into the evil category."

"If you say so." Carmen shrugged. "Now, if you don't mind. I'm tired. I'm going home."

Angie blinked. Carmen was right. There wasn't a lot they could do to her. They could stop her from calling the demon or letting it out. They could protect Mara and prevent Carmen and Grant from sacrificing her. But… They didn't have any authority over Carmen herself.

It was always the problem in this world. Humans just kept summoning demons. And all the hunters could do was prevent them from releasing those demons, maybe even keep them from getting killed by their own hubris. Carmen must have a strong will if she'd been summoning a Molder demon for any length of time. Which meant it wasn't likely to kill her yet. But Sebastian wouldn't have been called to this summoning if the demon wasn't on the edge of escaping. They'd likely saved Carmen's life. And yet, Angie had no doubt the woman would just call the demon again.

Carmen reached for the lantern. "I'll just have my property back," she said.

"No," Sebastian said.

"That's theft," Carmen said. "I could have you arrested."

Sebastian smiled. "You could try."

Carmen narrowed her eyes. "You don't know what you're holding."

"I have an idea," Sebastian said quietly. "That's why I'm keeping it."

Angie held her expression, not letting her curiosity show, but she very much wanted to ask Sebastian more.

Carmen let out a breath between her teeth. "It's not yours to keep."

"Sacrificing children is evil, and we're not going to leave you with something that helps you do that," Angie said, watching Carmen's reaction closely.

"I said before, I was *not* sacrificing that child," she snarled.

"You helped Grant to plan her sacrifice, then?" Angie asked, pushing harder.

"Of course not."

"That demon thinks it's getting Mara as a sacrifice."

"No, it doesn't—" Carmen cut herself off and cursed. "I don't have to justify what I do to you. Or explain. Give me back my lantern."

"No," Sebastian said again.

"No sacrificing kids," Angie said bluntly and matter-of-factly. Wondering just how far she could push Carmen on this.

"I was *not* sacrificing a child, you bitch. Shut up and give me back my lantern." Her voice deepened.

Angie felt her will, felt her powerful intent, rolling out in that tone.

Carmen held out her hand and stared at Sebastian as she said again, "Give me. My lamp."

CHAPTER TWENTY-TWO

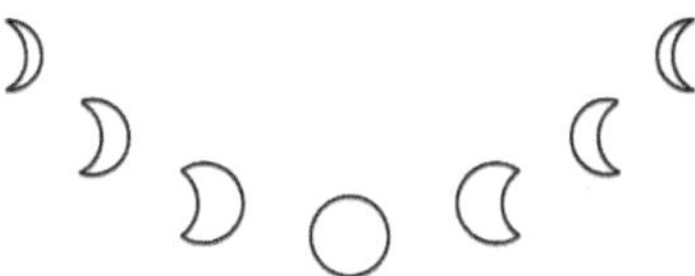

Sebastian held his ground, but he dropped his chin and his lip lifted in a slight snarl. "Not to movie quote," he said, his voice also very deep, "but my will is as strong as yours."

Angie almost smiled as she finished the line in her head: *And my kingdom as great.* It was from one of her favorite movies, *Labyrinth*, one she'd made him watch more than once. That he remembered the line made her heart happy.

But that was emotion for a later moment. The clash of wills was almost palpable. There wasn't much to the fight visually. They just stared at each other. The darkness under the trees masked a lot of their expressions. The sound of traffic just the other side of the copse was a quiet background hum.

Nothing visually or audibly indicated any sort of struggle was happening. But Angie could feel the undercurrents of it, just at the edge of her senses. And the tension between Carmen and Sebastian was obvious enough even a mundane human would have noticed.

Angie subtly put a protective circle around her psychic skills, and was tempted to build one around Sebastian to protect him from Carmen. But that might distract him and that was the last thing she wanted to do.

Distracting Carmen on the other hand…

"Why don't I just take that lantern to a witch friend for safe storage," she said. "Lot of dangerous artifacts in this world. Need proper storage. My friend is good at that."

Carmen turned her ire on Angie. "That's theft!"

"That's protecting the world from a dangerous artifact," Angie said in as mild a manner as she could manage in the face of Carmen's rage. "Shall we go to the police instead? Discuss the situation with them and see what they think?"

"You aren't going to the cops any more than I am," Carmen said, though Angie heard the slight waver in her tone. "You're just a loon who works as a supposed psychic at a Village cult shop. That's what the cops will think. They won't buy anything you say."

"They'll believe Mara, though," Angie said. "When we tell her you've been using her, helping Grant while pretending to be her friend…"

"I was not *pretending* to be her friend," Carmen shouted. "I saved her from that asshole. I kept her safe!"

"Doesn't look that way to me," Angie said with a shrug. "Won't look that way to Mara either after we explain all this." She gestured to the smudged circle in the dirt and the lantern.

"Bitch." Carmen lifted her lip and charged at Angie.

Angie had no idea what the woman intended, but she didn't wait to find out. She stepped to the side, and stretched out her hand to intercept Carmen's arm. The shock spell slipped out of her lips without conscious thought, modulated in power to send Carmen to her knees but not knock her out. The dance of subtle blue light over Carmen's skin briefly lit up the dark.

Carmen gasped and dropped, clutching her arm. "What the hell did you do?"

"Little jolt. You'll be fine. Don't attack me again. That's the mildest of what I can do."

To prove her point, she murmured one of the spells she'd been working to perfect over the last two years, holding her palm up and repeating the chant twice before the little ball of swirling fire formed in her hand. It wasn't a wizard bolt of energy—she couldn't do that with her type of magic—but she could call on the elements. And fire was one powerful ass element when thrown at an enemy.

"This isn't ordinary fire that you can roll in the dirt to put out," she said, holding Carmen's gaze as she flexed her fingers a little to make the small ball of flame dance. "I throw it, it burns until I put it out. Don't tempt me."

"You play demon games, witch," Carmen said. "They threaten eternal burning, too."

"For different reasons," Angie said, not taking the bait.

Her use of natural elements was *not* the same as what demons called upon or did.

And Carmen didn't need to know exactly how far she was willing to go.

Carmen's gaze kept jumping to the dancing ball of fire even as she tried to hold Angie's gaze and prove her defiance. "You won't use that. You consider yourself one of the good guys."

Angie shrugged. "Your choice. I believe in people making their own choices. And dealing with the consequences of those choices." She flexed her fingers again. The flames flared a little brighter.

"I never intended for Mara to get hurt," Carmen said.

"Since you're not going to 'bad guy monologue' and tell us what you did intend," Angie said, throwing out her own bait this time, "I'll just keep believing you meant the child harm. And I'll be sure to pass that information on to her."

Carmen snarled. Angie shrugged. Sebastian raised the bone lantern a little and looked at it closer.

"Wouldn't play with that, hunter," Carmen said without looking away from Angie and the fire ball still in her palm. "You gonna put that out or not?" she asked, nodding at Angie's hand.

"Are you going to attack me as soon as I do?"

Carmen relaxed back into the dirt, raising her hands in a kind of surrender. Angie didn't buy the surrender, but even if Carmen were supernaturally fast rising and attacking from that position, Angie would still have time to recall the little fire ball now that she'd called it once. That was the lovely part of this particular spell. It had a "sleep" option that meant she could reawaken the fire in a snap.

She murmured the "sleep" phrase that let the ball wink out of existence, though it hovered in the magical realm, waiting to be called into action. Carmen narrowed her eyes. Angie smiled.

"You going to talk about any of this yet, or are we at a standoff again?" Angie asked.

Sebastian lifted the lantern. "I'm very curious."

Carmen snarled at them both. "Curiosity killed the hunter."

"Depends on the hunter," Sebastian said, his voice very deep. He was letting his will seep out more. And if Carmen didn't talk soon, there was every possibility Sebastian would try to force her to.

Carmen seemed to recognize the tone. And since she hadn't won their clash of wills earlier, Angie had to wonder if she fancied her chances now or not.

Apparently, she didn't. But she didn't answer the unspoken question of what the lantern was. "I kept Grant in line," she said. "That was my job. To keep him doing all the wicked things that kept his corrupt little soul in line with my master's goals."

"The Molder demon is your master?" Sebastian asked.

That was a slightly different level of relationship than just a summoner asking for a favor from a demon. The master-minion relationship meant Carmen was getting something regularly from the demon—and vice versa—and that she worshiped the beast in an almost religious way. A typical human summoner didn't refer to a demon as their master unless…well, unless the demon was. Most didn't know enough to use that phrase. Those like Grant usually thought *they* were the masters in the relationship.

Until their part of the bargain came due.

"Do you know how many greedy, rich, white bastards there are in the world?" Carmen asked.

"Oh lots," Sebastian said without any hint of amusement. "Encounter them all the time. Occupational hazard."

Carmen lifted her lip a little, an expression halfway between a snarl and a smile. "I bet you do. Did you know that greedy white bastards never give their household staff a second glance? That particular brand of asshole just…lets their gaze skim right over the top of their staff."

"Hiding in plain sight?" Angie guessed.

Carmen smiled fully this time. "So so easy to be overlooked if you're a Latina woman working in a wealthy white man's house. No one thinks you understand very much. They don't think you have good English if you put on the right kind of accent—even if your English is better than theirs, accent or no. No one thinks twice about you except when they need something done. Oh, they're quick to send you away if they want privacy. Careful if they don't want to be overheard by the 'staff.' But never careful enough."

"Should I ask what drove you to this or is that too monologue-y?" Angie asked.

"Too monologue-y," Carmen said with a shrug. "All you need to know is the intent was never a child sacrifice." She narrowed her eyes at both Sebastian and Angie. "You two don't seem entirely stupid. I'm sure you can work it out."

"But why should we, when you can just tell us?" Angie said.

She'd already worked out some of it. The target was Grant and had been Grant from the beginning. And the why had to do with some sort of revenge goal against greedy rich bastards—at least on Carmen's part.

Angie almost couldn't blame her for that. She liked balance, and the greedy rich bastards of the world threw that balance off. They'd usually earned any bad consequences that came at them. Unfortunately, a lot of times they never received those consequences in this realm. Some people chose to believe there was another way in which punishment was meted out after death—Hell, or a bad reincarnation, or bad luck visited upon their descendants, or any number of outcomes used by religions to promote good behavior in this lifetime. For some, that wasn't enough.

Angie got the feeling Carmen was one of the latter.

"Let's just say," Carmen said slowly, "that you shouldn't worry too much about what happens. Mara is safe. Her mother is safe. Grant is…not worth worrying about."

Angie narrowed her eyes as something niggled at the back of her mind. She went with her instincts because she trusted them—in all things but romantic entanglements. "Did you know Mara called a demon? Did you…give her that idea?"

Carmen frowned and looked away. "Damn it, she wasn't

supposed to—" She pressed her lips together. "I take it you stopped her," she said to Sebastian.

He didn't respond, and Carmen's expression darkened. "That child should not be allowed to summon demons. Her will is strong now but not strong enough. She still needs—"

Again, Carmen cut herself off. But she'd slipped and they all knew it.

"Training Mara to take over where you leave off," Angie said more than asked. "How can you claim you weren't sacrificing her to a demon when that was clearly your aim? She enters a bargain, takes over your bargain, and she's lost."

"You think I'm lost, too, then? Poor little lost Carmen doesn't know what she's gotten herself into?" Carmen attempted a haughty, dismissive smile. It didn't quite reach her eyes.

"As I said, I believe in letting people make their own choices. You chose this? Or it was forced on you?"

"Choice," Carmen snarled. "A choice I'd make again."

"Then the consequences are yours, too. But is it a choice Mara would make without…manipulation?"

Angie knew the answer. She'd sensed a lot about Mara when she'd read her room. This sort of revenge life, subservience to a demon to wreak havoc on people who may or may not deserve it, this wasn't an innate part of Mara's nature. But at twelve, the girl's fundamental kindness could be manipulated, distorted.

From the beginning of her training, Angie had to learn where she drew her moral line and which side of that line she wanted to be on. All witches with real magic had to make that choice—and the choice always came with consequences, no matter what, good or bad. She'd had a good teacher, who helped her to clearly define that line, to make her own decision about what kind of witch, what kind of person, she wanted to be. Temptations to do harm were abundant in a world full of horrible people. Giving in to those temptations led down a path Angie didn't want to travel. She made another choice.

Carmen had chosen the do-harm path.

Mara should be left to choose her own path as well. But Carmen was giving her a push in a direction Angie suspected Mara would regret. And yet, in the end, it would be Mara's choice…

That didn't mean Angie had to let Carmen be the sole influence in that decision. In fact, she didn't have to let Carmen have any say in it at all.

"You can forget about manipulating Mara anymore. Find a new replacement. Or better yet. Don't. The world doesn't need more evil people. We have more than enough already."

"You would know, wouldn't you? Seeing into their souls with just a touch." Carmen shifted a little in the dirt, but didn't attempt to rise.

Angie noted the adjustment though, watched the way Carmen's gaze jumped to the lantern again. "I would," Angie said, her attention divided between the conversation and the small, subtle movements Carmen made. "Though to be honest, most of the people I work with are lost souls in need of guidance. I shine some lights that give them options." She adjusted the strap of her purse across her chest, letting the heavy part settle more comfortably against her hip.

"Shine light? What a load of bullshit. Witches always say things like that. Do you know what balance, real balance is?"

"Yup," Angie said without clarifying.

"It's people doing what I do, to balance the scales. I don't make them bargain with a demon. I don't *make* them wish harm on others through greed. They do that shit themselves. I just ensure they get what's coming to them."

"Been doing that for a while, have you?" Angie asked.

"Long enough. Long enough to see the good I do."

Angie's eyebrows popped up. "Good? That's what you think this is?"

"The horrid, evil men who would sacrifice babies for power and wealth end up punished. You tell me if that isn't good."

Angie shrugged. "It's their own doing. I won't argue with that. But they'd get that end without your help. They always do when they try to bargain with demons. Eventually."

"Except that your kind keep showing up and stopping the demons!" Carmen roared.

With a suddenness that shocked Angie, even though she'd been watching for it, Carmen thrust to her feet and charged—not Angie, but Sebastian.

And the lantern.

Angie recalled the little ball of fire into this existence, raised her hand to throw it.

Carmen reached for the lantern. "Give that back!"

Sebastian stood his ground. He didn't even move to one

side. He just stood there and raised the lantern high over his head, and said, "No."

There was a moment... A moment with Carmen hovering mid-reach, stretching, straining forward, but unable to move closer to the lantern. The faint red in Sebastian's eyes flared as his will washed over Carmen. Carmen's jaw clenched as she fought against his will with her own.

And Angie's gaze accidentally slipped to the space between them. To a tree with a natural "V" shape in its trunk.

To the demon world she could see just inside that "V".

CHAPTER TWENTY-THREE

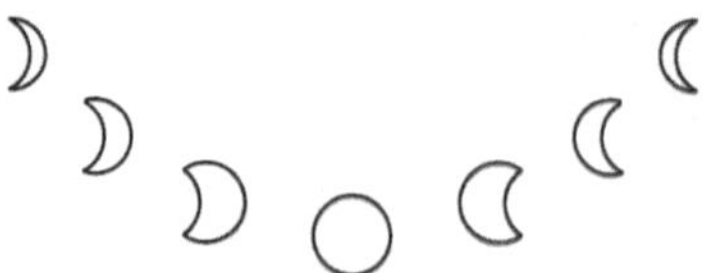

The sounds of chittering overwhelmed Angie as she took into the red heat, the glow, the sky like fire, the hiss and crackle of lava rock, the burning scent.

The demons passing too close to the opening between realms.

Caught. Caught. Trapped. No escape.

The fire ball in her palm winked out as she lost the concentration to hold the spell. Her gut tightened. Panic clutched at her throat. She hadn't meant to… She couldn't. Not now. Not right now…

Her fingers went automatically to the charm on her wrist, a little jolt of reassurance, of strength, of protection. She pressed hard into the pentagram, forcing her breath in and out.

A demon turned. Saw her.

Smiled.

All she saw were its teeth and the red glow of its eyes. She couldn't see any more, couldn't have identified the species, the realm. Panic had closed her mind down and she couldn't think.

A shiver through her arm from the charm, another little jolt.

She sucked in a breath. She had to turn away. Carmen. The lantern.

Sebastian.

She couldn't let this happen. Couldn't allow her fear to unleash this mess. Not again.

Never, never again.

She forced a blink. There, that was it. Just a blink. Just one more. Look away. Turn her head.

She heard Sebastian call her name, heard someone else say something. Carmen. Carmen was a threat.

She had to turn away.

The sounds of the demons inside the hellscape grew louder, the chittering grating along her nerves.

There was a laugh, and then the brush of something against her leg. That last sensation startled her and she glanced down.

Nothing there.

But it had been enough.

Keeping her gaze down, only glancing at the tree with her peripheral vision, she heard the sound of a screeching protest from inside the demon realm as the rip between realms sealed shut, the barrier hardening once more. The red light cut off. The little patch of woods fell into darkness again.

She blinked hard, trying to regain her night vision. The brightness of the hellscape wouldn't have affected the others. No one could see into the breach but her—unless a demon got out. Even mundane humans could see the demons once they broke into this realm.

But that hadn't happened. She hadn't let them through. She hadn't been sucked in. She was okay. The world was okay.

She looked up when Sebastian set his hands on her shoulders. It took her a good ten seconds to realize… "Carmen?"

"Got away, I'm afraid," he said.

"The lantern?"

He nodded down. He'd placed the lantern on the ground between them so he could still guard it, but so it wasn't touching her in any way.

"At least there's that." She huffed out a breath and closed her eyes. "I'm so sorry. I should have known better. I…" She shook her head, no more words to explain. She'd made a mistake. And that mistake had distracted Sebastian, allowing Carmen to get away.

"Carmen said something before she abandoned the lantern and ran off," Sebastian said quietly. "She seemed to know what had happened."

"How? She couldn't have seen into the realm breach."

Even during the years they'd worked together, Sebastian couldn't see directly into the demon realm she opened unless a demon had moved mostly out of it. He trusted that it was there because he had seen demons roll out of one of the openings before. He'd seen demons disappear back through the portal.

And once he'd reached into the breach to save her from a hellscape. Though he couldn't see it, he'd held it open with his will and reached in for her because...

Because he said he loved her and refused to let her die.

That had happened two years ago. And it had been the last straw for Angie and demon hunting—or at least she'd tried for it to be. She'd moved across the country to escape that world because she didn't want to experience that fear again. She still had nightmares about those moments being stuck in the hellscape and knowing the opening she'd made between the realms was about to close. Knowing she wouldn't be able to open another one because there were no trees inside the hellscape. Knowing the demons overwhelming her would kill her before she could even try.

The fear haunted her. It popped up at odd moments. It chased her through her nightmares. And despite how much she loved him, that fear of what had almost happened hovered in the back of her mind every time she looked at Sebastian.

She was almost glad when he'd dragged her back into his world a couple more times, enough to anger her, enough to make her so mad at him, she wasn't tempted to go running back to him every time she thought of him.

She shook off the fear, the memories, the past. "What did Carmen say that made you think she knew what I'd done?"

"She called you a demon witch, a realm splitter."

Angie frowned. "I've studied witchcraft for years. I've

even seen notations about my particular skill in one or two books, and how rare the ability is." It was a once-every-four-or-five-generations rare. So rare… "I've never seen it given a name before. And I haven't heard the term realm splitter before."

"Carmen might have been making up the terms," Sebastian said, though his gaze flickered briefly away from hers when he did.

"What don't I know?" Angie said, dropping her voice to a deeper, warning tone.

"The question is, what does Carmen know. And how?" He glanced down at the lantern. "And how did she get her hands on one of these?"

Angie wanted to stick to the original topic, to what he knew about those terms, what that flicker in his gaze meant. But the immediacy of the lantern drew her away. She had questions about that too, and they were more important at the moment.

"You know what it is? What it does?" she asked, though she already suspected he did. And she had no intention of letting him get by with a half-assed explanation this time.

"I haven't seen one personally before," he said, releasing her shoulders and leaning back a step. They both looked down at the lantern. "There are rumors of such things but you won't find them in most books on demons."

True enough or Angie would have a better idea what it was—she'd made a point of studying demons alongside her witchy studies.

"A bone lantern." He glanced up at her. "They're a kind of demon reliquary."

"A reliquary? As in a housing for religious artifacts?"

"In this case, a housing for demon artifacts. Demon bones." His gaze flicked down to the lantern again. "Demon god bones."

"Demon gods?" That was in the books, that there were demons of such immense strength and power they were essentially on par with gods. They were often worshipped as gods among demons. Rumored to be from realms most demons couldn't even access. And, like most human gods, considered myths by the hunters. Considered myths by a lot of demons as well.

Sebastian shrugged. "In reality, they don't require actual god bones, as far as I know. Like Catholic reliquaries often contain the supposed bones of saints? A bone lantern can contain the bones and essence of a powerful demon with specific gifts. Specialized magic. Something else unique that makes their lantern powerful."

Angie looked between Sebastian and the lantern. "This is really made from demon bones." She scowled. "And it has magic of some very specific variety. That's what you're telling me."

"It may well be why our Molder demon can move into this realm, in a host body, without sacrificing power. The Molder might not need all the usual blood bonding and sacrifice to make it happen."

"You're telling me that with the bone lantern, the Molder

demon can move into a host's body…easily?" She took a single step away from the lantern. The idea of a demon moving into her body, taking her over without effort, work… Consent.

She shuddered.

"That's one of the rumored possibilities with a bone lantern. But like the demon gods, hunters have assumed bone lanterns were rumors, too. I'm not sure even Aidan has seen one, and she's been fighting demons for a very long time."

"So…what do we do with it? How can we tell if it's a real bone lantern or just a prop used by the Molder demon to manipulate the humans its dealing with?"

The bones lining the lantern's sides could be plastic for all she could tell in the dark, without touching it. Seeing it in real life, rather than as a brief glimpse in a vision, she could at least study it better now. The top and handle were beaten wrought iron that seemed to support the bones running down the sides. The glass between the bones was warped, with visible bubbles in it, like it hadn't been properly blown. She couldn't tell what color the glass was with only ambient city light to see it by, but it was clear enough to see through to the center of the lamp.

She backed up another few steps so she could bend down and see inside without touching it. The center was just an open space as far as could tell. There didn't seem to be a candle or a place to insert one, certainly no modern plugs for light bulbs. The base was the same wrought iron as the top, shaped like a flattened wide brim hat, giving the lantern stability.

And it was old. Even without touching it, Angie could tell

it was old. It had the feel of something that had existed for centuries.

It crossed her mind to wonder if Laura could read the lantern's aura. She could read objects almost as well as she could read people, when she tried. The lantern was just the type of thing Laura should be able to look at and understand.

But Angie didn't want to bring her colleague and friend into this mess. Any more than she'd already been brought into it when the demon had tried to get information from her. No, better to keep this thing as far away from Dana's Cauldron as possible. She'd risked the lives and safety of her friends enough already just by getting involved with the hunters again.

With Sebastian again.

She shook off the thought to refocus on their current problem. "You can pick it up without it affecting you?" Angie asked him. "Are you risking a link with the Molder demon, giving it a way to move into you?"

He pressed his lips together. Neither of them had looked away from the lantern for very long. He continued to stare at it as he considered. "The demon would have to have a stronger will than mine to use me that way, even if I'm holding the lantern. But… For safety's sake, we'd better find another way to carry it. A box to put it."

She snorted. The idea of sticking the lantern into a shoe box flashed across her mind and she chuffed out a laugh. Somehow that seemed weirdly appropriate.

"I don't have a box," she said, motioning to her purse, "or the kitchen sink. But I do have a spare shopping bag in here."

She pulled out the folded, reinforced clothe bag she used for her groceries so she wouldn't have to use as much plastic. "Will this do?"

"It'll do for now. The less physical contact made with the lantern, the better."

"But that doesn't solve the problem of what to do with it."

He carefully spread the pale, clothe bag open on the ground next to the lantern. With careful precision, he lifted only the lantern's handle and put it into the center of the bag. Angie finally took a full, deep breath when Sebastian pulled the long handles up over the lantern, blocking it from view. The picture of a fruit and vegetable cart on the outside of the bag looked wholly incongruous with what the bag actually contained.

"Now it's out of sight," Angie said, still staring at the bag, "where do we take it? How do we keep the Molder demon and Carmen from using it again?" How had Carmen even found such a thing? Or had she been given it?

She'd wanted to train Mara to this work, to take over where Carmen left off, using the demon to mete out revenge against those Carmen felt deserved it. Did that mean she'd intended to pass the lantern down to Mara? And if so, did that mean the lantern had been passed to Carmen?

If that were the case, who had given Carmen the lantern? Why?

And were they still around? Or dead?

Sebastian considered the bag, his frown deep.

"What?" she asked. His look didn't actually tell her much of what he was thinking, only that he was thinking hard.

"We need to keep it. To stop the demon getting out again."

"I'm not putting that thing anywhere near people I love."

He looked up. "What about the witch who knows how to store artifacts?"

"I was bluffing. I don't know anyone who stores things like this."

"I do." He sighed. "But I'd rather not go to them yet."

"Them?" She narrowed her eyes. This was the first she'd heard of a "them" that could store dangerous artifacts. "The Bookstore?"

The magical store did contain specialized and dangerous books. There were spells—or something—on the store that kept those books in check and from harming readers. But as far as Angie knew, the owner didn't take in random artifacts, only books.

"Not for something like this," Sebastian said, confirming her own thoughts. "But... Well, at any rate, I'll have the people I know store this after we stop the demon."

"Wouldn't getting that thing as far away from Carmen and Mara as possible be a good way to stop the demon?"

"It can still come when summoned. Removing the lantern from the equation will only make its ability to move into a host body impossible."

"That sounds like a good thing to me," Angie said, with a lot of emphasis on the "good" part of that sentence.

"Except that losing that option means it will be more

inclined to just kill the human summoning it and escape into our realm," he pointed out reasonably. "It's on the verge of escaping anyway. That's why I keep getting called to it. We remove the lantern, it has no motivation to remain in its realm."

She wanted to ask what had motivated it to stay in its realm for this long anyway. What was its deal with Carmen? What did she get out of it? But Angie wasn't likely to get those answers from Sebastian, or anyone else for the moment. The demon *might* boast about its plan. While Carmen didn't want to bad-guy-monologue, demons loved to talk about all the horrible things they intended—those descriptions magnified the terror in their victims and they ate that fear as much as they ate souls, flesh, and blood.

But she had no intention of summoning the Molder demon to ask what its nefarious plan was.

She glanced at the bag Sebastian held. She should absolutely not, under any circumstances touch that lantern. Curiosity or not. Touching the lamp, for someone like her, could be disastrous.

There were answers there, though. She knew there were. If she opened herself to the thing, she'd understand what was happening, maybe learn how to stop it.

"No," Sebastian said, breaking into her thoughts.

"No, what?" she asked, her gaze still on the bag.

"No touching the dangerous lantern," he said. "No risking your life or worse for information."

She snorted. "What do you think I've been doing for the last two days?" She met his gaze and the slight flare of red in the depths. "You brought me in to uncover information. I'm here specifically to use my non-demon-related talents to help you. One of those primary talents is my touch."

"And your touch could get you sucked into the demon realm." He raised the bag. "This isn't a thing to mess with."

"I know. I have no intention of 'messing' with it. I was just…reconsidering my earlier objections to touching it."

"Your earlier instincts were spot on, and I'll not have you risking any more than you already have. Do I make myself clear?"

She raised her brows at his tone. Held his gaze until he looked away and pulled a face.

"Sure, professor," she said, teasing and sarcastic at once.

"This is for your own good," he said, not rising to her bait. "I will hand this over to the council before I let you touch it."

"The council? Who the hell are the council?"

He cursed under his breath, and a muscle in his jaw jumped. "No one," he said.

"Why are you lying to me? You've never done that before."

Or had he?

She'd assumed he'd kept some things to himself. The kinds of things someone in his job didn't like to remember. But this seemed like a bigger omission than not telling her about every demon he'd fought. His reaction made clear he'd slipped and revealed something he shouldn't have.

"We'll talk about it later," he said finally. She opened her mouth to ask more, but he cut her off with a gesture. "I'm taking you home. I'll deal with the lantern. We're done for the night."

"I don't think so."

"No more demon danger for now," he said. "The rest… Later. We can sort it all later."

She wanted to argue but he stalked off, back toward the road she could now hear clearly just the other side of the copse of trees. Not giving her any choice but to follow him or linger in the darkness, surrounded by trees and potential disaster.

Annoyed and grumbling, she followed him, but not graciously.

She carefully kept her gaze on the ground, though, until she'd left the small clump of trees behind.

CHAPTER TWENTY-FOUR

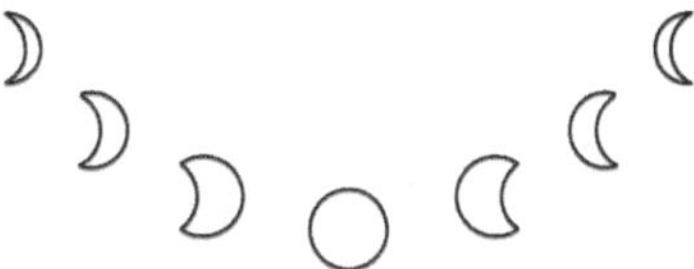

She'd assumed he'd head straight for the street and a taxi. Instead, he angled around the trees and back into the apartment complex, stalking through the open central area to the basement door of Ellen and Mara's building.

"You're going up there now?" Angie asked, jogging to keep up with his long strides. She didn't normally have to do that with other people. She had long legs and a rapid gate when motivated. Sebastian still covered the ground twice as fast, reaching the door before she could fully catch up.

Again, the lock wasn't an issue—a trick she sometimes did envy the hunters, especially when she left her keys behind in her apartment—and they entered the building quietly. There wasn't the same sense of dread this time, however. No anxiety that a fight was coming. No sense that a demon waited just around the corner. In fact, the sounds of the laundry machines whirling, the stronger scent of soap and dryer sheets wafting from the laundry room, gave proof ordinary life was underway here. The overhead motion sensor lighting turned on this time as well, blaring brightly after the outside darkness.

Angie blinked hard a few times to adapt to the brightness. The basement looked a lot less daunting, a lot more ordinary, even cheerful with all this light.

They passed the laundry room and Sebastian waved to the older woman sitting at the folding table, reading a book. She smiled and nodded back before returning to her book, as if she was greeting a neighbor she saw every night.

The elevators were more active tonight as well, one moving up, the other already on its way down when they pressed the button. Though Angie looked closely, there was no sign of the flame circle that had been there the night before. Not even any smudged ash. The floor was glossy and clean, its dark blue color unmarred.

Either the maintenance and cleaning staff of the building were geniuses—who might also be used to cleaning up after demon summonings given the building—or the buildings themselves allowed the evidence of their demonic focus to seamlessly fade back into the architecture, unnoticed to those with no interest in demons.

The rent in this place had to be really good, Angie thought as the elevator dinged open. A man in running shorts and a loose, pull over sweatshirt stepped out, putting earbuds into his ears.

He nodded absently at them. "Hey. Have a good night."

"You too," Sebastian said, holding the elevator door for Angie.

She shook her head as the doors closed. "You have real knack for blending." Which, of course he did. Still. Going from the confrontation with Carmen, the demon, accidentally opening a doorway between realms, and the information about the bone lantern, Angie was feeling off kilter and awkward around normal people.

Sebastian showed no signs of feeling similarly. He fit himself into his surroundings, walking through them like he belonged.

One of the reasons demon hunters were so good at what they did. No one ever noticed them, unless they wanted to be noticed. A demon hunter could walk through the world and be absolutely anyone at all, as innocuous as needed, as invisible as necessary. A neighbor you're sure you've seen before, even if you can't remember which floor he lives on.

Ellen and Mara's floor was quiet but for the occasional noise of activity behind the closed doors. The lights were bright again here, and the space felt very lived in and ordinary. The singe of the otherworldly didn't seem to reach up this high.

It only occurred to Angie as Sebastian knocked on Ellen's door, that although they were supposedly on the fourteenth floor, that was only because the building didn't have a thirteenth. In actuality, this was the thirteenth floor. She raised her brows. If she were superstitious, she'd worry about that. But—maybe oddly for a witch—she didn't go in for superstitions much. And she actually liked the number thirteen. It was one of those power numbers she often used in her magic work.

Ellen poked her head out the door and frowned at them. "What now? Grant's found us?"

"No," Sebastian said. "But we need to warn you about Carmen."

Ellen's eyes widened. "Carmen? What about her?"

"Can we come in?"

"Oh, yes, sorry." Ellen stepped aside, widening the door for them.

Mara was sitting on the couch, looking over the back of it at them. The TV was tuned into a cooking show. "What's wrong?" she asked. "Is Carmen okay?"

Sebastian waited until Ellen had closed and bolted the door before speaking. "Has she been in touch?"

"Of course not," Ellen said. "She doesn't know where Mara is. Unless you told her. And if you did, Grant will get it out of her." Ellen's scowl clearly promising repercussions if they'd told Grant where Mara was.

"We haven't spoken to Grant since finding Mara," Sebastian said.

"He hasn't been bugging you about whether or not you've found her?" Ellen asked. "That's not like him."

Sebastian shrugged, smiling a little. "He's no way to get in touch. I don't carry a cellphone."

Which wasn't exactly true. He had one. He just didn't give the number to people who summoned demons and tried to sacrifice babies to those demons.

"So…" Mara rose up onto her knees, leaning against the couch back now. "He doesn't know I'm alive still?"

"No," Sebastian said. "But I'm not sure that matters." He held Mara's gaze, frowning slightly. "How much time do you spend with Carmen?"

Mara shrugged. "A lot I guess. She's more like family than staff. At least with me. She's been the one taking care of me all these years. My… Bart—" she smirked at her mother's name for Grant, "—wasn't interested in being a real father, so he pawned off most stuff to Carmen. She was like my aunt."

"You didn't think of her as a mother?" Angie asked. Given her circumstances, and given Mara had thought her mother dead most of her life, it was a little surprising she hadn't put Carmen into the roll of surrogate mother, even in her own mind.

Mara shrugged. "I guess not. Not sure why. I just always thought of her like an aunt. A relative, but not a parent."

Angie wondered if that was down to the way Carmen treated her, or an instinct on Mara's part to keep some psychological distance between herself and Carmen. But she didn't suppose a twelve-year-old would have considered the idea all that deeply.

And now, here they were, about to tell this poor child that the one person in her life she'd thought she could trust, the one person who actually had taken her in and raised her and showed her familial love, had actually been working toward some sort of nefarious plan the whole time. No different from her father at the base of it. Oh, Carmen didn't want to see

Mara killed—Angie was inclined to believe Carmen about that—but she'd still intended to sacrifice Mara all the same, offering her up to the Molder demon as yet another disciple.

"Has Carmen been in touch?" Sebastian asked quietly.

Mara frowned. "How could she? She doesn't know where I am. Unless you told her."

"She helped you run," Angie said. Carmen had told them as much.

Mara's expression flickered, a hint of guilt in her light eyes. "I don't want her to get into trouble."

"You think we'd do that?" Angie asked. "Given what your father had planned?"

Mara winced at Angie calling Grant that, and Angie kicked herself for the slip. Her usual good sense and ability to deal appropriately with people was not on display tonight.

She gentled her tone. "You think we'd cause Carmen trouble for *helping* you escape?"

Mara's shoulders relaxed a little. "Sorry. Carmen… Carmen was like family, but she was still working for my… for Bart, and he could do awful things to her if he found out she helped me. Worse than just firing her. I don't want him to know she helped me."

So, there was a sense of loyalty there as well as affection.

None of that boded well for how Mara would take the news they had.

Angie decided to momentarily change tack, delaying the inevitable, but something had just occurred to her and she couldn't resist asking. "Do you know any of Grant's associates?"

Mara shrugged. "I guess. I see some of them at the house. Why?"

"What's all this about?" Ellen asked. "Why are we discussing Carmen, and why have you changed subjects?"

"Carmen, I'll explain in one moment. I just want to check something first. It'll clarify a hanging thread." To Mara she said, "If I describe someone, do you think you'd recognize them?"

Mara shrugged so Angie described the man who'd walked into Dana's Cauldron looking for her.

"Sounds like someone I've seen at the house," Mara said, frowning and wrinkling her nose. "I don't know who he is, but he kind of stands out with how pale he is and not having eyebrows. Makes his face look weird with his dark hair. He's never spoken to me."

"Does that answer your question?" Ellen asked.

"Enough," Angie said, not sure that it helped much. Knowing he was an associate of Grant's meant the man was a human who'd been inhabited by the demon when he'd gone to Dana's. Likely Carmen had somehow manipulated him—

"He's not a friend of Bart's though," Mara said, bringing Angie's thoughts to a screeching halt. "He comes to see Carmen."

CHAPTER TWENTY-FIVE

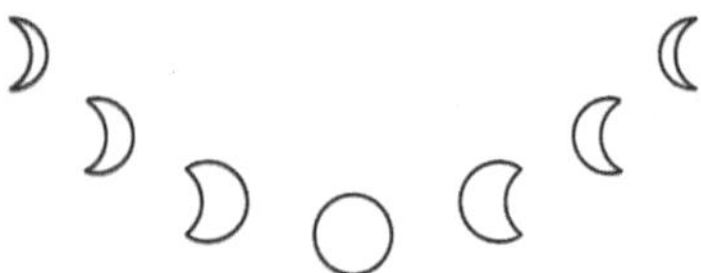

"Wait, the man I described came over to see Carmen?" Angie asked. Her heartbeat sped up, although she wasn't sure why. Except that it felt like more of the pieces were falling into place.

"He comes over to visit her," Mara said, glancing at her mother before looking back at Angie. "She's never introduced him to me. They usually meet when Bart is out, or when he's on the phone or something in his office. I thought once he might be her boyfriend, but they don't act like that."

Angie glanced briefly at Sebastian. "What do you mean?"

Mara rolled her eyes, but her cheeks turned pink. "You know. The way boyfriends and girlfriends and stuff look at each other and, I don't know, hold hands and stuff." She shrugged. "It's kind of weird since Carmen is pretty old, but I wanted her to be happy. But she wasn't happy when the guy showed up."

Angie ignored Mara's assessment of Carmen's age—old was a bit harsh since Carmen was likely only in her early forties, if that. But twelve-year-olds weren't great judges of adult ages. And frankly, it was possible Carmen tried to appear older to Mara so she wouldn't seem threatening, maybe even a little grandmotherly. "What was she then, if not happy when he showed up?"

Mara shrugged again. "I don't know. Not happy, but not really mad either. Like…intense. The way Bart gets when he's on the phone with a politician."

"Did Carmen seem to be…in charge? Or was the man in charge?" Sebastian asked.

Good question, Angie thought.

"Oh Carmen. He did what she told him to do." Mara grinned. "She was like a mother, or his boss or something, ordering him around. And he didn't even argue about it. Not once. He just did whatever she told him to do."

Mara's glee at Carmen ordering someone around might have amused Angie if Angie hadn't suspected some of the orders were demon-related.

"Did he visit often?" Sebastian asked.

"I guess. I don't know for sure. I saw him around maybe once a month or something like that." Her gaze narrowed. "Is Carmen in trouble? Did the man hurt her?"

"Why would you ask if he'd hurt her?" Angie asked.

"He was kind of scary. Intense." She looked to her mother. "I'm not sure how to say it. Like… Like if I tried to say something to him, he might yell or something."

"Did he yell at Carmen?"

"Oh no. Just did what she told him to do. But, like, Bart always looks like he wants to hit people who give him orders, only he doesn't give them that look until their backs are turned or maybe even after they've gone. I didn't see this guy often enough to see him look at Carmen that way, but…" She glanced down at the back of the couch. "I didn't like him much, but I never told Carmen. He scared me."

Ellen went to Mara and wrapped her arm around her shoulders, the couch back between them. "Why are you asking these questions? What does all this have to do with Bart and demons?"

Angie sighed and looked at Sebastian.

He held up the bag. "We discovered Carmen, in a stand of trees at the edge of the complex. She'd summoned the very demon we think is at the heart of this."

"Carmen?" Ellen said. "No, that doesn't make sense. She's just—" Ellen pressed her lips together, cutting off whatever she'd been about to say. "She's not a bad person. Bart is the one who called the demons before. I know he is."

"He's been summoning demons," Sebastian confirmed. "But he's not the only one. And might have had some help learning how."

Angie watched Mara closely during this reveal. The girl's eyes widened, her hands clenched tight into the worn material of the couch back. Her already pale skin grew paler. She looked at her mother but quickly away before making eye contact with her.

"Did you know?" Angie asked her quietly.

"No." Mara shook her head hard. "No. Not that she did… that."

"But?" Angie pushed as gently as possible.

Mara swallowed hard. "She's… I got the books on demons when Carmen took me to this library in the Bronx. And she said my…Bart wouldn't know about the books I checked out, that she'd keep this visit a secret. She knew the librarian pretty well. I just assumed it was near where she grew up or something. She told me she grew up in the Bronx."

Angie doubted much of what Carmen had told Mara was true, but the library in the Bronx was a detail she filed away. The hunters would have to visit that library—it held books that shouldn't be checked out by ordinary humans.

"Carmen didn't say anything about demons," Mara went on, "but she suggested the exact isle I needed to find those books. I thought it was coincidence. The shelf across from the demon books had graphic novels and YA books."

Angie almost groaned aloud. Of course they put the YA books right next to the demon summoning books. Of *course* they did.

Recruiting children. Vulnerable teenagers! Despicable.

"You didn't tell Carmen what kind of books you were looking for?" Sebastian asked.

His tone was also very gentle and there was a soothing quality to it that made even Angie want to relax and tell him everything. Not a feeling of being manipulated into revealing something. It was a sense of trust that you could say anything to him and he'd keep the secret, not judge you, make everything safe again.

That will of his was one powerful tool.

Mara shook her head. "No. I just told her I found something in the basement and wanted to look some stuff up."

"She knew what Grant was doing in the basement," Angie said, also keeping her tone gentle. "We think…" She glanced at Sebastian. "Based on what she said, we think she's the one who gave Grant the idea to summon a demon. Or at least helped him do it."

"No," Ellen said. "No. She couldn't have. She didn't come to work for us until after we were married for a year. She wasn't there at the beginning. And Bart only married me to get a baby to sacrifice to his demon. He was already messing with all that stuff before Carmen."

"They could have been working together before she came into the house," Angie pointed out. "There's no reason to think they didn't know each other before she started working for you."

"But *I* hired her. I'm the one who did the interviews. There were… I don't remember for sure, five or six applicants sent over from an agency. I could have chosen any of them."

"There are…tricks that someone versed in summoning demons could use," Angie said, thinking of the will Carmen had to have been dealing with a demon all these years.

"Carmen was my friend," Mara said, her voice so quiet she was hard to hear. "She tried to have me killed?"

"No," Angie said quickly. "She was adamant about that. She claimed she protected you."

"She helped me when I ran away," Ellen said, looking as pale as her daughter now. "I trusted her. When I let Bart… take custody of Mara, I trusted Carmen to take care of her."

"She did," Mara said. "She looked after me."

Holding the bag at its base, Sebastian let the top part of it open and fall back enough to reveal some of the lantern. "Have you seen this before?" he asked Mara.

She blinked a few times at the seeming change of subject and looked closer at the lantern. "That was in the basement. On the altar Bart used to summon the demon. The same picture I found in the book I got from the library." She frowned deeper. "Can't remember…"

"It wasn't in the picture," Angie said. "It was the only thing not the same as that picture."

"What does that mean?" Mara asked.

"Carmen was using this tonight," Sebastian said. "When she summoned a demon. It's for allowing a demon to move into a human host without having to sacrifice their power."

"Huh?" Mara said.

"It's a dangerous object," Sebastian said. "And it's very hard to come by."

"Did Carmen take it from Bart?"

"Best we can tell," Angie said, "Carmen's been using it for a long time. She may have allowed Grant to use it. Or used it against him. We're not sure."

"None of this makes sense," Mara said.

"Demon summonings usually don't," Sebastian said.

Angie had been thinking it all made better sense now. But for a girl who was just learning the person she'd been relying on for years was at the heart of the problem, this was a tangled mess.

"Carmen knows where you are," Sebastian said. "She was here summoning her demon. That's not a coincidence."

"She might have found out it was good for that kind of thing, the way I did," Ellen said. "It *might* be a coincidence."

"She has plans to train Mara," Angie said, "into the demon world, to have Mara take over for her in some sort of…revenge life." She shrugged, not entirely sure what to call it since Carmen hadn't seen fit to outline her nefarious plans for them. "She wasn't here on accident."

"She's coming for Mara?" Ellen's arm tightened on her daughter.

"Not to kill her," Angie said quickly. "But… Her intentions don't seem entirely *good* either."

"I don't want to be stuck with demons all the time," Mara said. "I don't want revenge on anyone. I just want to be normal and have my mom back."

"You've got me back already," Ellen said gently. "I'm not going anywhere now."

"I'm glad you're not interested in continuing Carmen's quest, whatever it is," Angie said.

"But that doesn't mean she won't keep trying to convert you to her thinking," Sebastian added.

"Or do something bad if she can't," Angie felt compelled to say. Mostly for Ellen's sake. Ellen needed to know her daughter was in as much danger from Carmen as Grant. Maybe more.

"Why is all this happening?" Mara said, leaning into her mother. "Why me?"

Ellen pressed her lips together, not answering. No one answered for a long moment. And in the silence, Angie considered...

"Mara," she said, waiting for the girl to meet her gaze. "I've told you I'm a touch psychic."

Mara nodded.

"I have a suspicion, a reason why Carmen has been trying to pull you into her plan. But I need to touch you and read you to confirm that. Touching your hand would be enough. May I have your permission?"

"What if I don't want to know?" Mara asked.

"Then I'll stay where I am. The choice is entirely yours."

Mara held her gaze. "Lots of people have been pretending I can trust them. And lots of people have lied."

"I know. And I'll understand if you refuse."

"How do I know you'll tell me the truth?"

"You don't. I've tried to be as honest with you as possible to this point. But you don't have any reason to trust me, and I understand if you're suspicious now. Don't worry. If you don't allow me to read you, I won't and we'll still keep you safe." Angie held her hands out to her sides, palms up. "The only difference my reading you will make is that it might—*might*—answer your question. Why you?"

Mara looked to her mother and Ellen held her gaze for a

long long moment. The resemblance between the two was so obvious in that moment, it nearly broke Angie's heart.

To help in her decision, Angie said, "If it makes you feel better, you can touch me. That works too. I'll hold my hand out and you can just touch the center of my palm. Or the back of my hand even, if that feels safer."

"Mom?" Mara said quietly, her voice quavering. She sounded very young.

Angie's chest contracted. Mara was very young. Too young to have to deal with all this. Angie understood the world, and life, wasn't fair. Things happened. Sometimes bad things happened to wonderful people. To children. But it hurt her soul every time she encountered that injustice.

"Can I stay close to her?" Ellen asked without looking away from Mara.

"Of course," Angie said. "It's best if you're not touching her. I don't want to accidentally pick up anything from you. But you can stay right beside her, close enough to pull her back if you feel she's unsafe."

"An explanation might help," Ellen said. "At least it will stop you thinking something is wrong with you. Nothing is wrong with you. Nothing at all. And this could help you understand that."

They'd obviously had that conversation before. Oh, Mara.

Another long moment passed as Mara stared at her mother. Then she nodded, very faintly. She met Angie's gaze, her bottom lip trembling slightly. "I'll touch the back of your hand. That will work, right?"

"Should do just fine," Angie said, stretching her arm out. She let her eyes droop close to closed so she could focus on opening her psychic sense, allowing her skin to accept that open sense of the hidden around her.

She felt more than heard Mara approach, a slight shifting in the air currents as the girl and her mother neared. Angie kept perfectly still—years of practice at her altar helped— and kept her gaze unfocused and half closed. She tried to look innocuous and harmless, but she didn't have the same knack for it that Sebastian did. She just hoped she looked harmless enough for Mara to take that final step.

A moment passed. Two. And then Angie felt the slight brush of soft fingers against the back of her hand.

CHAPTER TWENTY-SIX

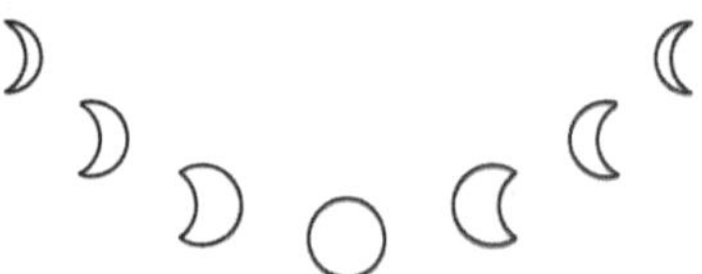

At first, Angie sensed nothing. Nothing at all. Which was a strange enough sensation she found it pulling her concentration.

And then…

The butterfly brush of Mara's burgeoning powers lapped against her skin like warm water, a gentle kiss of heat, accompanied by the soft flavor of citrus and vanilla and electricity. The taste of it surprised Angie. She didn't often experience taste in her visions. She'd have to do some research, but she suspected that added element would help her determine the type of magic growing in Mara.

Because there was, without a doubt now, magic there.

She smiled a little as she let the magic flow over her skin, as she studied it. Good, good magic. Sparkling and bright and, at the moment, so pure and clean. Like spring water, warmed in the sun's heat. Crystalline and fresh. The sensation of new magic was always a delight to encounter—at least this kind of magic. And Angie allowed herself the moment of hope and peace that came with acknowledging that new little spark as it grew into this world.

She was still smiling when she opened her eyes and met Mara's gaze.

"Well," she said, to Mara's raised brows, "you will need some training soon."

Mara frowned and looked between Angie and her mother. "Huh?"

"It seems you're coming into some magic of your own," Angie said. "It feels lovely. I'll need to research to determine what these first hints tell me about what you could be capable of. But, it looks like you're a fellow witch."

"Witch?" Mara's eyes widened.

"Aren't they evil?" Ellen said, reaching out to pull Mara close.

Angie quickly dropped her arm so she and Mara were no longer touching. Mara took a moment longer to let her arm drop back to her side.

"I'm a witch," Angie reminded quietly. "And no, they aren't any more good or evil than any other human being. The magic just is. Some witches don't even have magic. They're just...theologically inclined toward the pagan philosophies." When Ellen's frown deepened, Angie said, "It's their religion. They align with witchy philosophies but don't necessarily have any innate powers. Then there are those of us with actual magic. Like me."

"What kind of magic?" Mara asked.

"Mine or yours?"

"Yours."

Her curiosity had her leaning in a little closer to Angie instead of leaning away. That was a good sign.

"Beyond the touch psychic senses, I can create spells—using words and gestures—that…make things happen. That part takes a lot of study and practice." She always felt the need to emphasize that to a possible new initiate. Magic wasn't something you just started throwing around one day. It was a muscle that needed training or injuries occurred. Sometimes injuries occurred during the training. But if you had a good mentor, those were minor compared to what they could have been.

"What kind of things?" Mara asked.

Angie decided to show her a small spell, something obvious but harmless. She murmured the spell under her breath, letting the words flow in a practiced cadence as she twisted her fingers together in a brief pattern. She chanted the spell twice through, then opened her hand. A small sparkle of colorful light, shaped like a butterfly, appeared on the center of her palm.

Mara's eyes widened and she let out a sigh.

Angie held the illusion for a few moments, then lifted her hand and tossed it into the air. The light sparkling butterfly flitted around her head a few circles before landing back into Angie's palm. She flexed her fingers and the sparkles dissolved, the colorful illusion winking out.

"That's a small illusion spell," Angie said. "One of the first things a witch with my skills will practice because its harmless but visible. You know if you get it right or wrong pretty quickly."

"So, like a magic trick at a show?" Ellen said.

"Not quite. My illusions aren't tricks of light and shadow and some clever props. I don't pull rabbits out of hats." She shrugged. "Well, technically, I could, but the rabbit wouldn't have already been in the hat."

Ellen raised her brows, her look skeptical. "What else can you do? Besides harmless illusions."

"Less harmless things," she said, purposely vague. "Things I won't do here because they're dangerous, and I don't want anyone hurt. Another specific skill is my ability to scry for someone's location. That's how we found Mara here." She focused on Mara. "The kind of magic, how it manifests, what you can do with it, that will come out in training. If you choose to get that training. I recommend it, because without it, some witches get themselves into trouble. Witch magic is all spells and gestures and intentions. It can require a safe space and a lot of time. Sometimes, it requires potions and props. Those are some of the variations. But it's a natural part of you, like your height. Your kind of magic is the sort that comes on at puberty, so it may or may not grow and strengthen. The stronger it gets, though, the more you'll need to train it to stay safe."

"What could happen if she doesn't?" Ellen said.

"That will depend on what her base skills are and how strong the magic is."

"Can you train me?" Mara asked.

"No," Angie said. "You'll need a much more experienced

mentor than I could be to you now. But if you're interested, I can point you toward some safe people, witches you can trust to have your best interests at heart."

"There are bad witches?" Mara asked.

Angie's mouth tilted up a little. "Just like there are good and bad people."

"Black magic?" Ellen said and asked.

That was a trickier topic. "The popular idea of 'black' magic and 'white' magic is a little simplistic and doesn't really accurately describe things. 'Black' magic isn't necessarily evil, and 'white' magic isn't necessarily good. But for the record, because so many people see black and white in those terms, that's why I call myself a green witch. My particular brand of magic links heavily into nature and the natural world, so the term fits better anyway."

"Your magic links into the natural world and you live in New York City?" Ellen said skeptically.

This time Angie grinned. "You'd be surprised how much nature a witch can find in this city."

"Central Park," Mara said, as if that was obvious.

Which, Angie supposed, it was.

Ellen made a face at Mara's attitude, but let that go. "So, what does all this mean for Mara?"

"It might explain why Carmen is so interested in her." Angie frowned. "At least, it might explain why she's interested in training Mara now." She faced Sebastian. "But Mara is only just now starting to come into her power. Carmen couldn't have known about her, that this would happen, when she was a baby. Or before she was even born if she's been working with Grant that long. Why protect Mara before this?"

"The demon might have sensed it," Sebastian said. "When Grant tried to sacrifice her, the demon might have sensed the magic. Their perceptions of time aren't as strictly linear as ours."

"Could that be why the demon allowed Grant to live when he offered a child not of his blood to fulfill his bargain? Why Carmen continued to pose as the housekeeper for so long?"

Sebastian raised his brows in answer. Not an absolute yes. But Angie felt the rightness in the statement. More pieces of the puzzle falling into place.

"Are you telling me," Ellen said slowly, "that the demon…planned all this? Getting me out of the way… Mara staying with Grant. Carmen essentially raising Mara. All of this was a plan?"

"Demons are bastards that way," Sebastian said into the heavy silence that followed Ellen's statement.

Angie glanced that the bone lantern, which Sebastian had covered over with the bag again. She met his gaze. "And if the demon can move into a witch's body instead of just a mundane human's…"

"It would have powers beyond its own in this realm as well." Sebastian sighed. "Well, that's not good."

"No," Ellen said. "No, it's not! Are you telling me this demon wants to possess my child, my baby? And I left her in their hands this whole time?"

Ellen was practically screeching by the last sentence.

Angie didn't know what to say to that. But everything was starting to make more sense. Why the demon waited until now to act. What had changed with Grant and his relationship with the demon. The only question was…

Why had Carmen helped Mara get out of Grant's house, if the plan had always been for the demon to possess Mara's body once she came into her magic?

CHAPTER TWENTY-SEVEN

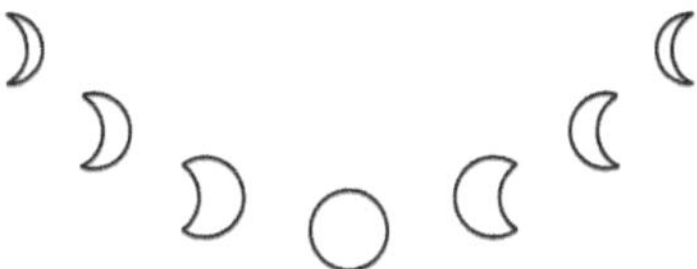

After getting Ellen calmed and promising to discuss magical mentors with Mara after they'd taken care of the demon, Angie and Sebastian left—warning Ellen not to take calls from Carmen or let her or the man she'd been working with into the apartment.

Angie wanted to warn them against letting anyone into the apartment, or even leaving the apartment to do laundry, until she and Sebastian had stopped the demon. But since Carmen no longer had the bone lantern, Angie didn't think the demon could move into a human host anymore. At least, not a stranger. She wasn't certain if the beast could occupy Carmen or her associate still.

So she asked Sebastian as they flagged down a taxi—no subways with a dangerous demon relic.

He considered the question quietly for a few moments. "Depends on the rituals they used, but as far as I remember, using the lantern to establish the bond, to facilitate the possession, means the demon can't possess them without it."

"Which was why Carmen was so desperate to get it back."

He nodded, lifted a hand without looking away from her, and a taxi speeding past screeched to a stopped, then did a U-turn to collect them. Angie smirked at him showing off.

As he held the taxi door open for her, he said, "This is all guess work as the lantern is supposedly a myth. But even myths have rules written into them, and those are the rules of the bone lantern."

Sebastian had the driver take them to a restaurant in the Upper East Side, not far from Grant's home.

She gave him a questioning look but he mouthed, *Later*, and she let it go until they had some privacy.

The ride took longer than Angie would have expected, given how late it was, but yet another accident caused a backup that left them crawling through crosstown traffic. By the time they arrived at the restaurant, Angie's anxiety levels had built so much she was fidgeting with her purse strap—though she wasn't entirely sure why she was so anxious. They had the bone lantern, Carmen couldn't use it. Ellen and Mara knew Carmen was a threat now. And Sebastian had bested the Molder demon once already tonight.

True, she'd accidentally opened a portal to a demon realm, and Carmen may or may not know what she could do now. That wasn't good. Carmen had gotten away, which wasn't good either. Though there wasn't a lot they could have done with her then anyway. They couldn't turn her over to the police for summoning a demon. Anymore than they could turn Grant over.

She stepped out onto the sidewalk as Sebastian paid for the taxi—she'd offered, but he waved her away and she was too jumpy to argue—and tried to pinpoint the source of her anxiety. She studied her surroundings. The restaurant was in the middle of a block, surrounded by bodegas, closed boutique stores, and a few other restaurants. She raised her brows at the still opened cupcake bakery across the street. That wouldn't settle her nerves but a cupcake sounded almost as good as a shot of Tequila right about then.

The street was quiet for New York, traffic stopped at a red light leaving the sound levels low and momentarily peaceful. The wind had kicked up, bringing the temperature down a bit more, hinting at winter cold. Two men stepped out of the restaurant behind her, and the scent of Italian food— garlic and olive oil and basil and tomatoes—followed them. The lovely smells made Angie's stomach growl. Dinner felt like it had been a long time ago.

Sebastian joined her and motioned her inside the restaurant. When he held the door for her, she chuckled. He was all old-fashioned manners and chivalry tonight.

The restaurant wasn't overflowing but many of the tables were full, even though it was quite late, well past even the late-night dinner rush. A man in a suit standing at the rear of the room talking with a woman in a chef's coat motioned them to take whatever table they wanted. Sebastian led her to one tucked into a corner that still gave them a full view of the main floor, where he could sit with his back to a wall and watch the door, and she could sit with her back to a wall and watch the restaurant and kitchen area.

They didn't need to discuss where they sat or the arrangement. And the realization that they'd set themselves up to watch things while they ate without having to talk about it was both strangely satisfying and a little disconcerting given how long they'd been separated.

Sebastian lifted his chin slightly and the man in the suit joined them to take their order. Angie ordered spaghetti with meat sauce. Sebastian got a carbonara dish. They didn't speak much until after the waiter had brought them waters and a bread basket. Angie tore into the bread as she let her gaze roam the restaurant.

"We're only a few blocks from Grant's house," she murmured when they were alone. "Why here?"

"We'll have things to do there soon."

"He's summoning tonight? Now?"

"Not yet. Soon, though, I'm afraid. We should still have time to eat."

"If... Why are you eating?" He didn't usually eat right before a fight. But since he'd had one already tonight, maybe he needed the energy?

"I find carbonara is settling." He smiled a little. "But mostly it's for you."

She raised her brows.

"You know you were going to share it."

She rolled her eyes but didn't argue. He was right. She would have asked to share. She ripped open another piece of bread.

"We should not bring *that*—" she nodded to the shopping bag he'd placed on the floor between his feet so he could keep in contact with it "—anywhere near Grant's house."

"That's why we're here. Beyond feeding you."

She frowned. "What?"

His soft grin made her heart flutter. That sensation was followed quickly by irritation when he changed the subject.

"How are you feeling after the tree incident?"

"Like crap because it was another mistake. But nothing got out, so that has to count." She focused on her bread. "Thanks for distracting me and pulling my focus. That brush against my leg, that was your will."

"You needed help."

She sighed. "Where are we going to store the lantern?" He'd been very vague about that so far.

"Someone will be here soon to take it," he said.

"What?" She straightened and met his gaze. This was news to her. He hadn't called anyone to arrange a meeting here. "You said you wanted to wait to hand it over to someone until after we got rid of the demon. You said without it, the demon would have no reason to remain in its own realm."

"The situation has…changed."

Which meant between their fight in the trees outside of Ellen and Mara's building and now, he'd sensed something he hadn't told her about.

"And you're right about us keeping it away from Grant," he continued without explain this *change*. "We can't take it to this fight. It'll be safer with the person coming."

"Who? Who's coming?"

"A…hunter. She'll take the lantern into custody, keep it well away from danger."

"Another hunter? She can help us fight the Molder demon."

"That's not her job. She's just coming to take the lantern."

"Not Aidan, then."

"Someone…else."

Angie frowned. He wasn't telling her something about this hunter. And she had the feeling whatever he was leaving unsaid was pretty damned important. Their food arrived then so she bided her time, waiting for privacy again, before saying, "Who the hell is this someone else? How do they know to meet us here since you didn't contact anyone? And why are you hesitating over who they are? Don't lie to me, Sebastian. Not now."

She remember his slip earlier, his mention of a council. He'd threatened to hand over the lantern to the council if she thought about touching it. Was this something to do with that? Was that what had changed?

"It's complicated," he said. "And something I'm not supposed to discuss with someone who isn't a hunter."

"There's things I don't know about the hunters?" She'd worked with him for two years. She'd assumed she knew most of what there was to know about demon hunters.

Obviously, she'd been wrong.

Rather than answer, he pulled her plate close to his and scooped most of his linguine onto her plate, spooning over extra sauce. She narrowed her eyes at him as he worked, waiting for his answer. When he pushed her now overloaded plate back to her, she pulled it close and started eating without taking her gaze off him.

He sighed. "I can't explain, Angie. I'm not allowed."

"How can you keep a secret from me about this? After all this time."

"You aren't a hunter. Even when we were working together, you kept insisting you weren't a hunter."

"I'm not."

"And I respect that choice and decision. It's not a job for everyone."

"If you respect my decision, you wouldn't keep coming back and dragging me into the demon world," she snapped.

He focused on his plate when he said, "I tried. I did honestly try." He looked up and his expression was carefully neutral. "In this world or not, you're not technically a hunter. So there are things you can't be told." He pressed his lips together in a tight line before saying, "I would have, if I was allowed. But you weren't a hunter. And I was…reminded repeatedly that until you accepted being a demon hunter, I had to keep certain secrets."

"Reminded by who? Aidan?"

"Yes. But she wasn't the only one."

"This person we're meeting tonight?" Angie ate another forkful of her spaghetti. It was delicious and tomato-y and had just the right amount of garlic and parmesan cheese. And she could barely enjoy it because her gut was churning with anger.

More anger than she should feel. Everything he said was right. She'd refused to accept the role as hunter. Even working with him, she'd refused that role. She'd been backup. Support. The one who could aid by opening a portal. And always, always a witch. Witchcraft *was* her calling. Nothing else. And she'd continued to insist on that distinction throughout their time together.

So why did she resent his keeping secrets so much now? He had a right to them. Especially if they had to do with his work. They weren't even a couple anymore. She had no real right to all his secrets.

That didn't seem to prevent the hurt tightening in her chest.

He didn't respond to her last question, just held her gaze. She couldn't read anything there. He'd shut down any hint of expression. And looking at him that way hurt as much as knowing he'd kept things from her.

She looked down at her plate and concentrated on eating so she could talk herself out of the hurt and anger. She didn't have the right to them, not now. She had to let it go.

They remained silent, him picking at what was left of his linguine, her shoveling in mouthfuls of pasta, until most of their meal was done. She still wasn't feeling great about this new bit of knowledge, but she pulled in a deep breath, prepared to talk again.

Only to be interrupted by a quiet throat-clearing. She looked up, expecting to see the waiter.

But it wasn't the waiter.

CHAPTER TWENTY-EIGHT

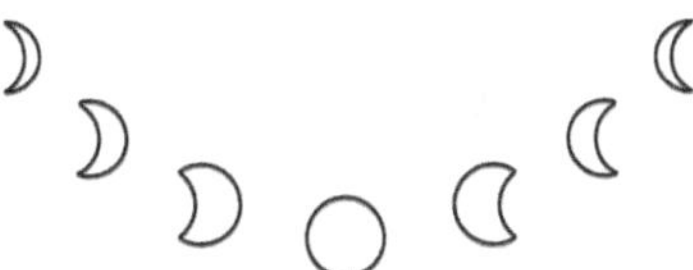

The woman standing beside their table was not particularly tall, but not short either. She *felt* average in height and build. A little thicker through the middle, with narrow hips and shoulders. But, overall, unremarkable proportions. Her hair was a steel gray color, pulled back into a tight bun at the base of her neck. Her light tan skin showed a few lines around her dark brown eyes and mouth. Her lips were pressed into a tight line, giving the impression of disapproval without having to say anything. She was dressed in black slacks and a long black wool coat, her hands tucked into the pockets. And she looked, for all the world, like a perfectly ordinary New Yorker.

If not for the faint red in the depths of her brown eyes, Angie might have been fooled into thinking this wasn't the hunter they'd been expecting.

"You got here fast," Sebastian said.

"I was in the area," the woman replied. Her voice was smoky and deep. A rival for Angie's own deeper octaves. And there was a very very faint accent, a sort of posh turning of the vowels, but Angie couldn't place it.

"Been in the area long?" Sebastian asked.

Angie glanced at him. There wasn't much in his tone to give away his emotions but there was a tightness around his mouth and at the corners of his eyes, a subtle sign of tension. Though a casual observer might not notice, she was very aware of the way he held his body with a kind of coiled intensity, ready to strike.

The fact that he held that much tension around another hunter was…interesting.

She narrowed her eyes at the newcomer, wondering who she was *exactly*.

"Long enough," the woman replied. She flicked a glance at Angie. "Is everything…settled?"

"I need you to take this into safe keeping," Sebastian said, ignoring her question. He handed the woman the bag with the lantern in it.

The woman took the handles of the reusable shopping bag and glanced inside without revealing the contents to the restaurant. Her dark brows arched higher, the only sign of emotion.

She closed the bag again and let her arms drop back to her sides, holding the bag as casually as if it carried nothing more serious than some groceries.

"That's a rare artifact," she said.

"And dangerous."

"You think you need to warn me?"

"It's been part of the Grant situation."

"Ah." The woman blinked. "Grant had it?"

"No. A woman working in his house. Carmen Ruiz."

Angie's turn to blink. She hadn't realized Sebastian had gotten Carmen's last name.

"She's working with another man," Sebastian continued. "The Molder demon has occupied him at least once that we know of."

"There's more?" the woman asked.

"For later."

She flicked another glance at Angie. "This needs to be settled."

Angie frowned. *This* meaning the situation with Grant and Carmen? Or something else? The way the woman kept giving her fleeting glares, it was hard to tell.

She wanted to demand an introduction, an explanation to the underlying conversation they were having. Instead, she scooped up the last of her spaghetti and ate it. If they weren't going to make introductions, she could pretend not to be involved or interested. All the better to observe them.

"We're done for now," Sebastian said.

And again, Angie wondered if there was more meaning to those words.

"This can't be left hanging, Sebastian. You know that. She must—" The woman's nostrils flared as she cut herself off.

Angie pretended not to notice the slip by taking the last piece of bread from the bread basket.

"The situation must be handled. You've been instructed."

"Warned?" Sebastian said.

"Requested," the woman countered. "This can't be ignored or left…out there. This is why you're here."

"No." Sebastian's tone made the woman straighten.

Angie wondered what he'd just said no to.

"I'm here for the Molder demon," he said as if clarifying.

The woman's shoulder's relaxed, but only slightly. "When this fight is done, if you survive, your presence is required at the New York office."

New York office? The hunters had offices? That was news to Angie. As far as she knew, outside of a once-a-year gathering to share information and mourn the year's lost or introduce the new recruits to the community, the hunters didn't meet. They worked alone for the most part, traveled alone. They didn't have *offices*.

Angie studied Sebastian from under her lashes, pretending most of her focus was on sopping up the rest of the red sauce on her plate with her bread. His jaw was tight, his mouth a hard line, his eyes narrowed slightly. The red in their depths flared brighter, though in the muted restaurant lighting that could have been an illusion. At least, that's what anyone who didn't know about demon hunters would think.

He sat a little hunched in his chair, and leaned back so he could meet the woman's gaze, but that coiled intensity, that sense that he was ready to strike, hadn't eased at all. In fact, he looked more ready to lash out than he had just a few moments ago.

"If I survive," he grunted. He did not sound happy about being summoned.

"An explanation is due," the woman said. "And we need a result."

"You've had the situation explained before."

"The result was not acceptable. You know it's not. Something has to be done. This has gone on long enough."

Sebastian pulled in a visible breath, and Angie waited for the explosion. He looked like he wanted to rip into the woman. His anger was a living thing between them.

And then, just as fast, all that anger and intensity vanished and he was a casual diner again, just speaking to a friend or colleague.

"Thank you for coming to get that." He nodded to the bag. "Tonight will go easier without it. I'll be in touch soon."

The woman held her place for a few moments even after Sebastian turned back to the table. The lines around her eyes and mouth deepened with her tight expression. And then she, too, seemed to let go all that intensity and her expression was once again casual if serious.

"Good luck," she said. Though it wasn't obvious, she flicked another glance at Angie. "With everything."

Angie watched her leave the restaurant. She was the only one who did. No one else even gave the woman a glance. She might have been a ghost moving past the tables, drawing no attention at all.

Angie turned back to Sebastian and raised her eyebrows. "Well, that was interesting."

Sebastian waved the meeting away. "She'll ensure the lantern is safe."

"Uh huh. And you're going to explain all the unspoken conversation to me, right?"

He opened his mouth, and she raised a hand to stop him.

"If you're about to lie to me, you can save your breath. I'm a little vain, but not so vain I assume all conversations are about me. But I can read body language. Very well. I know there was more in that conversation than was supposed to be obvious." She set aside the last bit of her bread, and held his gaze. "And I know at least some of it had to do with me."

CHAPTER TWENTY-NINE

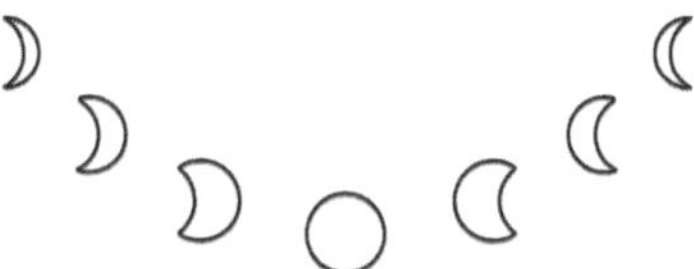

The waiter arrived with their check. Whether that was Sebastian trying to distract her or just coincidence, she wasn't sure. She and Sebastian both ignored the little slip of paper on the side of the table, though. And she didn't turn away from him, even long enough to acknowledge the waiter. Neither did Sebastian.

"Well," she said after a moment longer, when they were alone again.

He sighed. "I can't discuss this right now, Ang. It's complicated and we still have to stop Grant."

"Stop him doing what? What he's been allowed to do for twelve years?"

He dropped her chin. "We've taken away the Molder demon's one option for moving in this world inside a human host without losing power. It's not going to remain confined any longer. Tonight, it will escape. And kill. Grant. Carmen." He held her gaze. "Mara. Tonight is it."

Angie sat a little straighter in her chair. "How long have you known that?" And why was she surprised? Shouldn't she have realized? He'd said something had changed. Didn't she on some level know this final fight was imminent?

But she wasn't a hunter. Should she really have known?

"Not long after we took the lantern," he said. "Probably on the way up to see Ellen and Mara. Everything in me—all those instincts I can't quite explain—are assuring me this is the moment. This is the night."

Angie glanced at the remains of their dinner. He hadn't eaten very much of his while she'd cleaned her plate and sopped up any extra with bread. Her gut tightened as she stared at the plates, the low-level anxiety that had been with her since Sebastian's text to meet him at the Botanical Garden bloomed into full-blown panic.

"The woman, she said something about if you survive tonight. What do you know that I don't?" She glared at the table. "Was this some sort of last supper?"

"Not if I can help it," he said firmly. "But I can't tell the future." With a slight lift of his lips, he said, "Anymore than you can."

"I can infer from past information and body language, though." And sometimes she did get glimpses of the future. They were always just too nebulous to carry much weight. Too many things could change the future. Including getting a vision of it. "Your body language is telling me you're worried you won't come out of this," she said, her voice quiet.

"No," he said. "I can't be worried about that, or I'll fail for sure."

"That's what worries *me*."

"What do you want me to tell you, Ang?"

"That you'll survive so we can continue this fight tomorrow," she snapped.

His smile softened. "I always have enjoyed fighting with you," he murmured, almost too quietly for her to hear in the hum of restaurant noise. "I know you hate the fights, but… I've always loved doing anything at all with you."

She swallowed. Hard. "Seb…"

"We'll argue about that tomorrow, too," he said.

"Promise?"

He reached across the table and gripped her clenched fist, squeezing gently.

It wasn't an answer.

Before she could drag the promise from him, though, his expression changed. He stood abruptly. "I need to go." He glanced down at her. "You can stay. Last chance."

"Right," she said. "We've had *that* argument already."

She dropped money onto the bill, enough cash to cover the cost and a healthy tip. She'd have cringed a little at the money, but it was for food, and at this rate, she might not have to worry about her retirement fund anyway.

She followed Sebastian from the restaurant.

He stood on the sidewalk frowning.

"What's wrong?" she asked quietly.

"I'm not… This isn't happening at Grant's house."

"Shit. Where?"

He started trotting up the street and turned down a side road, heading toward Central Park.

Shit, she thought again. The Park after midnight. This wasn't going to be fun.

As she trotted after Sebastian, trying to conserve her lung capacity—she wasn't a runner—her second thought was that there were a lot of trees in Central Park. A lot of potential for disaster. She spent time occasionally in the Park. It was glorious, that patch of green in the middle of the city. But always in the daylight, always when she could be careful of the trees.

Night was more difficult. At night, it was easier to get caught.

Just as she'd already gotten caught once tonight.

Sebastian picked up speed and Angie stretched to keep up with him, holding her purse in one hand so it wouldn't bounce against her leg, concentrating on her breathing. She fell behind a bit, and got caught at a traffic light Sebastian raced through. She watched him disappear into the Park without her and cursed under her breath. A quick glance at signs told her they were at the 76nd Street entrance. Lots of trees here.

She counted to ten, impatiently waiting for the light because despite the late hour there were still a thousand cars on the road. Why the hell were there so many cars suddenly? Why was the light taking so long? Argh!

Rubbing the pentagram on her bracelet, she counted to

ten again. And the instant the lights changed, she charged across the street, still nearly getting clipped by a driver running the red light. She muttered one of her more colorful profanities under her breath and didn't slow down as she barreled into the dark park.

Low wattage lamps lit the path past one of the iconic playgrounds and deeper into the heart of the Park. This time of night, no one was around. The place felt empty and more like the deep forest than the middle of the city. The paving beneath her feet did little to dispel that feeling. The smells of pine and damp dirt overwhelmed the now faded scents of cooking nuts and city crowds. Still a touch of mustiness, but mostly just the scents of nature and night. A night bird hooted. The faintest sound of running water. Even traffic noise as it rose and fell seemed distant, more like a breeze through canyons than anything manmade.

Angie might have enjoyed the serenity. The quiet. She might have even been fooled by the peaceful surroundings…

If she wasn't so aware of the predators ahead.

Careful to keep her gaze lowered and not on the trees bracketing the path, she listened for any noise that would indicate which direction Sebastian had gone, following instincts. He was too far ahead of her for her to actually hear anymore, but she hoped she'd be able to intuit a direction. And when instincts didn't provide any good answers, she paused and put her hands on her hips, scowling into the darkness.

Panicking and charging off into the depths of the Park without a clue where she was going wasn't going to help. She sucked in a deep breath, pulled in the loamy, woodsy scents around her, focusing on those smells. She let her pulse calm, though it took a considerable effort, and time that if she focused on would make her panic again. She gave her pentagram one last rub, then let her arms drop to her sides.

The tracking spell wasn't one of her best. She was still practicing it. But it did work better when she knew the person she was trying to track. She hadn't ever practiced the spell in a life-or-death situation, though, and fear kept clogging her throat, making her concentration slip.

Fisting her hands once, hard, and then relaxing, she breathed out, letting her eyes drift almost entirely shut even as her awareness of her surroundings opened. The sounds of a light breeze moving through the trees. The brush of cold air against her cheek. The rustle of a small night creature in a nearby tree. Even the barely perceptible changing light as the clouds moved overhead, covering the waxing moon, changing the shadows across the path.

And very very faintly, a scent like sulfur reached her. Elusive and impossible to follow. But there.

She murmured the words to the spell, letting her mind fill with an image of Sebastian. With him, this part was easy. His beloved face crowded out the fears, that flash of his smile, the wicked twinkle in his dark eyes when he was thinking things that made her body tingle. She let the very essence of his soul fill her, everything she knew and didn't know about him.

Him.

And then she twisted her fingers in a pattern that, from

the outside, probably looked like someone pretending at sign language. She murmured the final words of the spell, letting them out on a soft exhale, formed a triangle with her first fingers and thumbs, then released both the spell and her hand gesture, splaying her hands forward.

When she opened her eyes, a faint blue illuminated line ran ahead of her into the darkness.

She let out a slow breath and followed the line, grateful she hadn't gone too far afield before initiating the spell. She had to double back to a small side path that led into a thicker wooded area, but that correction only took a minute.

Letting her awareness stay open, she hurried down another paved path, this one covered in dried leaves and a few fallen branches so it was hard to tell it was paved. She kept her gaze on the blue line, her focus on the spell, and hoped no muggers jumped out to disrupt things. She was well into the middle of the Park now, heading into the Ramble, the night deepening as the trees crowded around her. At the very edge of her hearing, she caught a slight sound of something like a ringing bell. Her heartbeat kicked up, though she wasn't sure why, and she picked up speed.

Beyond that faint, deep gong, the Park had grown remarkably quiet around her. No more birds. No more night sounds. Even the breeze had died and the leaves were still. She sensed her surroundings pause, like Nature was holding her breath. Angie's fear ticked up another few notches.

She was nearly at a full run by the time she heard the fight, still hidden by the trees, but impossible to miss now that she was this close. No longer in need of the guiding spell, she let her focus on it drop. The blue line winked out of existence. Without the faint illumination, it took a few minutes for her eyes to adjust to the normal night light. The shifting darkness and that faint red city glow overhead. Clouds rolled in, covering the moon.

When she felt she could see without tripping on a branch, she rushed forward, again, prepping a defensive shield spell, running through the words in her mind so the spell would be ready to trigger.

But before she got within sight of the fight she could clearly hear now, a large, pale shape stepped out in front of her.

Angie skidded to a stop.

And triggered her shield spell.

CHAPTER THIRTY

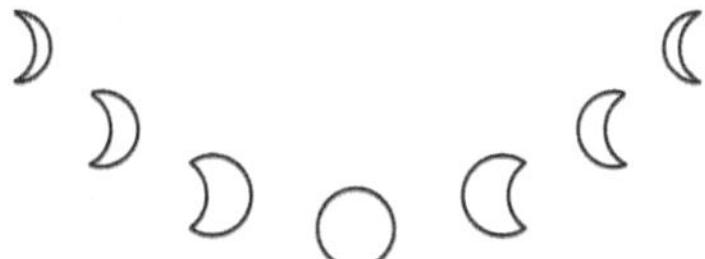

a dome of faint blue circled Angie, though she knew from experience no one else saw the shield but her.

The pale man standing before her smiled. "'Bout time you got here." He stepped forward and hit up against her magic, getting a jolt of energy that made him curse and step back. "Bitch," he hissed.

"Witch," she corrected. "You sound different when you're not hosting a demon."

The man was just as she'd seen in her vision at Dana's—short and painfully thin, pale skin, skeletal facial features, brown hair, no eyebrows. But his eyes were an ordinary brown, not black with a hint of red in the depths. And everything about him seemed…less.

Not less threatening, just less…

Demonic.

"He wants you now," the man said. "And Carmen's happy to give you to him."

"Him who?"

The man frowned. "The Master."

"The Molder demon isn't a 'he,'" she said. "That particular species doesn't come in distinct genders. We use 'it' because that just seems more appropriate with a demon. Although, sometimes I still slip and use gender pronouns. I'm working on that, which is why I bring it up. If you're going to be working with a specific species of demon, it's important to understand their basics."

The man blinked. Angie grinned. Sebastian did that sometimes, lectured someone in the midst of a confrontation. Nothing like throwing an opponent off their game.

And while he was confused by her calm lecture, she murmured the fire spell, calling the little ball of heat and flame into her palm.

The man's gaze flicked to that. "She warned me about you," he said. "Warned me you could call the fire like a demon."

"Then you know trying to fight me is a bad idea. I'm going to go help my friend now. And if you don't get out of my way, I will let you burn."

Someone shouted around the corner. She couldn't tell if it was Sebastian or not because more noise, the sounds of something whooshing through the air, a scuffle, all competed with the shout. Not knowing what was happening, what kind of trouble he might be in, filled her with dread and panic. She had to get around this asshole, and fast. He might be dangerous under normal circumstances. But with a demon just beyond the next clump of trees, he seemed a nuisance rather than a threat.

Until he grinned.

Her attention snapped back to him. That grin worried her.

"I ain't here to kill you," he said. "The Master wants you. I'm here to stall you." His gaze lifted as if he could see behind him without having to turn his head. "Sounds like I stalled just long enough."

He stepped aside as Angie barreled past him, dropping her shield to move fast. She kept the little fire ball in her palm, which slowed her down because if she ran, she risked accidentally dropping or tossing it. Though it wasn't *technically* a physical thing she touched in her hand, it was linked to her in a way analogous to holding. But the hold was tenuous when she was moving.

She skidded into a clearing, leaving the path to reach the patch of dirt and leaves. In the middle of the clearing, the Molder demon laughed, its pointed gray teeth against black gums so obvious even in the dark it was like the beast glowed from within, a ghastly apparition in the dark clearing. Carmen and Sebastian were clenched together in a physical fight, and it only took a moment for Angie to realize Carmen was his match. She was a head shorter, but stronger than she looked, and obviously trained because she was holding her own against the much larger man. When she punched Sebastian in the kidney, Angie hurt the hit and winced for him.

She wanted to intervene in the physical fight, but *she*

wasn't trained for that, despite all the fights with her brothers over the years. She could hold her own in a dirty, kicking, biting fight if she had to. But getting between Sebastian and Carmen right then would likely get her a head-spinning punch to the face or breath-stealing gut punch, and none of that would help Sebastian.

But she could banish the demon.

The Molder demon picked that exact moment to shift its gaze and stare at her. Its smile widened grotesquely, making its teeth look even longer. A split in the side of its gray, skeletal face dripped a thick black liquid like tar. Or blood.

Maybe she could banish the demon.

The man who'd slowed her down, his words came back to her. That he was stalling. That the demon wanted her. *Her.*

She didn't have to think too hard to figure out why. If it could possess her body, it would be able to open demon realms and let loose a torrent of chaos onto this realm. But she wasn't making any deals with it. And it no longer had the bone lantern.

Keeping out of the way of Sebastian's fight with Carmen, she approached the demon, studying the containment circle Carmen had drawn to summon the beast. This one was built from salt but no chalk this time. The area around it had been swept clear of leaves, and when leaves blew past in the breeze, they stacked against one side of the circle without crossing the line.

In her mind's eye, Angie could see the faint reddish color of the circle, a light not visible with the eyes. She let her gaze soften long enough to ensure the circle was intact. Carmen might be mad for revenge, but she wasn't stupid. She'd built a solid circle that was holding.

Unless Sebastian had to kill her.

That worry nagged, but she carefully kept the fear from her face as she met the demon's black gaze. Looking into that darkness was like staring into a bottomless void and she wasn't immune to the vertigo. She was just good at ignoring it. She'd stared into that void more than once.

"You don't have the will to banish me, witch," the demon murmured. "You know you don't. It's why you haven't joined the hunters."

Its voice hissed out, full of Ss, sibilant with an undercurrent of something sharp that grated over her nerves like nails on a chalkboard. She kept her wince to herself.

"My will is strong," she said. "It's just focused on something more—" she bounced the fire ball in her palm, "—magical." She grinned back at the grinning demon. "And if you think I'll let you use me, you're wrong."

"I know you fear me," it said. "I felt that when you touched the book. When we met in the realms of memory. You fear me, but you know me."

"Nothing personal, but I'd rather not know you." She didn't argue with the fear. It would be pointless. She was afraid. Very very afraid.

She was also determined.

"Your fire will not burn me," the demon pointed out.

"This? This isn't for you. This is for your minions." She

thought of the hunter who Carmen had killed while the hunter had been trying to defeat this demon. She hoped not to make the same mistake. Carmen's associate was still behind them somewhere. "You… You will require something else."

"A fight?" The demon laughed. "A bargain?"

"Oh, no. I'm not bargaining with you. I know what you want already. And it's not on offer." Once Carmen uncovered her secret, Angie knew the demon would understand what it meant.

"You would be more powerful," it said, the lilt of a lure in its voice. "Power beyond your imagining."

It lunged close to the edge of the circle, a move that startled her despite herself. Like having a cockroach fly at her face. She bit back the screech, but cursed under her breath.

"You would never have to fear being trapped again," it whispered.

Trapped. Trapped. They're coming. Scrambling over glass-sharp rock. Blood. Heat. Fire. Burning. The chittering of demons. Close. Too close. Overwhelming her. The spark spell not enough. Tearing at her. Breaking through. No! The portal closing. Trapped. She was trapped.

"You would control your gift fully," the demon whispered.

She clenched her teeth and forced down the memory that haunted her nightmares. Her heart pounded so hard in her chest it hurt.

"No bargains," she said, her voice deep, her throat raw as if she'd been breathing the sulfur air in the demon realm.

Damned demon, hitting on just the right nerve, pressing

just the right button. It knew her fear, knew her deepest terror.

Or at least, it thought it did.

Somewhere behind her, she heard a grunt of pain and then some cursing. Not all of the cursing was Sebastian's, which was good. She hoped. The demon laughed at her and moved back a little. It rose higher, floating just above the ground like a ghost. There was a lot about this type of demon that hinted at ghost, and that only added to its insidiousness.

When it towered over her, forcing her to drop her head back to look into its face, it pointed a long, skeletal, black claw-tipped finger at her. "You think you have stopped me from passing into your world, don't you?"

"I don't see another bone lantern lying around the place," she said with a shrug. The gesture made the fire ball hovering over her palm sway. "I hear they're quite rare."

"They are," it confirmed with a nod.

It glanced behind her and despite herself, she looked. She couldn't not, even though she suspected it was a trick of some kind. Sebastian had Carmen in a choke hold, a slow squeeze around her neck, her head tilted to one side as he pushed her toward unconsciousness. She'd seen him do this before—to get a human summoner out of the way for their own good. She knew he could knock Carmen out without killing her, trusted him to do so. But once Carmen was unconscious, the circle holding the demon would be more… breakable.

Angie had a choice in the moments remaining before

Carmen passed out. Build a personal shield. Or a protection circle.

She faced the demon again, and startled back a step. It was right at the edge of the circle, again, its face close to hers. Smiling.

"I will have you," it whispered. "You will be mine. And then I will control everything."

"No," she said.

It laughed. "You think you're safe from my possession? Because there is no longer a lantern?"

"Because I won't welcome you in," she said. "And I'm not some wet-behind-the-ears child witch. Not anymore. You can't come in without an invitation."

"You've already invited me," it said.

She knew she hadn't. Oh, it was tempting to ask how, when, but if she did, she risked showing the demon her hand.

It already knew enough.

"No," she said again.

Inside her head, she murmured her spell, setting it up, rolling through the words. Because the fire in her palm prevented her from forming the appropriate hand gestures, she tossed it into the air and put it to "sleep", letting it hover inside the magic realm, no longer present in this one.

The demon narrowed its eyes at her. "You think *I* can be tricked?" It chuckled. "I make fools of others. No mere human witch can fool me."

"Fair enough," she said, only half paying attention to it now. Her focus was on properly building her spell, on the rhythm of the words, the motion of her fingers…moving now, forming the final link in the chain of her magic.

Movement behind her. She ignored it. Sebastian was there. He'd guard her back.

The demon rose higher above her again. Hovering. Looming.

She ignored it, too.

"You cannot use magic on me," the demon intoned.

She didn't comment. She was too deep in the chant, in the building of her spell. She let out a slow breath through her nose, releasing all the air in her lungs before filling them again. Once. Twice.

And the final word whispered out.

She raised her hands, palms facing the ground. Finally, she looked up at the demon. And jerked her hands downward.

A flare of blue light momentarily lit in her minds eye, giving assurance the spell had set.

She smiled.

"What have you done, witch?" the demon hissed.

"Safeguard," she said. Without looking away from the demon, she said over her shoulder, "Is Carmen out?"

A soft grunt. And then Sebastian said, "She'll sleep soundly for a while."

"Good."

The demon laughed. "You've released me?"

"Of course not," Angie said. "She's not dead."

"But her will no longer binds me. And I'm still here."

"You can leave now," Angie suggested.

"Her will was weakening. She'd grown soft. For the child."

"Which is why I'm here," Sebastian said.

"Your will cannot bind me either, hunter."

"We've gone over this before," Sebastian said, stepping up to Angie's side. "My will is strong enough for any fight you offer."

"Are you sure?" It moved like a snake, fast and suddenly, its face dropping from above to line up with Sebastian's. "When I possess your witch, you'll crumble. You can't hurt her. I *know*."

If Sebastian had a button, Angie knew this was his. And demons were very very good at pushing buttons. Weakening wills. Tricking humans into ignoring their instincts. Sebastian had hunted them for decades now, and was hard to fool. But the demon had hit on a truth. And that truth was Sebastian's one weakness.

Her own trauma after getting caught in a demon realm hadn't been the only reason she'd tried to push him away. That might have been the initial reason. The impetus for finally letting go of their love.

But it wasn't, in the end, the only reason.

"Don't let him in," she murmured.

She glanced at Sebastian. He smiled at her. And winked.

The gestures made her heart swell and her muscles relax with relief. Maybe he knew…

"Now," Sebastian said, "I believe we're to the banishing point of the evening. And it's time for you to go." He stepped in front of Angie, close enough that he and the demon were practically touching.

The beast chuckled and reached for Sebastian. Sebastian met the black gaze without flinching, ignoring the claws reaching for him. He started to chant, in Spanish, letting the words of the banishing echo in the clearing. Once again using the method Carmen had used to summon the demon to banish it.

The demon hissed words that weren't part of any human language and struck out at Sebastian. Its hands came up against a wall of light that flared blue in the visible world. Its black eyes narrowed and it faced her. "You. What have you done?"

"Backup safeguard," she said with a shrug. "I thought I said that already. Is there something wrong with your memory? You might need help for that."

The demon wasn't the only one capable of pressing buttons. Her comment, ridiculous of course, but it was such a very human issue that the suggestion of it would deeply offend a demon.

From the way the demon lurched at her, all ghostly gray rage, she had to assume she'd hit a soft spot.

Sebastian continued to intone the banishment chant, the spell rolling out of him in a deep, reverberant tone full of power and the strength of his will.

Even Angie felt his will, like actual magic, filling the area and controlling the demon.

The beast howled, throwing its head back. The gray strings of its garments swirled around it in a breeze she couldn't feel. It lifted higher above them, and the stench of sulfur and rot increased. The demon screeched in ear piercing rage and a thick, snake-like tongue thrashed from its gapping mouth like a completely separate entity attempting to escape.

Satisfaction and relief started to relax Angie's muscles. Started to release all the tension she'd been holding.

Until…

"If you don't stop," Grant said quietly from behind them, "I'll shoot the girl."

CHAPTER THIRTY-ONE

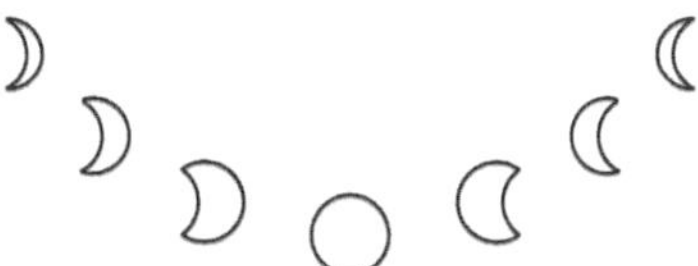

Silence descended over the clearing. Angie turned, very slowly, keeping the demon in the periphery of her vision but focusing on the horrible tableau behind her.

Grant stood with Ellen in front of him, a gun to her head. She was bound and gagged, her hands tied behind her back, and tears streaked down her cheeks even as she glared at everyone.

The pale man who'd supposedly been Carmen's associate stood to Grant's left. He had a hand on Mara's shoulder, pushing her ahead of him like a shield even though she was just a little shorter than he was.

Mara was also bound and gagged, though her hands were tied in front of her. She was pale, and even at a distance, Angie could see she was trembling. But unlike her mother, she wasn't crying. She wasn't glaring. She wasn't wide-eyed with panic and fear.

Her blue eyes looked…hollow. Like she'd resigned herself to her fate and wasn't aware enough of what was happening to struggle anymore.

That, more than Ellen's terror and anger-fueled tears, broke Angie. Broke her heart, but also some vital element of restraint she held close to keep a check on her own anger.

"What do you expect to happen here?" Sebastian said. He'd stopped chanting and the demon had stopped screeching.

"I expect you to move out of my way so I can finish what I started," Grant said. "You think that maid was in charge?" He snorted. "She was in over her head from the start."

From the corner of her eyes, Angie saw the demon hovering closer, smirking, but she kept her attention mostly on Mara. She was also keenly aware of Carmen laying vulnerably unconscious nearby, too. While Angie hated what Carmen had been doing, and wanted her punished in some way for summoning demons and putting Mara at risk, she didn't want Grant to kill her while she couldn't defend herself. Angie couldn't be certain he'd bother with that. But she couldn't be certain he wouldn't either.

As subtly as she could manage, she mentally said a small confusion spell, folding her fingers into the correct pattern before brushing her hand in Carmen's direction. The spell would hover over the prone woman, making her hard to see, hard to focus on. Easy to overlook and ignore. It wasn't bullet-proof—Angie couldn't build bullet-proof shields with her brand of magic—but it would hopefully keep Grant unaware of her. Unless he literally tripped over her. But she was far enough away that shouldn't happen.

Once she'd assured herself Carmen was safely out of the way, she refocused on Mara. She was staring at the demon hovering behind Sebastian now, her gaze still hollow, her expression blank. There wasn't anything there, like Mara had gone off somewhere else in her head. Angie recognized that for what it was, too, and her anger pitched higher.

"Let Mara go," she said, her always deep voice almost an octave deeper. Anger, and swelling magic, did that to her.

Sebastian didn't glance at her, but she sensed him adjust his stance, moving just a little closer to her. She wasn't sure what his will could do against a gun. They'd never faced one in their years of battling demons together. If they survived, she'd have to ask him if guns were a threat to a hunter or not.

Grant laughed. "I will have my reward, my bargain fulfilled. The demon wants her now. I finally have my sacrifice." He pushed Ellen forward, keeping the gun at her temple. "No thanks to this bitch."

The closer he got, the more Angie realized how decrepit he looked. The light at his back in the study yesterday had prevented her from getting a good look at him, but she'd swear he hadn't looked this bad. Now, even in the dark clearing, with only the ambient city glow turning the overhead clouds red and the ghostly gray glow of the demon, he looked like he was wasting away, decaying before her eyes.

His hair seemed thinner. His cheekbones were hard lines

under tightly pulled skin. His eyes were circled in dark smudges and sunken back into his skull. And when he smiled, the expression reminded her of a dead man's rictus. Because he held Ellen out in front of him, Angie couldn't see if the damage spread everywhere. He wore gloves, which could have been to prevent fingerprints, but also to hide further wasting.

After only one day? Had he used some sort of magic or illusion spell yesterday to disguise the decay? Or had the last thirty hours gone very badly for him?

Whatever deal he'd made with the demon, it was eating away at him, destroying him visibly. That would make anyone desperate. A desperate man with a gun was not a good thing.

"Thanks for leading me to my daughter, by the way," he said, smirking at them.

The comment had Ellen shouting something around the gag in her mouth, angry words Angie was sure were aimed as much at her and Sebastian as they were at Grant. She cut off her tirade abruptly when Grant jerked her arms and dug the gun into her temple.

"You didn't find her through us," Sebastian said, his tone calm and assured. As if none of this was a problem. "Carmen led you to them. And the demon led her to them." He paused, tilting his head to one side as he considered Ellen. "But how did the demon know?"

Angie didn't ask aloud how he knew all this. Sebastian often gleaned information in ways she'd never fully understood. Like he plucked the information from the air. Like he was the psychic. But in truth, she had a feeling it was something to do with his skills as a hunter. That his intuition, fueled by a will to know, was just that good.

And he often made connections she missed, which only added to the feeling he knew things in strange and mysterious ways.

She really wanted to survive so she could grilling him about it again.

After a few moments, Angie noticed Ellen's gaze drop, and she knew Sebastian had hit a button of some kind.

"Ellen summoned the Molder demon? A second time?" she asked him quietly. Had Ellen tried to call the demon even after she realized her will wasn't strong enough, after she'd made the deal with Grant and given him custody of Mara? But...why?

Sebastian continued to stare at Ellen, not responding to Angie's questions. But the demon behind them laughed.

"She was desperate," it hissed. "They are all desperate."

A shiver along Angie's shoulders and movement in her peripheral vision told her the demon had jumped closer, close enough to test the edges of her containment circle. A faint flare of blue light in her mind's eye confirmed its test, but her binding held.

"They are all desperate," the demon whispered, close to Angie. "You see it. You see he is wasting. The child... Think of the child."

Oh, the demon was clever. Trying to use her compassion

to trick her into doing something rash. She had no idea what the demon wanted in the end of all this, not what its ultimate game might be, but she knew it was enjoying the fear and tension, eating up the desperation. She was feeding the damned thing as much as the others, too, and she knew it. Except for Sebastian. She was certain he wasn't giving the demon anything to work with.

But…

But the demon knew she was Sebastian's weakness.

"Mara," Angie said, playing into the demon's game to see what it would do. "Are you okay? Can you look at me?"

The girl blinked once and looked at Angie, but her gaze was still hollow and resigned. She wasn't really there at the moment. Angie wasn't sure if that was a blessing or not, but such hopelessness in a twelve-year-old's expression was devastating to see. Letting her gaze soften, Angie reached for another spell, a soft, gentle, reassuring spell she used sometimes with extremely anxious clients. The spell was simple, easy to do, and would hopefully give Mara some measure of reassurance. Like a gentle calming of the senses, a breath of air to ease the pain.

Mara blinked a few times and some life came back into her gaze. She looked more fully at Angie then, her brows lowered.

Angie nodded. "I'll explain later," she promised the girl.

"Your tricks won't save her," the Molder demon whispered to Angie. "She's been mine from the start. My servants didn't know, but I saw her potential."

Grant narrowed his eyes at the demon. He didn't

comment, but obviously, he wasn't aware of Mara's potential as a magic wielder. The demon failed to mention that part.

"Who dies for you to possess the child?" Angie asked the demon without looking away from Grant.

"Everyone," it said with a chuckle. "Everyone will die."

CHAPTER THIRTY-TWO

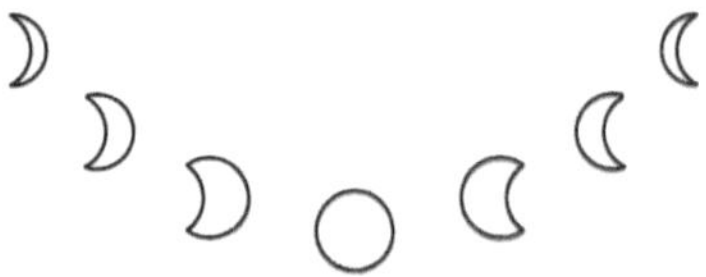

"No," Grant barked.

The silent clearing echoed his shout around the trees. If there'd still been birds or animals in the area, that noise would have sent them skittering away. But the presence of a demon had done that all earlier. Overhead, the cloud cover glowed a deeper read, reflecting city light down through the tree branches.

"You promised," Grand said, snarling at the demon, still nearly shouting. "I've served you for all these years with a guarantee that you would reward me! You made a bargain. You can't back out now."

"You will be rewarded," the demon said, its tone never changing. "A very thorough reward."

Grant's shoulders relaxed at that. Angie raised her brows. He hadn't heard the demon's double meaning? Was he that stupid?

Mara must have heard the threat in the demon's words, though, because she cast a look at Grant that was a cross between incredulous and disgust. It was such a teenager expression, so full of annoyance with the idiocy of adults, Angie had to press her lips together not to smile. There she was, there was the real Mara back with them again. The ache in Angie's chest eased a little.

"No one dies," Sebastian said. "You return to your realm, and this ends here."

"No," Grant shouted again. "I must have my reward. I *will* have my reward."

Sebastian shook his head. "You've never been in charge, you know. Not with this one. Why did you survive handing it a sacrifice not of your blood? Why do you think it's talking of possessing Mara and not killing her?"

"He needs a body. He always needs a body." The gun in Grant's hand wavered.

Angie tensed.

"Is that why you look like crap?" Sebastian said. "Been letting a demon take a ride? That kills humans you know? Or didn't you? Were you too stupid to look that part up? Did you think you would be the exception?" Sebastian's derisive laugh echoed in the clearing. "No wonder the demon continued to use you. Stupid minions are the best, aren't they?" This last he directed over his shoulder to the demon.

The demon didn't answer, but it didn't refute Sebastian's comment either.

Grant glared at them both.

Angie took a single step away from Sebastian. Easing a

bit closer to Grant and Ellen. She would have to jump in front of Sebastian to get to Mara, but since the pale man didn't have a gun, he felt less of a threat. The gun was the most unpredictable part of all this. Grant had to be disarmed.

She started another spell, quietly under her breath.

"What have you done?" Grant hissed at the demon. "What's he talking about?"

The demon's chuckle was like ants crawling over Angie's skin. She tried to ignore the sensation, but it broke her concentration and she had to start her spell over. Damn it. She took another step toward Grant and Ellen.

Grant's full attention was on the demon now. "You used me!"

"Of course, human. That was always part of our bargain."

"Not the possessions, you used me to get at my daughter. Why? Why not just kill her the first time? What don't I know?"

"So many things," the demon said on a sigh.

Its tone was so condescending it made Grant growl.

And the gun moved away from Ellen's temple.

"You promised," Grant hissed. "You made the bargain. Immortality. Freedom from the early death. You promised me."

"Oh, I will give you immortality," the demon said. "A bargain is, after all, a bargain."

Grant's shoulders relaxed a little. "You said we'd all die. You didn't mean me. I see. I see."

The demon chuckled again. Angie held her concentration on the spell this time, but only barely.

"You're missing a lot," Sebastian said to Grant, taking on his lecturer tone, the academic schooling the ignorant student. "Do you know what a demon will do with an immortal human body? The torture and pain it will inflict? And you won't die. You'll continue to suffer, over eternity. This is part of the problem with making demon deals. There are many layers and humans frequently miss the loopholes. Your lack of understanding is to be expected, I suppose, but really, after all these years." He sighed. "You should have done better research."

Grant swung the gun toward Sebastian. The end shook in Grant's trembling grip.

Sebastian smiled faintly.

Angie knew, in her gut, why Sebastian was doing this. But even still, watching the wobbly tip of Grant's gun directed at him made her heartbeat triple and her palms sweat. She wanted to cry out a warning, do something to protect him, but she didn't dare offset the balance or distract either man. She murmured the last words of her spell, completed the final hand gesture just before setting the spell. And waited for her opening.

"*You* don't understand," Grant growled. "I have spent years 'doing my research.' Why the hell do you think I'm here? I will *not* succumb to the same fate as my father and his father. Do you hear me? I will not die that way."

"No," Sebastian said with a sad sigh. "If I left you to your fate, you would die in a much worse way—or in this case, not die. But suffer. Greatly." Sebastian flicked a glance at Mara, then back to Grant. "I'm tempted, you know. To let you suffer. Because you offered up a baby. Because you purposefully tried to conceive that baby just so you could have the demon kill her. Far as I can tell, you've earned your demonic 'reward.'"

"You don't know," Grant said, his voice low, the gun wobbling more as he jerked his arm out toward Sebastian. "You don't know anything."

Another sigh. "More than you do, mate. More than you do."

Because she was fully focused on Grant, Angie saw the flex of his finger on the trigger, the tightening of his jaw. She was moving before the retort of the gun sounded in the clearing, already grabbing his wrist in one hand and roughly shoving Ellen away from him with the other. Ellen helped by rolling away, jerking free of Grant's hold. And the instant she was no longer touching Grant, Angie pushed his arm upward and triggered her spell.

Grant's entire body seized as the shock went through him, the currents of electrical charge so strong, every muscle clenched tight. She heard the crack of teeth and blood trickled from between his lips where she was sure he'd bitten his tongue. His finger tightened on the trigger a second time and another shot fired overhead. Angie prayed no errant night birds, or anything else for that matter, had been directly over them and the bullet would fall harmless to the ground—likely to be lost in the Park's detritus unless some curious leaf comber discovered it.

She cut the spell, ending the waves of electricity, and the instant his body started to relax, she pried the gun from his fingers. When she had the weapon, she jumped away from Grant, putting enough distance between her and him that he couldn't easily launch an attack.

Only then did she look around to assess what damage had been done.

And saw Sebastian staring at a bullet as it hovered in the air a few inches from his nose.

CHAPTER THIRTY-THREE

ngie gasped and took a step toward him, but he raised a hand to still her without taking his gaze off the bullet.

Under his breath, he murmured, "My will is as strong as yours. My kingdom as great."

She nearly cried hearing him quote *Labyrinth* to her at a time like this.

She swallowed hard. She'd never seen any of the hunters stop a bullet before. Though, as she thought about it, she wasn't sure she'd seen any hunter have to deal with a gun in her time working with Sebastian. And she realized suddenly that, in this country at least, that might have been unusual. It was entirely possible they dealt with guns a lot more than she suspected.

He wasn't sweating. He didn't look worried. Just focused. Very very focused.

She, on the other hand, was sweating hard now and her heartbeat couldn't hammer any harder or she'd pass out. She couldn't look away. She knew Mara was still in trouble. The pale man was still there. Grant would recover soon. The demon hovered only a foot behind Sebastian. Too many threats still. Too much could go wrong.

But she couldn't look away.

After another breathless moment, Sebastian reached up and plucked the bullet out of the air. His hand jerked, as if he absorbed some of the bullet's residual momentum. But other than that… He was fine.

Angie let out a breath, her shoulders slumping. "Fucking hell," she muttered.

Sebastian chuckled. "Haven't needed to do that in a few years," he said, studying the bullet. "Had a good run without guns." He tucked the bullet into his jean's front pocket and winked at her.

She huffed, relief making her giddy. A touch of irrational anger at him for scaring her robbed her of a proper comeback. She finally turned her attention to the pale man and Mara. Ellen struggled to her feet, even with her arms behind her back and lurched toward Mara, ignoring Grant where he'd crumpled to the ground.

Angie hissed a warning at her. Grant was down now, but she hadn't used enough of a jolt to actually kill him. She'd just wanted to get the gun away from him. The bastard was still a threat.

The pale man hadn't moved, hadn't taken his hand off Mara, and didn't seem even a little bothered by the passing events. Not even the fact that Sebastian had somehow stopped a bullet with just his will. He looked on as if all this was expected and he was just waiting for…something.

"Let the girl go," Angie said. "None of this ends good for you. If I have to, I will kill Grant to protect her." She adjusted the gun in her hand and pointed it toward the pale man. "And you too."

"You know how to shoot?" Sebastian asked. "Should have guessed. Americans."

She pressed her lips together to keep from snarking at him. In truth, her father had taught her and her brothers at a target range only so that he could impress on them that they didn't want to mess with guns, that guns were dangerous, and that she, in particular, was already dangerous enough without one. As her witch's creed was—at least an attempt—to do no harm, she'd agreed wholeheartedly with him.

But that didn't mean she wouldn't use the weapon now if she needed to. Even if she really just wanted to melt it into a useless knot of metal so it couldn't hurt anyone ever again. She hated guns. And she hated them even more now that she'd watched Sebastian face down a bullet.

The pale man smirked at her. "You shoot me, you risk hurting Mara and we both know you won't do that. I'm not as easy to distract as Grant, so that—" he gestured at Grant's prone body— "whatever you did to him won't work either. Won't let you get within touching distance. I know you have other spells up your sleeve, witch, but I also know with Mara here in the way, you'll be reluctant to use them." He nodded at Ellen. "Pushed her away first. I notice these things."

"You're outnumbered," Sebastian pointed out. "And the demon can't help you."

The demon chuckled. "So you assume, hunter."

"So I will it," Sebastian said in a deep voice, without looking at the demon.

The beast hissed but Sebastian still didn't turn to look at it. "Best to let it go. Take Carmen somewhere far away. And maybe, if you don't summon any more demons, you won't have to see me ever again."

Angie heard the unspoken threat and it sent a shiver up her spine. She had no idea what Sebastian might do to the pale man and Carmen, what his threat implied *exactly*. Just that it was a threat. And the fact that she wasn't entirely sure how far he'd go, how much he could do to them, was both upsetting and illuminating. But not in a good way.

Grant started to stir, his body twitching. The pale man glanced at him. "He's not dead? Huh." He looked back at Angie. "You that kind of witch? 'And it harm no other...' type?"

"Depends on the circumstance," she said, not letting the gun waver. She wasn't big on permanent harm. She didn't like the idea of taking those kinds of stains on her soul. "A child in danger would be the 'harm is okay' kind of circumstance, though," she added.

He shrugged. "Of course. Noble people tend toward the predictable. Me, see, I'm not noble. Not like Carmen in her quest to destroy arrogant rich men. Not like you and the hunter, out to stop demons from escaping, rescue kids, all that. I'm just here for the money." He paused, then, "Well, and to watch the show. This has been one hell of a show, I've got to tell you. Before Carmen, no idea there were demons. And having one walk around inside you is…interesting."

"Bad interesting or good interesting?" Angie felt compelled to ask.

"Powerful interesting. I can see why people jones for it."

"You?" Sebastian asked.

The man shrugged again. "Could take it or leave it. Wouldn't call it addictive. For me anyway."

"Who's paying you, then?"

"Both of 'em." He nodded to the twitching Grant first then Carmen. "Lucrative work. But…" He glanced at the back of Mara's head. She was staring at the demon, no longer with that dead expression in her eyes, but there was something else there, something more than the fear. The man couldn't see it, but Angie frowned, wondering what she was thinking in the middle of all this.

"But," the man said again, "I'm about done with this job. One last part, one last arrangement, then enough money to retire." He glanced at the demon. "Right?"

"Of course," the demon murmured.

"And no killing me since that wasn't part of the deal."

The demon chuckled. "We do have a bargain."

Angie sighed. "Everyone making deals with this fucking beast."

"What's left to do?" Sebastian asked the man.

Angie darted a gaze at Grant and Carmen. Carmen was starting to stir now, too. In another few moments, there were going to be more bad guys than good again. Ellen glared at the pale man, but she was still bound and gagged. And unless Angie wanted to lower her gun, she couldn't free her. Angie needed to find a spell that would loosen bindings, damn it. Never considered she might need it… Oversight.

She stepped closer to Sebastian so she could keep all the potentially dangerous people in view. Ellen took a step closer to Mara, but the pale man shook his head.

"Nope," he said. "You get too close, I'll just toss her to the demon without ceremony."

Ellen froze. Angie narrowed her eyes. Mara wasn't exactly a tiny child, but he might just be able to follow through with his threat. And the problem with the type of containment circle she'd built around the demon—it was designed to keep the beast from getting out, not others from getting in.

"What now?" Sebastian asked quietly. He subtly adjusted his stance, a movement Angie felt more than saw.

"Now," the pale man said. "The demon gets the body it's been wanting. And the witch opens up a demon portal. And the rest of you can deal with the hordes. I'll be off to an island in the Pacific. Far far away."

"You know…none of this will go the way you want it to, right?" Angie said, frowning at him. How did people *not* see that their bargains were barbed and designed to work only in the demons' favor?

The pale man shrugged. "Got me a house picked out and a plane ticket already. Not sure how it couldn't."

"You don't have a lantern," Sebastian said. "The demon can't possess her without that."

The man smirked. "Yeah, well, see, what I haven't mentioned before is my previous profession. I'm a thief. A good one. A really excellent one. And, you know, it's easier to put together a fake bone lantern than you might think."

While still keeping a hand on Mara's shoulder, he reached over his own shoulder to a backpack Angie hadn't noticed, the straps so black, they blended in with his coat. From the pack he pulled out a lantern that looked identical to the one Sebastian had handed over to the other hunter just an hour earlier.

Angie's heartbeat sped.

"Now," the man said, "I know what you're thinking. This could be the fake lantern. You've secured the other, I assume?" When no one answered his question, he nodded. "But see, Carmen never looked at the thing real close. She's been using it so long, it just didn't occur to her to study it every time she carried it off to commune with her demon. She might have figured it out earlier tonight, if you hadn't stopped her. But you did, and she didn't, and that sure did make my life easier."

The man met the demon's gaze. "Bargain complete?"

"With one last effort," the demon assured.

Angie took a step forward. "Drop the lantern or I shoot," she said.

"And risk hitting the girl?" The man shook his head. "Nope." He even moved farther behind Mara, blocking any shot Angie might take. "Nope, I'm going to finish what was started." He stared at the demon again. "So it is done," he said in a more formal tone than he'd used before.

And then, with a grunt…

He threw the lantern.

CHAPTER THIRTY-FOUR

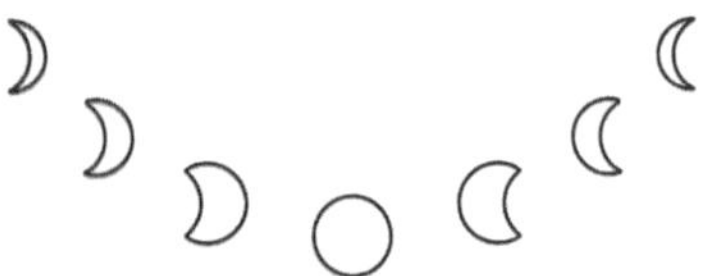

$\mathcal{A}$ngie reacted without thought. If she'd thought, if she'd stopped for even a moment to consider what she was doing, she'd have made a different choice.

Unfortunately, she didn't think. She moved. Reaching out and catching the lantern as it barreled toward her head.

For a full ten seconds, she stared wide-eyed at Sebastian, holding the lantern by its handle in front of her like she couldn't quite believe it was there in her hand.

Then the visions hit like a baseball bat to her skull.

Death and blood, so much blood, spilling, slicing, screaming. Burning. Heat. Pain. Power. Rotting stench. More pain. Always more. Always more. Screams. Blood dripping. Skin splitting open. Melting. Rotting. Stench. Heat. Burn. Pain…

Angie lost all sense of self, all sense of everything. She was the pain, the burning, the power and heat. She was immersed in blood and broken bones and screams. She might have screamed herself. There was too much, all around her, filling her, twining with her. She couldn't run away, couldn't escape. There was nowhere to go.

So many people, so much torture and suffering, all the greed, all the power and longing and pain.

She wanted to burst apart with it all, drowning in the lava flow of suffering. She couldn't find herself, couldn't remember she was an individual. And nothing stopped the torrent, nothing slowed the blood.

Something moved. Darkness. Darkness filled her. Then everything turned gray. Colors washed away to be replaced by gray and black and…a void.

After the torment, the void was a relief. She breathed. She could feel herself breathe. For the first time. She could relax into the darkness, into the gray void. Let it go. Let go.

Let everything go…

She felt her eyes blinking open. Strange. She could feel herself again, but vaguely. She was there somewhere. Her body anyway. She floated in a soothing void of emptiness. Oh so soothing. So calm. No more pain or heat.

Something… Her mouth moved. Sound came out. Was that her? That didn't sound like her.

Laughter. No. That wasn't her laugh. But she felt her body shake with it. The sense of triumph, that felt foreign to.

What was happening?

Nothing, the void whispered. Come back and rest.

Yes. Rest. Cool and gray. No more pain. No more blood.

Except…

Blood? Why did she feel hunger? She smelled something. Something bad, like rotting eggs. She pulled back from the void to look through eyes that didn't feel like hers, but she could see through them. Strange. Visions usually played out like movies for her. She wasn't inside the skull of anyone in her visions. She watched. She was watching now, but from the inside of…someone.

"Ah," that someone said. "So much more power than she knows." More laughter. She felt the laughter like it came from her. "A perfect vessel."

There were trees. A clearing. Oh, the clearing she'd been in before her world shattered and broke, and now she needed to be in the void to rest.

But…

The clearing. The park.

No. Rest. There was too much. You've seen too much. The darkness will sooth you. Rest.

She wanted to close her eyes, take the advice. But her eyes remained open, she remained inside the vision.

"Release her," a deep voice said, a voice with power and strength.

And she felt that power, felt the strength of…will. In her bones. In her soul. No! It would not take her, not will her away. She was here now. She would stay. She would own this world!

Wait. What? She…

No, not her.

But her mouth moved. The voice came out of her. "You will die first, hunter."

Hunter? Was that a name? Did she know who that was?

"You will leave her and be gone," that same voice, full of strength. So strong.

A laugh. Her? Something else? "This is my world now, hunter. None of you can stop me in this body."

Angie felt the spell more than heard it. Something familiar. She knew the words. Hands moving. Her? No. Not hers. She didn't want to call the flames. Why would she need the fire when she just wanted to sink into the void?

Flames on her hand, building. Not there yet. But building. Didn't burn. That was good.

"Angela Jordan," that same voice of strength said, "drop the lantern."

What? She wasn't holding anything. But the voice willed her to do… That voice. Angela? Who was Angela?

"Angela Jordan, you will drop that lantern. Now."

Her fingers flexed. She tried to open them. She wanted to open them. Didn't she? She wanted to let go. Yes. Yes. Let go. Into the void.

No… Not the void. Open her hand. Let go.

Flames built. Somewhere. She could feel that. But… No. The hand movements were wrong. That wouldn't work. Only one hand. Needed the second hand to make the spell work right. Why wasn't she using her other hand? Oh, yes, holding something. Had to release.

No!

A hiss. What? Why not?

"Angela, you will drop that lantern."

Angela. No one called her that. Except her mother when

she was in trouble. Her mother. Her mother called her that. But that wasn't her mother's voice. No. Too deep. The accent.

Sebastian. Sebastian hadn't called her Angela since…

Since they first met. When he'd teased her. In the beginning. Annoyed her. Before the love. Before she loved him.

She loved him.

Sebastian.

"Open your hand, Angie," a murmur now. "Let the lantern drop. Come back to me. Come home."

"No!" Fire on her hand. No heat. Flames. She could see the flames.

No! She needed to look at Sebastian. See him. There. There he was. Oh. It was him. His eyes were glowing, faintly red, but it was him. She could feel him. Feel the love. Feel the will. She wanted to be with him. Not in this void. Not in this grayness. Wait. Red in his eyes. She could see through the gray. She could…

"Die, hunter," a voice from her mouth. The flames raised. Her hand? No! She couldn't…

She *wouldn't* kill Sebastian. Something stirred in her gut. Anger, but more. Solid. Hard. Her chest felt the tightening of that sensation. Like what Sebastian fed her.

Will.

Will. And love.

No. She wouldn't hurt him.

She forced air into her lungs, took control of her breath.

Yes. That's me. I'm breathing. I'm here.

I. Am. Here.

She stared at her hand, at the ball of fire. She willed it away. Ended the spell. No need for you now. You can rest. Thank you for answering my call.

The flames winked out.

A scream. A curse. The air around her grew hot, but inside she became ice. What was happening? She was losing again, losing herself into the void. No. She didn't want the void. Not now.

She fought back, willing her body to heed her. Couldn't focus. Damn it. Stop screaming. She scrambled. She'd been here before. No. She hadn't. But... No. She could do this. No. She wasn't going to succumb. No. She was in here.

She would do this. She had to stop this. She had to...

Let go.

She felt the breath leave her, felt her heartbeat slow, felt the panic ease. Darkness and soothing quiet. And a deep deep voice said, "Let go."

So she did.

CHAPTER THIRTY-FIVE

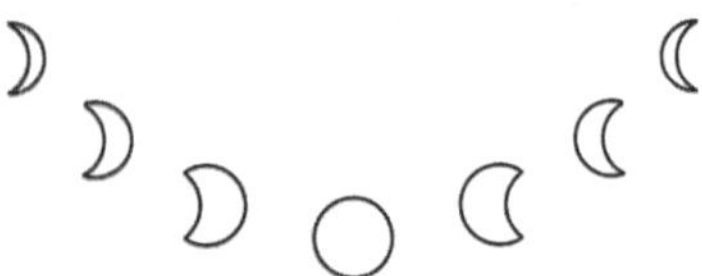

ngie opened her hand. For a long moment, all she heard was a shriek of denial. She took another deep breath. Let it out slowly. Relaxed back into her body. Her body. Her place. No passengers allowed.

"Leave," she commanded, and this time heard her own voice aloud, heard the deep resonance. This was the voice she used to command the elements and work her spells. She felt her powers welling up, felt control and focus and peace. Felt the magic embrace and envelope her. Yes. This was her place. This was her home.

Magic.

She opened her eyes. She was surrounded by a circle of blue light. She'd built a protective circle without conscious effort. And the lantern lay outside the circle now. Several feet away. She chuckled.

Inside her skull the demon screamed. She felt its claws,

scrambling at her soul, felt the heat and anger, heard the whispered denials, the temptations to give in and let it have her body.

She shook her head. "No." She pulled in all that made her her. Not so much the will, though there was that, but her magic. Her magic, her peace and her place. This was *her*. She let it well up inside her, and used it to push out the invading enemy.

The separation hurt, like being pulled in two. The demon didn't abandon her easily and she had to close her eyes again to finish the task. Focus and concentration. A quietly murmured spell of protection. The demon tried for her mind, tried for her visions. Showed her things she didn't want to see. She let the images roll past, not really seeing them, letting them go. And as she released them, she built another protection circle around her psyche, kept that part of her safely inside a cool cool haven of blue light. Away from the demon.

Another scream, but she repeated, aloud and over the noise, "Leave."

A flash of pain that left her breathless. Felt blood dripping down her nose. She touched it. And opened her eyes.

The demon hovered a foot in front of her, its black eyes glowing red in the depths, its anger and venom a physical thing between them.

"How?" it hissed.

"Don't ever come to this realm again," she said, quietly, but with the force of will that flowed from her magic. She set a second circle inside her own, this one around the demon. It lunged for her only to come up against the barrier.

"No!"

"Yes," she said. Slowly she turned, looking for just the right kind of tree.

"Angie." Sebastian's voice, soft and strong.

She faced him.

"There's a perfect one here." He gestured to a tree with just the right sort of shape, a natural V formed from the trunk. Through that V she glimpsed the demon realm. She didn't focus on it, didn't open it. Yet.

She dropped the circle around herself and stared at the demon. "Time to leave."

"I will not abandon all I have built, witch. You will be mine. All of this will be mine."

"No," she and Sebastian said at the same time.

"No," Mara said.

Angie blinked at the girl. She was on her feet and staring at the demon. Angie realized the pale man had vanished. And Mara and Ellen had managed to get their hands unbound. Ellen held a knife in one hand—where the hell had that come from?—and was standing at her daughter's back, facing the now conscious Grant, the knife pointed at him like she knew how to use it.

Angie took a moment to look for Carmen. The spell she'd put over the woman to conceal her from the others had dropped when Carmen moved, and Carmen had moved at some point during the fight. She stood near Grant, but behind him, her gaze jumping from the demon to the lantern a few feet from Angie.

Before Angie could issue a warning, though, Sebastian scooped up the lantern, keeping it out of harm's way.

Carmen huffed out a curse and glared at them.

"No more, Carmen," Angie said. "This is done. For good."

"I'll just call another," Carmen said.

"We have a deal, woman!" the demon growled. "We made a bargain. You will allow me in so I can destroy these humans. Or you will die."

Carmen sighed. "We all have to die one day," she said.

"No!" Grant yelled. "You promised. You promised you would give me immortality." He started to rise to his feet, but Carmen gave him a quick kidney jab that Angie barely saw and the man dropped again, hard.

"Sit," she ordered. "If I don't get to keep the demon, you don't get immortality." She snarled at him. "Bastard. Trying to kill a child just to outpace your own genetics. You could have been enjoying what life you had."

"There's a story there," Sebastian murmured. "But perhaps for later."

Angie turned back to the demon. It was testing her circle, pressing its hand against the edges. Blue light flared around it with each contact.

Angie considered the tree from the corner of her eyes. "You push, I'll open?" she said to Sebastian.

He winked.

"I will not be so easy to banish," hissed the demon.

"If I banish you to a realm not your own, that should keep you busy for a few millennia," Angie said.

"What? No. That's not possible."

"You know what I can do. That's why you wanted my body. But, the trick is, I don't open *your* realm just because you're here. I open whatever realm the tree connects to." She nodded to the tree Sebastian had found her. "Sometimes it's the right one. Sometimes it's not."

"I will own whatever realm I am in."

"Yeah, I doubt you'd have spent so much time working on cultivating a way in here if that were the case. Earth and humans are easy pickings, not the kind of place anything truly powerful really wants."

The demon snarled and lunged at her. The blue light of her containment circle flared bright enough to light up the entire area, like a flood light had gone on suddenly. And just as suddenly dropped.

Angie blinked against the spots in her vision. For the most part, that blue light was a metaphysical thing, showing up only in her mind's eye. But that contact with the demon had flared in the physical world, she realized, because even Mara and Ellen had tried to shade their eyes.

"Mara," Sebastian said. "You feel up for helping me banish a demon?"

"What?" Ellen said. "No. She can't…"

"Oh, she's got the will," he said quietly. "That's part of the problem." He chuckled. "But I think that will will be used for something other than demon hunting in the future."

"Like magic," Angie confirmed.

There was a very very faint glow around Mara. Not an aura as such since Angie couldn't see those very well. But a pale pale blue light that appeared in Angie's mind's eye. An instinctive bit of protection Mara had built around herself. It wasn't strong enough to hold against real magic. Or any kind of physical world harm. But the fact that Mara had instinctively built that shield without even knowing how was a good sign she'd need training soon.

Mara looked between them. "I don't know if I want magic, but I do want this demon gone for good."

"We can help with that," Sebastian said.

The demon laughed. The laughter drew all their attention.

"I cannot be banished forever, humans. I will be back. I live in your nightmares. Your fears and anguishes. I whisper your deepest secrets and shames. You will call me again. Like it or not. You all call me."

Sebastian sighed. "I'm done with this one. Off you go."

The demon lurched backward as if it had been hit. "No," it snarled.

Sebastian merely said, "Yes." And the demon lurched backward again, coming up hard against the containment circle. To Angie, Sebastian said, "Let me know when you're ready. You'll need to drop your circle."

"Right." She faced the tree fully, finally, staring into the V, staring at the hellscape beyond. A fire and brimstone realm. The crackle of hardening lava, tinkling over the rolling liquid heat. Flames burst in the distance from unseen fissures. The sky was a deep red, and dark like the sun had just set. Stinking steam rose around the doorway Angie opened.

And in the distance, she heard the high-pitched, nerve-scraping chittering of approaching demons.

"Time to go," Angie said without taking her gaze from the breach. She dropped the circle around the demon, cutting it with a swift mental gesture, and from the corner of her eye, she saw the demon lunge for her.

Sebastian stepped between her and the demon. He was holding a long sword that glowed with a reddish light.

"And where did that come from?" she asked, without expecting an answer.

She wasn't disappointed.

The demon pulled up short, but still too close to Sebastian. Sebastian jabbed forward, a direct hit to the center of the demon. It screeched and grabbed at the sword.

There was no blood, no obvious jagged hole, not that Angie could see. But steam rose around the wound, with a stench that made her bile rise.

"Well, that's gross," she murmured. For once in her life, it took an effort to keep her gaze on the realm breach she'd opened rather than having to force her gaze away.

"Be gone, beast," Sebastian said with all the strength of his will deepening his voice. The power filled the clearing. A magic all its own.

"Be gone," Mara added, and though hers was still a child's voice, a child's will, the strength was there, waiting to be built and developed.

The demon screamed and clawed at its chest even as it backed away from them. Sebastian moved closer, forcing it back as he chanted under his breath, a banishing spell in a mix of Latin and Spanish, the same chant he'd used before but with a few added elements Angie wasn't familiar with.

The demon reacted to the spell, though, screaming and clawing at the air as it was slowly, relentlessly forced backward, like the opening into the hellscape dragged it closer. A gravity well of pain and suffering, pulling the demon in.

Angie winced as the sounds of approaching demons from beyond the portal grew louder. They'd be here soon.

"Faster," she murmured, her voice lost in the Molder demon's shrieking.

Sebastian stalked forward, and with every step the demon dropped back, closer and closer to the breach.

"I will return," it hissed. "I will have this realm."

"No," Mara said at the same time as Sebastian said, "Be gone, beast."

The Molder demon hit the edges of the portal and was sucked through with a horrendously awful, squishing noise that made Angie wince.

There was enough screaming and high-pitched denials that she wanted to cover her ears. She blinked slowly, prepared to look away, to close the opening between realms, to let the barrier that separated her world from the hellscape solidify again. Focused on pulling her gaze away. Willed herself to turn from the tree.

A flash of movement to her left and another series of screams.

She couldn't look away in time. Grant lunged through the gap, threw himself into the hellscape at the same moment as Angie forced her gaze to the ground.

Too late to stop him from going through.

CHAPTER THIRTY-SIX

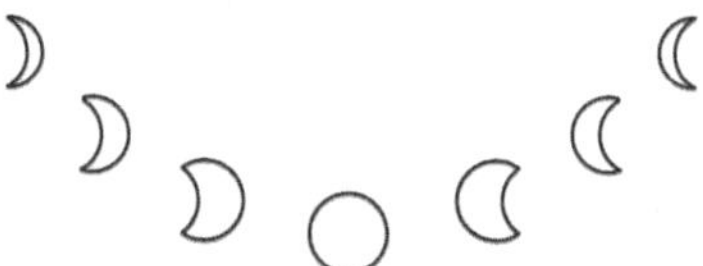

The opening between realms closed with an audible snap.

Angie blinked hard at the ground. "Shit. Should I open it again? We need to get him out."

"Leave him," Carmen said in disgust. "He deserves what he gets."

Angie looked to Sebastian. She'd almost been trapped in a demon realm once before. Only gotten out because Sebastian had managed to hold the doorway open with his will and pull her out. He'd reached through that portal and rescued her. If not for him, she would have been trapped. And she'd been too panicked to defend herself well. The demons had been on her. She would have died.

She wouldn't wish that terror on anyone. Not even Grant.

But he'd gone through willingly, run into the realm, not

been dragged there. He would die in a horrible way, but it was his own doing.

Sebastian looked to the tree. He wouldn't be able to see into the hellscape. He couldn't even when she tore open the boundary between worlds.

"Open it for a moment, not long," he said quietly. "If I can pull him out, I will."

"No," Carmen said, nearly barked. "Why risk it? He's a baby killing bastard."

Angie agreed he was a bastard, but…

She forced her gaze up and stared into the tree's natural V, brought the realm beyond into view.

And knew it was too late.

The screams. The blood. She gagged and dropped her gaze, dropped all the way to her knees as her stomach rolled.

Almost worse than the images from the lantern and the demon's own psyche.

"Well, that's going to cause a lot of nightmares," she murmured as Sebastian dropped down next to her and pulled her into his arms.

She went without protest, hugging close to his heat.

"He earned that," Carmen said.

"Yes," Ellen agreed. "He did."

Angie couldn't echo their sentiment. They hadn't seen. They didn't know.

And maybe it was better for everyone that way.

She looked up at Carmen. "Why did you give up the demon?"

She made a disgusted face. "I didn't have much choice, did I?"

"You'll do this again?"

"The people I go after deserve what they get."

"You could use your will to a better purpose," Sebastian said.

"Like you do? Stopping demons?" She snorted. "No."

"There are people who will want to talk with you," he said.

There was a bite in Sebastian's tone. And Angie remembered that Carmen had killed a hunter. The others wouldn't let that go. What they'd do with Carmen, Angie had no idea. But they'd want justice for their fallen.

"If they can find me," Carmen said. She glanced at Ellen. "Don't leave your daughter with demon-summoning assholes anymore."

Ellen pulled Mara close, glaring at Carmen.

Carmen turned to Mara and her expression softened. "I wouldn't have let him hurt you," she said.

Mara leaned into her mother without answering.

Carmen sighed and nodded. "Be good, little girl. Train that magic so you don't hurt yourself." She glanced at Sebastian again. "If your people come looking for me, I will fight back."

"We wouldn't expect any less. But they will be looking for you."

"Fair enough." She gave him a little solute and disappeared into the darkness under the trees.

"You're just letting her go?" Ellen demanded. "She's one of the bad people."

"She won't get far," a new voice. From beyond the tree Angie had used to open the demon realm.

The hunter they'd met in the restaurant, who'd taken the lantern—or fake lantern as it now seemed—stepped from behind the tree. She looked at Angie. "What you can do is terrifyingly impressive," she said without preamble.

"If you say so. I find it a pain in my ass more often than not."

"What are you doing here?" Sebastian asked.

"The lantern…" She gestured to the real lantern, on the ground within Sebastian's easy reach.

"You figured out the other was a fake?" Angie asked, wishing they'd realized as quickly.

"It wasn't," the hunter said.

Angie and Sebastian sat up straighter, though he didn't pull his arms from around her.

"They come in pairs," the hunter said.

"Why didn't I know that?" Sebastian asked.

"It wasn't relevant."

"Not relevant?" Angie snarled. "If a hunter comes across one, and doesn't know it's part of a pair, they won't look for the second one. What a dumb ass thing to say. Not relevant. Of course, it's bloody relevant."

Sebastian's hand flexed on her shoulder.

"They're impossibly rare," the hunter said without any signs of unease. "There are only six pairs. And we have four of those in our possession already." She shrugged. "Over the years, the pairs have been separated. There was no way to know if this pair had remained intact or not."

"I'm not buying that even a little," Angie said. "Or you wouldn't be here."

"Buy it or not, it's the truth," the hunter said. "I didn't know the pair was intact. But I did sense when the second one activated. That's why I'm here."

"Why did Carmen's associate say he'd replaced the other with a fake then?" Angie asked, realizing she had no idea what the pale man's name was. He'd be harder to track now.

"Don't worry about him," the hunter said as if reading Angie's mind. "The police are picking him up now. Anonymous tip. He's quite the thief, you know."

"Mm hmm. Why did he think he'd replaced a real lantern with a fake?" Angie wouldn't be distracted, but she was glad to hear he'd be arrested. She didn't like the idea of loose ends running around, especially ones who'd spent time hosting a demon. Carmen walking away was bad enough.

"Carmen will be taken into custody too," the hunter said, again as if reading Angie's mind, but also answering Ellen's earlier question. "She's a history of stealing from the rich men she destroys. She's cleaned up most of her… fingerprints, if you will, over the years. But not all." The hunter's eyes flared just a little redder as she said, "Killing one of ours comes with consequences."

"Well that's all nice and neat," Angie said, but not with any rancor. In truth, she was relieved. She'd have been frustrated if the scales hadn't been balanced. She knew they couldn't always be, that sometimes, bad people got away with their crimes. But oh how she loved a balanced scale. And this way, the appropriate level of justice would be done.

Images of Grant's screaming husk rose to haunt her. She wasn't sure that had been appropriate justice, even if he'd done it to himself. Maybe even if it was what he'd deserved. She just... Some things were just so damned horrible, even for evil bastards.

The hunter approached the lantern with care, studying it without touching it. "You have an affinity for demons," she said to Angie without looking at her.

"No," Angie said.

"You didn't require any sort of...process before the demon could use the lantern to possess you. There's usually some sort of process involved."

"Is that why it went for me instead of Mara?" Angie asked. She knew the beast had intended to possess Mara, because of her magic. It had only changed its interest to her because of her ability to open doorways into demon realms. But in those moments before the lantern had been tossed at her, they could have as easily forced Mara to take the demon. Unless doing so required more time.

"They had already prepared Mara to be a host. Though she wasn't aware of it."

"What?" Ellen screeched. "How do you know that? What did they do to her?"

The hunter sighed. "We haven't let Grant go unmonitored," she said slowly.

"Yet you didn't stop him. Or Carmen." Ellen took a step toward the hunter, violence in her eyes.

"Actually, we did," the hunter said. She widened her hands. "You'll notice neither of them got away with their plans."

"Not for lack of trying," Angie muttered.

"And they nearly did," Ellen added.

The hunter shrugged. "It's all worked out. I'm not sure why you're upset."

Ellen snarled and started toward the woman again, but Mara held her back. "Let it go, mom," she murmured. "They're all gone now. We can start over."

Ellen let out a harsh breath. "So much time lost," she whispered.

"But it's over now. We can start over." She touched her mom's shoulder and Ellen turned to face her, her glare dropping away as she looked at her daughter. "I want to start over. Maybe somewhere…else."

"If you're open to suggestions," Angie said, "New Mexico is lovely. And I have a friend there who is very good at training budding witches. She mentored me when I was new."

"There," the hunter said. "Everything is properly sorted. Now, I'll take this lamp." She looked at Angie. "And we'll expect you before the council in the next week. After you recover yourself." To Sebastian, she said, "Assure she's there. After what I witnessed tonight, we can't allow this… estrangement to continue."

"What the hell are you talking about?" Angie said, half rising.

The hunter waved at Sebastian. "You're free to explain now. The time has come."

"'Bout bloody time," he muttered under his breath.

"Explain what?" Angie said her voice rising.

"Goodnight, Angela. Sebastian." The hunter scooped up the lantern and dropped it into a reusable bag she pulled from her coat pocket—not the same bag as Angie had sacrificed to the other lantern. "We'll see you both at the end of the week."

"Wait," Angie said, her voice deepening with her anger. But Sebastian put a quelling hand on her shoulder even as the hunter walked away, heading down the path that would lead toward Strawberry Field and an exit from the Park.

"I'll explain everything later," he murmured, close to her cheek.

Angie realized belatedly that the hunter *had* distracted her, and she still didn't know why the pale man thought he'd replaced a real lantern with a fake. So much for balance. Damn it.

"Let's get Mara and Ellen home," Sebastian said. "They've had a bad night."

Angie looked at Mara, her face pale and worn. She was drooping, hanging heavily in her mother's arms now. And Angie remembered the will she'd used to help Sebastian. The instinctive shield she'd built around herself. The girl was using powers she was new to and had no real control over. Add to that she'd been kidnapped and nearly handed over to a demon tonight. Of course she was exhausted.

Angie let Sebastian help her back to her feet, but whispered in his ear so only he would hear, "You have a lot of explaining to do later. And you owe me a bottle of Tequila."

"Yes," he said. "To both."

CHAPTER THIRTY-SEVEN

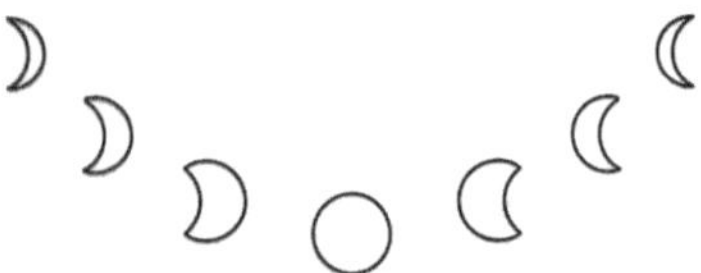

Angie woke with her head aching. Damn, she should have had more water before bed. Live and learn.

Live.

She was alive. She didn't have a demon inhabiting her body. Some dangerous artifacts had been removed from the careless hands of human society—at least she hoped. And most importantly, Mara had survived and found—again, Angie hoped—a loving home.

She really really hoped Mara and Ellen finally found some piece and normality. Hard to live under the reign of a demon for all those years.

She rubbed at her face and rolled over in her bed, staring at the brick wall. She loved this little apartment. Loved the single brick wall that ran through the long, narrow space. Loved the continuity of that. Her landlord had let her paint the walls, so she'd given everything a soft, sandy color with a few highlights of turquoise and burnt orange. The rugs were Navajo, sent from her parents. And her no-longer-working fireplace in the living room held a collection of flowering cacti.

Living room—where Sebastian had crashed on her couch. She'd have to face him soon. She glanced at the clock and groaned. Almost noon. She had work tonight too. And she and Sebastian still had a lot to say to each other.

They hadn't talked about anything important at all last night. They'd picked up a bottle of Tequila in an all-night liquor store, come back to her place, gotten ripping drunk, and he'd passed out on her couch while she'd stumbled into bed to pass out.

They'd spent the night arguing over the philosophy inherent in their favorite movies. That philosophy had seemed deeper and more profound the more Tequila they drank, too. The messages of hope and love in *Die Hard*. The existential crisis at the heart of *The Highlander*. How it would have been a crime against humanity if anyone *but* David Bowie had played the Goblin King in *Labyrinth*.

The release of the last couple of days, the freedom to just get drunk and enjoy an old friend's company had been so wonderful.

And the fact that they'd managed not to complicate things by falling into bed together, despite a very near moment, an almost kiss, was also a relief this morning.

It had been a close thing, though. That moment, leaning in, holding his gaze, knowing exactly how his mouth would feel on hers, how he would taste…

But that would have been much too complicated when they still had so many things to discuss.

Unfortunately, with light streaming in through the crack in her curtains, she knew it was time to face that discussion, like it or not. No more hiding in Tequila and movie philosophy.

She rolled out of bed with a groan, her head swimming, and stumbled to the bathroom in the vain hope that a cool shower would somehow help her hangover.

She did feel less spinny and gross by the time she came out to the living room, but her head still ached.

Sebastian was sitting on the couch, looking rough around the edges, cradling a steaming cup of tea.

"Is it helping?" she asked.

He smiled up at her. "I could will the hangover away, but I feel like I deserve it."

"Thought the same thing in the shower. I earned it. I have time for it. I need to live with it."

"You have the good tea still." He raised his cup.

She breathed in the strong scent of English Breakfast tea and smiled. "You ruined me for the ordinary stuff."

She sat on the opposite end of the couch from him, carefully, so she didn't jostle him. He was still wearing his t-shirt and jeans, all looking the worse for wear since he'd slept in them, but he'd neatly folded the blanket she'd slung over him last night and set it on the back of the comfortably overstuffed couch.

Tucking her toes up under her, she faced him. "We better talk now. I have work later."

"You don't want breakfast first?"

She groaned and put a hand to her stomach. "No food. Not yet."

"The only time you ever pass up a meal. When you've been deep into your Tequila." He sipped his tea. "You want to start with the questions, or will I just carry on with the answers?"

She waved a hand for him to carry on. The questions were all pretty obvious.

"The hunter you met, who took the lanterns, she's a member of the demon hunters council. Our governing body."

She raised her brows. "You have a governing body? Why didn't I know?"

"No one but the hunters know they exist. No one we work with. No one we love. You have to be a hunter to know about them."

She let that sink in for a few minutes before saying, "I'm not a hunter."

"No," he said with a nod. "You're not."

"What happens? Now that you've told me. Why have you told me?"

"They've been…" He looked away, staring at the cacti that turned her otherwise useless fireplace into a mini desert garden. "They aren't happy that you've been left unmonitored for the last two years."

Everything in Angie stilled. She only remembered to breath after her lungs started to burn. "Monitored?"

He didn't face her. "My job, after we first met, when Aidan and I came to you for help, and…"

He didn't need to go into detail. She remembered their first meeting.

She'd met Aidan at five, when Aidan had saved her after she'd accidentally unleashed demons onto the world by looking into a V in a tree. She'd been a child and Aidan had seemed like a white knight. Over the years, Aidan had ensured her safety, introduced her to her magical mentor, Esmerelda, and when she was old enough, had come to her for help with a demon loose in New Mexico.

She'd brought one of her protégé with her.

Sebastian.

Angie didn't really believe in love at first sight. But there had been something between her and Sebastian from the start. A spark she couldn't dismiss. Something he didn't act on at first. Not at first. But he and Aidan showed up a few times that year, always asking for her help. Eventually, he started showing up without Aidan, and not always for help with demons.

He rubbed a hand over his hair, his gaze still on the cacti. "I was ordered to watch you. To make sure you didn't start calling demons into this realm en masse."

She swallowed down her reaction because she wasn't entirely sure what that reaction was yet. Only that it involved a lot of cuss words.

"I tried to convince them you weren't the type," he said. "But your skill is so damned rare, and so dangerous, they didn't trust you."

"What did Aidan say?" She'd been there first, at the very beginning. Did she know about all this? "Why didn't they tell

Aidan to monitor me?" She tried not to snarl the word "monitor" but failed.

"She wanted them to leave you be as well," he said quietly. "She assured them you were on a different path. You wouldn't be a hunter. They didn't believe her." He finally met Angie's gaze. "I didn't stalk you, if you're worried about that. I kept tabs, from a distance at first, after Aidan introduced us, to ensure you were safe. And that they left you alone. After that first time, that first fight Aidan brought you into, I knew…you weren't on our path." He nodded at her bracelet. Angie unconsciously rubbed the pentagram. "The council didn't…accept that conclusion."

"Our relationship?" She had to ask. She had to know.

He held her gaze steadily. "Not part of the plan. Not even a little bit. In fact, they…reprimanded me for it. I was to keep you from unleashing a demon apocalypse, not fall in love with you."

She swallowed hard, not sure if that made things better or not.

"Even Aidan warned me against it. Complicated things."

"Yeah it did. While we worked together?"

"The council hoped you'd choose hunting over magic. After their initial anger, they decided to encourage our work. Even our relationship. It…" He did flinch now. "Kept you in line."

"In line." She pulled in a deep breath. Let it out slowly.

"Not my intent. I fought back as much as I could. But…"

"But?"

"But I wanted you. I loved you. I didn't want them trying

to force us apart. Which they would have. So eventually, I…
let them think I was going along with them."

"When I left?"

"My feelings about that had nothing to do with the
council and everything to do with losing you. I would have
let you remain out of the demon world until you were ready
for me to be in your life again. I would have handled the last
two years…differently. I still love you, Ang. And I wanted all
this to go very differently."

She felt the pain in her gut, felt the tears threaten. She
held everything carefully at bay, buried deep so it didn't
overwhelm her yet. "What do they want from me?"

"They want you to align with the hunters once and for
all."

"Or what?"

"They want me to train you properly. To bring you
through the process that will finally make you a hunter."

"Or. What?"

He leaned forward and set the tea mug on her coffee
table. He didn't face her for a long moment.

"They'll try to have you locked up somewhere. 'For the
good of the public.'"

Angie shot off the couch, her hangover headache and
rolling stomach forgotten—or more to the point, she was now
nauseous for a very different reason.

"No," she snarled at him. "I will not be locked up by
anyone. Who the hell, who the *hell* do they think they are?"

Her voice deepened and she felt her magic rise in a way it
rarely did these days. She had too much control for this. But

the thought, the mere thought that these…*strangers* thinking they had some kind of control over what she did… Livid wasn't a strong enough word. Her anger crackled in the air, and sparks actually ran over her fingertips before she controlled the reaction. Her apartment was too small to call any of the elements. She'd risk setting the whole building ablaze.

That this council had been *monitoring* her for years. That all of this had been part of some scheme.

And that Sebastian had been part of it…

She wanted to scream. It was on the tip of her tongue to demand he leave.

He would too. If she told him to go, he would go. He would leave and fight his council on his own, trying to keep her out of the world she didn't want to be part of.

How she knew that…the fact that she did know that, helped calm her rising anger. Enough she could rein in the crackle of magic rolling through her.

"No," she said again, more calmly this time. "I'm not a hunter, and I will not be commanded or manipulated by this council of yours. No."

"I've assured them of your position on this. They want another answer."

"They aren't getting one."

He held her gaze for a long moment. The red deep inside the brown of his eyes banked and faint. "You know about them now."

She narrowed her own gaze. "What does that mean?"

"No one outside the hunters knows they exist."

Hands on her hips, she glared. "If you don't explain what you're trying to say, right now, Sebastian, I'm going to throw you out of this apartment physically."

His lips twitched but he didn't smile. Which was good because in her mood, she'd likely slap him with a shock spell if he did.

"They've pulled you in, like it or not. Against my wishes," he added. "Against Aidan's warnings. They've pulled you in. And the only way out now is through."

"Through? Meaning?"

He stood and very slowly approached her, watching, waiting for her to object. She surprised herself by not objecting. Not even when he settled his hands on her shoulders. Though she didn't drop her hands from her hips.

"I thought about this a lot, after to you left. They won't let you go. I've tried. Aidan's tried. They won't let you go."

"They don't have a choice," she snarled.

"They'll make your life miserable. They'll keep dragging you back. And they'll find a way to keep me from being there to help you. They'll force your hand, and I won't be able to get between them and you anymore."

"You have been?"

He nodded. "But they're forcing my hand now, too."

"What did you mean by through?" She finally dropped her hands to her sides, but she didn't otherwise relax her stance.

"You allow yourself to be taken into the hunter fold," he said quietly. "Trained as a hunter. Part of our world, not just peripherally like you were when we worked together. Fully integrated into the world."

Angie felt the tremble of denial rise through her, but she kept it in check. Sebastian's gaze, intent, held more than the words he spoke aloud. There was something behind the faint glow of red, something more to his plan.

Still, she asked, "And then? What? Give up my true calling to be one of you?"

"Then..." He pulled her close, his gaze holding hers as his voice dropped to a murmur. "When the time comes. We bring it all down."

Thank you for reading BONE LANTERN WITCH! I hope you enjoyed the first book in this urban fantasy romance series. If you haven't read it already, don't miss *Moonlit Strange*, the short story of the moment when Angie hit her breaking point and tried to quit demon hunting.

If this is the first of my books that you've read, Angela Jordan was originally introduced as a secondary character in one of my other romantic urban fantasy series featuring Protector Cary Redmond. Angie is one of Cary's best friends, and her past—the events of the Demon Witch series—are hinted at there, but never fully revealed. This series arose out of my desire to explore Angie's past and see what *really* happened.

If you're interested in reading the Cary Redmond series, the first novel is The Trouble with Black Cats and Demons. Continue reading for an excerpt. There are also a lot of short stories around the series, including Cary and Angie's first meeting in When Cary Met Angie, and a story where someone from Angie's past comes back to disturb her peace Cary and the Demon Witch.

For more information on all my books, new releases, and occasional freebies, as well as ramblings about books, baking, and balcony gardening, join my newsletter. Subscribers receive two free, exclusive short stories, one from the Cary Redmond series, *When Cary Met Ariel*, and one from my Tiger Shifters paranormal romance series, *Mate Run*. *Mate Run* is quite hot for such a short story, just so you're forewarned. You can also check for new release updates at my website, or follow my author page at your favorite vendor.

Thanks again for reading!

~Kat

KAT SIMONS

THE TROUBLE WITH
BLACK CATS AND DEMONS

A CARY REDMOND NOVEL

THE TROUBLE WITH BLACK CATS AND DEMONS

A CARY REDMOND NOVEL

EXCERPT

CHAPTER ONE

"Not again." Cary Redmond ducked as another fireball clipped over her head. "You don't think fireballs are a bit over the top," she shouted up at the ceiling then had to duck again as a dagger whispered past her ear.

Close. Her heart pounded. Way too close.

She needed to find the damned cat and get out of here. She scanned the apartment from her dubious cover behind a table piled high with unopened mail. Fireballs, daggers, gusts of preternatural wind, freezing hail, and the occasional lightning bolt dropped around her, roaring through the living room in a bright cacophony of magical mayhem.

The lightning bolts flashing in the small confines were pretty spectacular. If they hadn't been trying to fry her, she might have enjoyed the show.

"Jaxer, I'm going to kill you for this."

Normally, this kind of thing was just a part of her job. She was a Protector and literally got paid to run around keeping people safe, mostly from magical bad guys. Not that she'd asked for the job, but that was another story. It *was* her job, so she faced off against dangerous stuff because the Nags—her bosses—told her to.

Tonight, however, was not an official assignment. Tonight, she was just doing a favor for her demented faery mentor. The bastard knew exactly how to get to her. All he had to do was mention a defenseless little black kitty cat and she was done for. How could she refuse to help a kitty? People did rotten things to black cats on Halloween.

Except Jaxer had forgotten to warn her about the fireballs.

She screeched through her teeth and dove behind the couch as one of the aforementioned fireballs barreled toward her. She cursed Jaxer as she took a quick look under the couch for the cat. Where the hell was it?

She'd called out to it when she'd first entered the apartment but hadn't gotten any irate kitty responses. After her lurching hunt of the living room and kitchen, the only place left was the bedroom.

She pulled in a deep breath as she contemplated the long space of unprotected ground between her hiding spot behind the couch and the bedroom door. Once she found the cat, this would be easier. When she was actively protecting something, very little of the magical dangers could get to her, and nothing deadly would touch her. She just had to *find* the cat first. And quickly. They had to be out of this cursed apartment before midnight. Before the wizard got home and all hell broke loose.

Again.

She ducked flying objects and ran to the bedroom, squealing when a lightning bolt hit the ground right behind her. Crossing her fingers that there were no nasty spells waiting for her, she lunged through the half-open door and cringed in anticipation of magical repercussions as she fell onto a red-carpeted floor. She held perfectly still, waiting. Nothing. She let out a breath and pushed herself up onto her hands and knees, shaking her head. All this for a cat. That bastard Jaxer had a lot to answer for.

She rose to a crouch, trying to calm her racing pulse, and froze.

In front of her sat a huge bed, which she barely noticed because the naked man lying in the middle of the enormous mattress stopped her heart.

Holy shit.

He was absolutely magnificent. Tanned skin, well-defined muscles, thick, black hair hanging down over his forehead. He was lying against a giant headboard with his head hanging forward so she couldn't get a good look at his face, but his golden eyes seemed to glow up at her from under his brows. Piercing and stunning and breath-stealing.

Cary swallowed. Hard. Because even the captivating gold of his eyes wasn't enough to keep her gaze from wandering over the breadth of his naked chest, the corded muscles of his shoulders and arms, the flat expanse of his stomach. It took a great deal of will power not to follow the line of dark hair arrowing down his abdomen…lower.

The man straightened and Cary heard the clink of chains at the same time as she got a look at his neck—and the thick collar covering most of it.

What the hell had Jaxer gotten her into?

"Who're you?" she asked, breathless and embarrassed.

"Who are you?"

His voice carried a deep reverberation that made her spine tingle. Oh boy.

"I'm looking for a black cat," she said, knowing the explanation sounded inane. Jaxer had told her about Sheldon the Wizard, but this? This was something else all together. What was this guy doing here? He wasn't Sheldon, she was sure of it. But then who was he? And where was the cat?

She blinked and a black leopard lay on the bed where the man had been. She sucked in a sharp breath, blinked again. And the man was back.

"Whoa." Cary swallowed. "*You're* the black cat I came to rescue?"

Oh, she really was going to kill Jaxer now. He hadn't said anything about a fully grown man who happened to be a leopard shapeshifter. He'd made sure she thought she was after a little, harmless kitty cat, not a deadly dangerous big cat who shifted into a beautiful, naked, very large man.

The faery was dead. Not that she knew how to kill him, but that was beside the point.

"Jaxer sent you?" The man's eyes narrowed and his

features took on a dangerous edge. He hissed a curse under his breath and shook his head. "Stupid."

"Hey!" She stood, the better to face his gorgeous disgust. No one should look that good while insulting you. "You could have done worse, buddy."

She took a step toward the bed, wiping damp palms on her jeans. The chains she'd heard earlier linked the collar on his neck to the headboard, which was brass and made-up of a scrawl of symbols she didn't recognize but looked like they might mean something if she stared at them long enough. He wasn't bound anywhere else that she dared peek, and the chains appeared flimsy enough. So obviously the power keeping him confined was in the collar.

"What is that?" She gestured with her head toward the thick band of metal.

"A binding ring," he said slowly, as if speaking to a child.

She frowned, both at his tone and the news. "But you just shifted."

"It's been designed to contain both my forms. Any other questions before you get me out of here?"

"Yeah, what crawled up your butt and put you in such a pissy mood?"

"Being held captive for sacrifice by a wizard and having a child sent to rescue me has dampened my day a bit," he said.

She grinned and enjoyed watching his eyes narrow suspiciously. "Child, huh? You know, at my age that's a compliment."

"How old could you be? Twenty?"

She shook her head. She'd actually turned thirty-one last April. But when she got tricked into becoming a Protector at twenty-five, she'd stopped aging at a normal rate. One of the few things about the job that didn't irritate her.

She took a quick moment to glance around the rest of the room. The red carpet wasn't the only gaudy element. Lots of black leather covered the walls and an animal skinned rug, which she was afraid to think about too closely given the captive on the overlarge bed, was tossed across the floor in front of what she thought might be a closet. A wood and metal trunk sat against one wall, red silk drapes covered the single window, and the overhead light was covered by thick, dark metal chains which gave the room strange shadows.

Fortunately, there were no nasty attack spells in here, which meant Sheldon the Wizard didn't want his captive accidentally hurt by a stray lightning bolt. That worked in her favor, giving her time to solve the binding ring problem without being pelted by hail.

Though even if there had been spells in here, now that she was officially protecting someone, she could keep them both safe.

She did wonder why Sheldon would care if his shape shifting captive got hurt before the midnight sacrifice. Obviously, he didn't want him dead. You couldn't sacrifice something that was already dead. But an additional warning spell in here probably wouldn't have killed his prisoner. Maybe. If Sheldon had enough control.

If he didn't, and was as powerful as Jaxer claimed, they really needed to get out of here. Fast.

She eased up to the bedside, still leery of traps, and leaned in close to the leopard man, trying to ignore the yummy, stomach-fluttering male scent of him as she studied the binding ring. It was a thick band of silver and copper intertwined in a complex pattern of twists and turns. Over the silver, tiny runic symbols danced and shimmered so they were nearly impossible to read.

"Oh good," she said, "a hard one."

The prisoner shivered, a low growl rising from his throat. The sound made Cary's heartbeat jump.

Speaking of hard ones.

She could feel his glare on the side of her face, but she resisted looking. She had other things to worry about at the moment.

Like how the hell she was going to get this damned magical containment brace off his neck without alerting the entire mystical neighborhood.

"You did that on purpose," the man snarled.

"Huh?" She glanced at him. "What are you talking about?"

"Don't breathe on me again," he said.

She scowled. "What am I supposed to do? Hold my breath until I get your collar off? Just relax, big guy. You'll be out of here in a minute." To herself, she mumbled, "Wouldn't have gotten this much grief from a proper black cat."

"You some kind of witch?"

"No." After a moment, she sighed and shook her head. "Well, there's no help for it. I'm gonna have to use brute force. It'll take too long to get this off subtly."

"We don't have much time. It's nearly midnight now."

"Gee, really?"

He ignored her sarcasm. "Brute force?"

"Hold onto your valuable body parts," she said and tried not to think about his exposed valuable parts. Then she wrapped her hands around the collar, easing her fingers gently under so the backs pressed against his neck. His skin was warm and another shiver danced down her spine.

"Wait."

She met his gaze.

"What the hell are you doing? If I can't break that with my bare hands, you can't—"

He stopped short when she tugged and the collar came away with a quiet click.

"I'm not without some talent," she murmured.

"Who *are* you?"

"Come on. We have to get you out of here. I just made a lot of magical noise with that little stunt."

"Hold on."

He grabbed her hand. The feel of his warm palm wrapped around her fingers sent tiny sparks of electricity dancing over her skin. He dropped his hold, but she saw his eyes widen with the same shock she felt. He inhaled deeply, and against her will, she watched the strong muscles of his chest rise and fall.

"What's your name?" he asked.

"Cary."

"Cary. I'm Deacon."

"Nice to meet you." Did that sounded as stupid to him as it did to her given the circumstances?

He smiled, a slow, deadly grin that made her pulse race. "Nice to meet you, too."

She blinked and shook her head. "Come on, Deacon. We need to move."

As he slid to the edge of the mattress, Cary turned her back to avoid embarrassing them both—despite the temptation to look over every inch of him. The sound of material moving over skin behind her didn't help curb her less polite impulses, though, so she hurried to the door to see how the lightning bolts and fireballs were doing.

Slipping into his jeans, Deacon watched the woman as she peeked around the edge of the doorframe at the living room and the still popping spells Sheldon had set to keep help from reaching him.

She wasn't the rescue he'd been expecting. He'd expected the damned faery to come himself.

Jaxer had convinced him to let the wizard "capture" him, so they could find out *why* Sheldon was kidnapping shifters. They'd only found a few of Sheldon's victims—their bodies anyway. And they'd been little more than desiccated husks. The rest of the missing shifters... Even their bodies had vanished.

Wizards didn't typically go after shapeshifters for sacrifice. They were too hard to contain, and most of them didn't have the kind of magical energy an average human wizard could absorb through ceremonial magic. Shapeshifting wasn't typically magic. It was just a species trait.

Deacon knew none of the shifters killed so far had had any actual magic. He was a different case, but he was pretty sure Sheldon didn't know that. Jaxer did, which was why he'd come to Deacon in the first place, and Deacon had felt obliged to help even though none of the shifters taken had been leopards.

He suppressed an irritated growl. This was the last time he'd let the faery use him for bait. He'd been chained to that fucking bed all day with no sign of help. Then Jaxer went and made things worse by sending in this…woman to rescue him instead of coming himself. How dare he endanger someone else when this crusade against Sheldon was his own personal business? Bad enough he dragged Deacon into it.

But as Deacon watched the woman straighten away from the doorframe when a lightning bolt flashed, he realized there *was* something about her. He couldn't deny the power she must have to break through the binding ring. Yet she looked and smelled like a normal, human woman.

Her light brown hair hung in long ponytail her back over a battered brown leather jacket. She wore jeans, hiking boots, and a purple t-shirt with a glittery Happy Halloween emblazoned over a maniacally grinning jack-o-lantern. Her blue eyes had sparkled when he'd called her a child, then flashed with irritation when he'd insulted her. And for reasons he couldn't quite understand, he'd found it hard to look away from her, especially when she'd knelt next to him on the bed.

Something about her…something about her scent tugged at his instincts.

Who the hell was she? *What* was she? She had to be more than human, but none of his sense picked up anything particularly preternatural about her. So where did all that power come from?

Jaxer had some serious explaining to do.

Deacon shook off his preoccupation and walked up behind her to stare at the living room over her head. Black scorch marks marred the hardwood floors, and a layer of frost covered one side table. The air was heavy with electricity and the smell of burning ozone.

Despite the multiple magical eruptions, the apartment was in remarkably good shape. As he watched, a dagger flew toward the bedroom, dropped harmlessly a foot from the doorway, and disappeared as if it hadn't existed.

Clever. Less clean up. And a testament to Sheldon's power.

He couldn't blame Jaxer for being worried about the little shit. But given a choice, Deacon would have taken a more… active approach to getting rid of the wizard.

Unfortunately, and he was reluctant to admit this even to himself, his approach probably would have gotten him killed. The bastard wizard was powerful. How Sheldon managed to be so powerful at his age was a mystery. But maybe that was the reason Jaxer was so obsessed with finding out the *whys* behind Sheldon's actions.

If Deacon got out of this apartment alive, he'd ask the faery. In the meantime, he and this very human woman in front of him had to navigate the bespelled living room and get away before Sheldon got back.

Deacon drew in a slow breath and was hit again by Cary's scent. Vanilla and cinnamon. And something else. Something that shot jolts of lust and need through his gut, making him lean closer to her just so he could feel the heat of her skin. He felt a possessive growl rising in his throat and swallowed it back, fisting his hands by his side to keep from reaching for her.

What the hell? He had more control that this. A lot more. He had to or people got killed. Resisting a woman, even one that smelled like heaven, had never been a problem before. With Cary, it took an effort to resist pulling her close and burying his face in her neck to soak up her essence.

If he didn't know better, he'd think she was a witch, casting a lust spell on him.

His nostrils flared. That scent of hers…

It reached down inside him, calling to a deep instinct. As he breathed her in, his leopard whispered, *Mine*.

Out in the living room, wind-lashed hail whipped toward the bedroom without actually coming through the doorway. And behind that, a lightning bolt sizzled the floor.

"Sheldon didn't make this easy," he said, quirking a brow when she jumped at the sound of his voice.

"Are you dressed?" she asked without turning around.

He couldn't help smiling at the slight panic in her voice. "Yes."

"Okay. Stick close. Stay behind me and don't try to dodge around me. Got it? That's how we'll get out of here alive."

He frowned down at the top of her head. She must have some pretty powerful shields to get through that mess. But she wasn't a witch?

He grunted a noncommittal response, and she swung around to face him. The flash of heat in her eyes made his pulse kick.

"Listen, buddy," she said, her chin tucked back as she glared at him, "if you don't let me protect you, we're both dead. Okay? Don't go trying to be a hero. Just stay close and let me do what I came here to do."

She mumbled something unflattering under her breath as she turned back to the living room, and he had to fight a completely irrational urge to kiss her.

Over the course of the long day, with no sign of help from Jaxer, he'd had to face the possibility of his own death. His reaction to Cary might be a result of that, a need to reaffirm he was alive.

But as he breathed in the heady scent of her again, he wondered…

Don't Miss The Trouble with Black Cats and Demons
Book 1 in the Cary Redmond Series
Out now!

BOOKS BY KAT SIMONS

Demon Witch Series

Howling Dreadful

Moonlit Strange

1-Bone Lantern Witch

2-Spiderweb Witch

3-Storm Shadow Witch

4-Darkling Mist Witch

5-Apocalypse Witch

Urban Fantasy

The Cary Redmond Series

Cary Redmond Short Stories and Collections

Joan of Kerry Series

Friday's Curious Shop Series

Paranormal Romance

Dragon Thief Series

Seven Families: Wolf Series

Tiger Shifters Series

Destiny Cats Series

Romancing the Leopard: A Tiger Shifters-Cary Redmond Crossover Novel

ALSO BY KAT SIMONS

Contemporary Fantasy

Haunts and Howls Collections

**Tombstone Wizard * The Unshattered Sword * Going Out of Business: Everything's for Sale * Anger Management * Demonic Dates * The Museum of Small Art's Everyman * Burning Inside a Stone Circle * Bored Questless * I Just Ate a Bug * Ting Ling * Sophie Saves the World * Black Water Hawthorns * To Dance in Fallow Fields at Midnight * The Troll and the Dressmaker*

Stories from the Café

The Café Collections

Stories from the Café: Volume One

Pick Your Genre Collections

Who Steals a Dragon

Contemporary Romances

Designed for You

Poinsettias and Possibilities

Mystery and Thriller

ROSS AND O'NEILL ADVENTURES

Galileo's Pendulum

ABOUT THE AUTHOR

Kat Simons earned her Ph.D. in animal behavior, working with animals as diverse as dolphins and deer. She brought her experience and knowledge of biology to her paranormal romance and urban fantasy fiction, where she delights in taking nature and turning it on its ear. She writes urban fantasy, contemporary fantasy, and paranormal romance in series which combine action adventure, the otherworldly, and a frequent dose of sexy romance.

The newest book in her bestselling romantic urban fantasy series about Protector Cary Redmond, The Trouble with Shifters and Fae Courts, sees a new direction for the intrepid Protector, her sexy leopard shifter mate, and the entire crew. Kat also launched a new novella length Urban Fantasy Romance series that follows the adventures of a magical thief and the dragon shifter prince she just can't seem to shake—and really doesn't want to. The first season of the Dragon Thief series released throughout 2024. Season Two begins in 2025 with The Crown of Kingship Job.

For something a little different, Kat also publishes fantasy, science fiction, and the occasional hockey romance under the name Isabo Kelly (https://www.isabokelly.com).

After traveling the world, living in places like Hawaii, Germany, and Ireland, Kat now lives in New York City with her family and a library's worth of books.

For more on Kat and her future books

Website: https://www.katsimons.com/
Newsletter: https://bit.ly/KatSimonsNewsletter

KatSimonsBooks

https://www.katsimonsbooks.com
https://www.TheCafeatKatSimonsBooks.com

Social Media

Facebook Page: https://www.facebook.com/
KatSimonsAuthor
BookBub: https://www.bookbub.com/authors/kat-simons
Bluesky: https://bsky.app/profile/katsimons.bsky.social
Instagram: https://www.instagram.com/isabokelly/
Threads: https://www.threads.net/@isabokelly

Join Kat's Newsletter

Stay Up-to-Date

On all Kat's News, Updates, and fun extras

New Subscriber Get Two Exclusive Stories Just for Signing up!

bit.ly/KatSimonsNewsletter

KATSIMONSBOOKS

Mystery

Urban Fantasy

Romance

And More!

KATSIMONSBOOKS.COM